The Big Day Deceit

A Romantic Story of Lies, Passion, and Second Chances

ANN FAIRWAY

About Ann Fairway

Ann Fairway writes contemporary romances grounded in reality, laced with humour, and brimming with themes like switched identities, forced proximity, and the quirks of serendipitous connections.

A lover of richly layered characters and heartfelt yet relatable stories, Ann Fairway explores how love and personal growth often emerge from life's messiest, most unexpected moments.

She lives in the South of England, surrounded by woods and wonderful people. Ann is equally happy lounging in her garden, taking lunchtime walks, or soaking up the sun on holiday.

To find out more about Ann

- visit her website at https://annfairway.com/
- follow her on TikTok: @annfairwayauthor, X: @annfairway, or Instagram: @annfairwayauthor
- or like her page on Facebook: https://www.facebook.com/AnnFairwayAuthor

To Neil, with whom I can be myself ...

The characters and events portrayed in this publication are fictitious. Any similarity to real persons, living or dead, is coincidental and not intended by the author.

Copyright © 2025 Ann Fairway
Ann Fairway asserts the moral right to be identified as the author of this work.

All rights reserved. No part of this publication may be reproduced, stored in a retrieval system, or transmitted in any form or by any means, electronic, mechanical, photocopying, recording, or otherwise, without express written permission of the publisher.

Cover design: 100covers.com

ISBN: 978-1-917786-00-3
Imprint: Stargazing Turtle
Edition: First

Contents

Chapter 1 1
Chapter 2 12
Chapter 3 20
Chapter 4 31
Chapter 5 42
Chapter 6 53
Chapter 7 75
Chapter 8 89
Chapter 9 96
Chapter 10 104
Chapter 11 128
Chapter 12 137
Chapter 13 147
Chapter 14 156
Chapter 15 170
Chapter 16 183
Chapter 17 193
Chapter 18 199
Chapter 19 209
Chapter 20 219
Chapter 21 228
Chapter 22 239
Chapter 23 246

Chapter 1

Annie's slightly curled brown hair shimmered in the light as she slid another hairpin into place, securing her crown. She could feel the weight of the pins on her scalp as they tugged at her hair as she adjusted them. Her nose wrinkled at the pungent smell of hairspray she'd applied, the chemical odour lingering in the stagnant air of the dressing room on the first floor of the wedding hall.

She stretched the skin around her eyes, attempting to flatten the light wrinkles that formed in the corners and on her forehead. Something that Louise, Annie's seven years younger sister, with her perfectly smooth skin, wouldn't have to worry about just yet. Under normal circumstances, Annie normally wouldn't care, but today wasn't about vanity. Today, she needed to cover every wrinkle and erase every telltale trace of herself.

From a small pot, Annie loaded the tip of her finger with a soft pasty primer and filled all the gaps, hoping that Louise's make-up artist friend knew her job well enough so she could pull it off.

A dry laugh escaped her throat as she glanced at her reflection, tilting her head from side to side. She barely recognised herself, which meant the plan might actually work. Her grin spread wider as she imagined the chaos that would erupt in less than an hour, especially her mother's reaction when she realised it wasn't Louise wearing the veil.

"You wanted a wedding, Mother? You'll get one you'll never forget." Annie smirked, tucking a stray curl behind her ear.

Much better.

A sparkly white purse belonging to Louise glittered in the dimly lit room as Annie rummaged through it for the foundation. Her fingers brushed against the corner of a stiff envelope, and her breath caught. She pulled it free and stared at the cream-coloured flap, the edge already too familiar.

So lucky he had to leave home early that day.

It wasn't the first letter that had arrived from her sister, but the only one Annie had intercepted.

The memory of that morning still churned in her stomach. She'd found the stash of other letters addressed to her, shoved carelessly into Darren's top desk drawer, their seals broken and their contents read without her knowledge.

If only she hadn't been so consumed by grief back then—so focused on building the perfect life, the perfect lie. She hadn't noticed the little signs at first, not until it was too late. Annie pressed her lips into a hard, thin line. Darren. That man. That liar. That piece of garbage.

"Men. All they care about is power and money." She hissed and squeezed a dollop of foundation—a tone darker than her natural complexion—onto her index finger, then and dotted it across her face, like bigger brothers to her sun freckles.

Letting fingers of both hands dance all over her heart-shaped face, she tapped the foundation in, covering the freckles, the pale skin, the prominent cheekbones, and the wrinkles, making her look more and more like Louise.

After wiping her hands with a tissue, Annie pulled at the corner of the white envelope peeking out from the purse. A stiff card fell out, and Annie traced the embossed letters with a finger wrapped in a tissue—"Louise and Conrad, 7th of May 2022."

Her jaws clenched. "Over my dead body," she murmured, staring at the wedding invitation.

If only she had known sooner, it all could have been avoided.

***

A week before the wedding …

Annie took a sip of peppermint tea, cleansing her mouth and exhaling with relief, then pulled the blanket tighter around her body and sank deeper into the weathered, burnt sienna leather sofa.

"Thank you, sis. This is exactly what I needed."

Louise plumped her tall and slim body onto a sofa arm, swinging her leg while taking a sip from her mug full of steamy hot chocolate. Normally, Annie would be the one having that hot chocolate instead of a cup of tea, but in her current state, peppermint was a godsend. "What did Meggie say about the wedding?"

"Oh, you know." Louise stood up and strode to the panoramic window, setting her mug down on a work desk covered in Post-it notes. She slid the window open, letting the aroma of fresh blooms mingle with the scents of mint and chocolate.

"No, Lou, I don't know." Annie turned the cup in her hands, watching her sister's slumped shoulders, clearly outlined by the bright morning light outside. "I bet she wasn't happy, but … "

Louise gasped and hid her head in her hands, and then a muffled, shaky voice reached Annie. "I didn't tell her."

"What?" Annie jumped to her feet so quickly that she had to steady herself on the arm of the sofa as a wave of nausea and dizziness from earlier washed over her. She took a few deep breaths, hoping for the weakness to disappear. "When do you plan to tell her? The wedding is in a week!"

"I know." Louise shifted over to the desk and stretched her neck from side to side. "I know, but how do you tell someone you love that you're going to marry someone else?"

Annie cringed, watching her baby sister struggle. She reached her in two careful steps, placed her cup on the only coaster on the desk and touched Louise's shoulder, wrapped in a soft fluffy jumper. "I didn't know you had strong feelings for Meggie, I thought it was just a fling."

Louise smiled in that sad way that reminded Annie of a puppy in the pouring rain. "No, this was always serious to me. I was just too scared to admit it."

Annie shook her head, furrowing her eyebrows, then put her hand on Louise's shoulder and pressed lightly to make her sister turn and face her. "So, why on Earth have you agreed to marry this guy?"

Louise opened her mouth, then pursed her lips again.

"Was it Mother?" Annie searched for a confirmation in her sister's eyes and the slight nod was all she needed. "I knew it! They forced you to do it."

Louise sighed. "No, they didn't force me. And they are right, you know. This is for the best."

"The best!" Annie threw her hands out into the air, rolling her eyes. "What did she tell you?" Annie focused her gaze on Louise's eyes like she wanted to look inside her sister's head.

"Well ..." Louise cocked her head. "Gosh, you're pale. You're sure you don't need a doctor?" Louise reached out to her back pocket, retrieving her phone. "I can call—"

"I'm fine. Stop stalling." Annie ambled toward the sofa as she started feeling more dizzy again. "I'll simply lie down for a bit while you tell me everything."

Louise followed her sister to the sofa and sat on the edge. "There is not much to tell. They need that cottage from him to unlock the inheritance, and this is the only way to get it. It's a good deal."

Annie smirked. "For him it is. He's getting a pretty young wife. How old is he? Forty?"

"Forty-four, but—"

"Forty-four! Damn it! He's seventeen years older than you."

Louise shrugged. "What does it matter anyway? I'm not into him."

"Exactly." Annie made a swooping gesture with her hand and then, in a much gentler tone, asked, "So, what about you?"

Her sister sighed but said nothing.

"What about your life and dreams?"

Louise rubbed her face. "Look Annie, I love you, but you weren't here."

"I know. I'm sorry." Annie touched her sister's arm as tears welled in her eyes.

"No, no, I don't mean it like that." Louise patted Annie's hand. "What I meant is that I'm at their mercy as I can't support myself yet without their money." She raised her hand in resignation. "And Conrad is rich and when we had that coffee date, he seemed nice and promised to help with my gallery." A low, sad chuckle escaped Louise's mouth. "I would finally be free from our parents, you know."

"But honey, it's simply trading one set of chains for another—you won't be happy. And what about Meggie?"

Louise's whimper tore Annie's heart apart.

"I know but what else can I do?" A whisper as light as a feather reached Annie's ears.

"You can say no." Annie extended her hand and stroked Louise's long, sleek copper-brown hair.

The head under her hand shook. "I tried. They don't listen."

Annie perked up. "So, you told them you don't want to get married."

"Yes, but they didn't take me seriously." Louise buried her head in her hands.

"Look at me." Annie lightly touched the olive skin of her sister's hand. "If you don't want to get married, they can't force you."

Louise looked at Annie with her glistening puppy eyes. "You know Mother, I can't just say no. She wants me to get married and she will make me. Besides, if they cut me off, then I'm screwed."

Louise swallowed hard and her gaze wandered toward Annie's belly. A small smile softened her facial features, making her look less haggard.

"And how am I going to help you and my niece or nephew when I won't have money for rent?"

Annie dismissed the comment with a wave of her hand, although she had to clear her throat and blink away the sudden moisture in her own eyes. The warmth around her heart expanded. She wasn't alone. And there was no reality in which she would let her baby sister suffer at their parents' hands. One daughter was enough.

"I've got an idea."

Annie clasped her hands, and her face cracked a mischievous smile, accompanied by light wrinkles and freckles.

"I give them a hell of a wedding, one they will never forget, and there will be no way for them to wriggle out of this one." A low growl escaped her throat. "And I'll tell them it was all my idea, which, frankly, would be true, so they won't have a reason to act it out on you. Plus—" Annie lifted her finger. "Mother will probably need to leave the country to avoid the humiliation."

***

A buzz from her mobile phone jolted Annie back to reality. She checked her smart watch—half an hour to go. Then she tapped at her phone and read the text message notification.

Lou: Just landed. It's gorgeous here and hot. On the way to the hotel now. Good luck sis xx

A wide grin cracked Annie's face, and she giggled like a little boy who had just pulled off the best prank of his life. The Canary Islands trip had been Meggie's idea, but it worked well with Annie's plan. Much easier to keep her sister out of their mother's reach when she wasn't physically here and could not be dragged back like a misbehaving child.

"Oh Mother, you'll wish I was never born." Annie sniggered as she darkened her long eyelashes, making her emerald green eyes stand out even more.

"Selling Lou like an animal on the market!" She spat out before covering her lips with a raspberry-shaded lip gloss. "Real Catholic, my ass."

As she finished applying her makeup, Annie could hear the muffled sound of church bells ringing.

The bright sunlight streaming in through the window cast elaborate patterns of light and shadow on the old-fashioned dresser, highlighting its intricate carvings and adding depth to the space.

"And you too." She flicked at the wedding invitation with a smirk. "A filthy rich man buying his wife. I bet you're a real jerk if no woman wanted you, mister."

Annie rose from the stool, her muscles sighing in relief, and slipped into her crimson stilettos—the only high heels she owned. There was no way in the world she could wear her sister's wedding shoes, which were at least a full size too big.

The deep shade of the shoes contrasted sharply against the pale cream colour of the wedding dress. It was a miracle the dress fit. While Louise was slim and tall, Annie was the one with the curves and full body; however, the last six months had taken a toll and for once, she was the skinny one.

Annie touched her belly. Not for long, though. It would start showing in a month or two.

She squinted, shading her eyes, and twirled around. The skirts swooshed, and the myriads of tiny zirconias twinkled in the bright afternoon sun. It wasn't her style, but it was never about style with her parents. Appearances. That's what they cared about. Especially Mother.

"What will people say, Mother?" She laughed, inhaling the musty smell of the old dressing room, with a worn-out sofa and an old-fashioned dresser complete with a mirror that was a little cloudy around the edges but still served its purpose. Heavy volumes filled the bookshelves, their spines worn with age, smelling of leather and dust.

The room darkened. Annie glanced through the wide panoramic window—a tiny cloud on a pale blue sky.

Her high heels clicked on the wooden floorboards, echoing through the empty room, as she glided toward the window, the rustling of the dress's fabric against her skin creating a soft, whooshing sound that filled the space.

She gazed at the breathtaking view of the surrounding lush green parks stretched for miles, enhanced with flower beds and benches under old oak trees promising a lazy afternoon in the shade.

"What a perfect day." She chewed on her lip until the artificial raspberry taste of lip gloss made her stop.

A sudden shiver ran through her, so she draped the white lace shawl around her shoulders and arms. The softness of the delicate fabric against her skin did little to the goosebumps on her bare forearms. Annie rubbed her hands together to warm up a little.

The sound of approaching footsteps made her rush back to the mirror.

"I'll be a minute."

She shouted toward the door with pins between her teeth while battling a layered veil—the only thing that would make the charade work long enough.

After pulling the veil over her face, she picked up the purse, shoved the invite and the phone in, and winked at her reflection, like it was her buddy in crime. The door squeaked, and her mother's face, as distinguished and perfect as Annie could remember, appeared in the cracks. Annie could feel her heart racing and her palms sweating as she tried to keep her composure.

Showtime.

***

Conrad glanced at the pitch-black titanium smartwatch secured on his left wrist with a black leather strap. The old-fashioned clock face showed five past two in the afternoon.

Where the hell was she?

Brushing off a speck of dust from his custom-made jacket, he scanned the crowd gathered in the Roman chapel. The only people he knew here were his distant cousin Tom, an older lady who had been with the company for generations, his accountant doubling as his witness, and Colton, his driver—someone who probably knew Conrad better than anyone else.

The people in the pews, dressed in their finest clothes, murmured to each other in hushed voices.

What if she changed her mind?

Candles flickered in the gusts coming through the open main entrance. Conrad shivered, shifting his body weight from one leg to another. The overwhelming scent of freshly cut flowers couldn't cover the musky smell of the old and damp chapel. The columns filtered the little light coming through the stained glass windows, casting long shadows.

A priest appeared at the side door and strolled toward Conrad.

"How're you doing, son? Nervous?" His jovial tone, round face, and intelligent eyes watching from behind rimmed glasses reminded Conrad of his old college professor. The only difference between the two men was the embroidered white robe worn by the priest.

"A little bit." Conrad tapped his watch. "How long before we start?"

The priest joined his hands in a praying gesture. "Soon, with God's help."

"Is there a problem?" Conrad felt a knot form in his stomach.

The priest put a hand on his shoulder. "Nothing to worry about, my son, I'm sure. The mother of the bride went to check on her and when Mrs Simmons sets her mind on something, nobody can stop her." He chuckled, and Conrad joined him with a faint smile. "And now, if you excuse me, I need to prepare a few things."

Conrad watched as the priest made his way to the altar, his white stole billowing behind him.

His mind wandered to that day several weeks ago when Richard, the father of the bride, had approached him with an offer to buy his cottage.

As much as Conrad needed the money, the no-sell clause on the cottage meant he couldn't do it. Unless …

Unless he considered a most ridiculous proposal. Richard had offered his daughter's hand for the cottage. It had sounded preposterous at first.

Him getting married? And to whom? A woman he had never met and who was way too young for him?

But Richard had had a point. Conrad couldn't sell the cottage, and Richard and his wife, Maureen, needed it to unlock the inheritance from Maureen's late mother, Grandma Ann. They had thrown Louise's trust fund to make up for his loss, which had been set to mature on the first month's wedding anniversary.

A bit too old-fashioned if you asked me.

Like the whole emancipation thing had never happened in that family, but hey, not his place to comment on other people's lives. They had requested the fund to be invested in a prosperous countryside club. Well, Conrad had other ideas about spending the trust fund money, but they didn't need to know about that.

It all made sense on paper. Under any other circumstances, adding such a gem to his chain of family inns would be a dream come true, even at the expense of the cottage. Under any other circumstances, he would not consider the arranged marriage, though. As pathetic as it might sound, he believed in relationships out of love. Under any other circumstances …

Not that he planned to get married, ever. What was the point? To have his heart broken in a more expensive way? At least this deal was honest—a financial arrangement. No hiding behind pretend feelings of love that were never there.

Conrad blinked and checked his watch—quarter past two.

What if she didn't show up? What if she saw through his motives and ran away? He couldn't afford to lose this opportunity.

Nah, it's just my nerves talking.

Louise had seemed fragile and kind of lost in that oversized jumper of hers, and a knitted vest on top, when she had sat in the coffee shop's corner where they had met four weeks ago. The age difference between them had been apparent. Her defect-free, soft, youthful face and shiny, sleek hair had compared starkly to his weathered face and short salt-and-pepper hair. From the moment he had met her, Conrad had had this protective feeling, like being her older brother.

And that, actually, had decided it for him. A companionship. Someone he could care about without expecting anything back. Conrad spent his days working anyway, so he could make such a marriage work if she was willing to. And she had seemed okay with this crazy idea, God knows why. Although he suspected that his promise to help with her photo gallery, which he intended to keep, was the tipping point for her.

Well, the only promise he could afford to keep. If she showed up.

Conrad scratched his chin.

Besides, they didn't need to stay married forever. If she was really unhappy with him, Conrad wouldn't stand in her way. As long as he had the fund money, so a month would do. Was he asking for too much?

As Conrad stood there, deep in thought, a sudden movement caught his attention. The father of the bride dashed for the door, pretending he wasn't running. Conrad's heart sank even further.

I knew it.

The silence was deafening as they waited for the bride to appear. His palms began to sweat, so he took a deep breath, trying to calm his nerves. The chapel was still chilly despite the warm May day outside. The old Roman walls kept everything in the shade, defusing the light and making everything look gloomy.

After a few more minutes that seemed like hours, the organ music boomed, and the bride began her walk down the aisle. She held her head high, her movements exuding beauty, defiance, and—was that stubbornness?

Richard, her father, scuttled at her side, struggling to keep pace. The failed attempt to link arms didn't escape Conrad's notice, nor did the fake, strained smile plastered across the older man's face. But that didn't hold his attention for long. No, it was her—the bride.

He watched as she walked toward him, her veil covering her face, and his heart began to race. There was something different about her. The way she moved, for one. Confident, deliberate, as if daring anyone to challenge her presence. Her hips swayed in a rhythm that made his pulse quicken, the curves of her body filling out the dress in ways he hadn't expected. The tight bodice framed her chest, highlighting every detail of her femininity, as though the dress itself struggled to contain her.

Conrad blinked, momentarily stunned. Was this the same woman he'd met in the coffee shop? The one who'd sat at the far end of the table in baggy clothes, shrinking into herself, her eyes fixed on her mug as if it were a lifeline? He remembered her then as pretty, yes, but reserved, almost timid. This woman, walking toward him now, was someone else entirely.

Maybe it's the dress? He scratched his chin. *Or the makeup?* Makeup could do wonders, couldn't it? The smoky eyeliner, the bold lipstick, the contouring—all of it made her look older, more striking. More confident. Or maybe she was warming up to the idea of their marriage, finding strength in the decision.

A spark of hope flickered in his chest at that thought as his gaze locked on her every step.

When she reached the altar, Richard took her hand and placed it in Conrad's. Her slim hand was warm, her grip surprisingly firm for someone with such delicate fingers. Conrad clasped it in his own rough, callused hand, and for a moment, he felt something unexpected—a spark of connection.

The priest stepped forward, clearing his throat, but Conrad couldn't tear his gaze away. The bride lifted her veil, and everything else in the room fell away.

Emerald green eyes locked onto his, fierce and unflinching. They sparkled under the candlelight with a fire he hadn't noticed before—no, a fire that hadn't been there before. Her full lips curved ever so slightly, promising more than he dared to dream of. She looked mature, self-assured, and entirely unlike the shy woman he'd first met.

For a moment, doubt tugged at the edges of his thoughts.

Why does she seem so different? Was this just the glow of the wedding? A trick of the lighting? Or maybe—

Maybe she's finally showing me who she really is.

A rush of primal admiration overtook him, silencing the questions in his head. He had never noticed her charm like this before, and he inwardly cursed himself for being so blind. Brotherly? There was nothing brotherly about how he felt now.

You lucky bastard.

Chapter 2

Annie lifted her veil with a triumphant smile as she looked straight into his face. Conrad's strong jawline and piercing blue eyes made her gasp. She didn't know what to expect, but not that. For some reason, she had imagined him to look more like a younger version of her dad, round, baldy, and with a second chin. Instead, the man in front of her was at least six inches taller than her, in a fitted jacket that suggested well-maintained firm muscles. The slivers of grey in his hair and the bushy eyebrows, together with smile wrinkles around his eyes, made him look mature, but in a way that made Annie's heart race.

He looked back at her with a glint in his eyes and a mischievous smile, almost as if her presence amused him.

"You look absolutely stunning."

His deep voice made her all tingly. Despite her efforts to focus on the job, his big working man's hands confidently holding hers made Annie imagine them expertly—without a doubt—exploring her body and finding pleasure points she didn't know existed. Annie licked her dry lips, forgetting about the artificial taste of the lip balm she had probably all eaten by now.

What was wrong with her? She shook her head and tugged her hand away from his grip. It must be the hormones. It had to be. Never—not even in the best of times—had she had thoughts like this about Darren.

He must be a real jerk.

With a face and body like his, this was the only reasonable explanation for his being single. As hard as it was for Annie to admit, this man could have any woman he desired, especially with his money. She could bet he had a new girlfriend every weekend to show off around, one prettier than the other. But here he was, marrying a woman he didn't know.

Maybe he's the controlling type?

She frowned, her stomach tightening at the thought. Men like Darren always seemed perfect on the surface, too. Charming smiles and big gestures didn't always mean kind hearts. Annie's fingers brushed her wrist absentmindedly, the ghost of an old bruise she'd hidden from the world for far too long.

Is he hiding a darker side as well?

The priest cleared his throat, interrupting her spiralling thoughts, and raised his hands. The organ music stopped abruptly, the silence enveloping the room like a cosy blanket.

"Dearly beloved, we are gathered here today in the sight of God, and in the face of this company of witnesses to join together this man and this woman in Holy Matrimony."

As he spoke the words, his voice seemed to echo in the high ceilings.

Annie glanced toward her parents, hidden from Conrad's view. Her mother's expression made Annie chuckle. Mother would break the farce any second now. But her father's unyielding smile and hushed whispers to her mother left Annie feeling uneasy.

Would she?

Why was this still happening? Someone should have been able to tell she was not the right person; surely, she looked nothing like her sister. Annie scanned the faces of people gathered in the church, many distant relatives she only remembered from the photographs. A few met her gaze with a delicate, encouraging smile, but none showed any sign of surprise.

Oh, come on!

The priest's voice filled the chapel once again, solemn and dignified.

"Conrad, will you have this woman to be your lawful wedded wife, to live together after God's ordinance in the Holy Estate of Matrimony? Will you love her, comfort her, honour and keep her in sickness and in health, and forsaking all others keep you only unto her as long as you both shall live?"

Annie's mouth opened in protest, but no sound came out as Conrad took her hands in his, making her heart beat faster while her knees threatened to give out beneath her. His gaze locked onto hers, his eyes the colour of the ocean on a clear day, and she found herself lost in their depths.

His full lips kept moving, but Annie couldn't hear what he said. She stared at him like a teenage girl on her first date, betrayed by her own body's physical response. This had to end, now. But she stood there unable to pull her hands away like they were tied with his by an invisible thread, a thread made of thoughts she should never have in the church.

"Louise?"

Her sister wasn't there. Why would the priest call her name? Annie cocked her head and blinked. The priest repeated, "Will you, Louise?"

Annie realised he was talking to her. "Yes?"

"I'm now pronouncing you husband and wife."

Wait? What? How did that happen? Annie's brows furrowed in confusion and dismay. It wasn't supposed to go that far.

She sensed his fingers on hers as he slid a cold ring onto her finger. A glance down confirmed it—a gold wedding band shimmered in the muted light.

Her throat closed up from panic, and she couldn't make a sound. Her eyes darted around the chapel, looking for someone to help her, but all she saw were smiling faces and cheering guests.

"You can kiss the bride."

Those full lips met hers, silencing anything she might have wanted to say until a wave of dizziness washed over her. In desperation, she tried to free herself, but it only made him pull her closer, his hands on the lower of her back, searching. His greedy lips exploring hers and her own body responding, betraying her.

Oh, screw it.

Annie parted her lips, letting him in, her cheeks burning, with an ache in her belly for more, like a force awakened from a long sleep. She only tasted a little before he released his grip and the pressure on her mouth weakened, taking away this gorgeous dessert.

The crowd erupted into cheers, drowning out the organ music.

For crying out loud.

This was the hormones talking again. She came here to end this malarkey, not indulge her fantasies, about being swept off her feet by a handsome stranger.

Conrad's firm hand on her upper back propelled her toward the exit.

The noise in the chapel rose to a deafening roar as the guests shouted their congratulations to the couple.

"I need to tell you something!" The chanting drowned her voice.

Shaking his head, Conrad pointed to his ears, leaned toward Annie and put his arm around her, closing the distance between them without breaking his pace.

Painfully aware of his fingers caressing the skin on her bare arm, short of breath, Annie managed to utter, "Wait, it wasn't supposed to happen." But she couldn't even hear herself in the cacophony of raised benches and boots stomping on the stone floor.

Conrad shook his head again and pointed at the chapel exit doorways as he released his embrace.

Annie wobbled without support and latched onto his arm as her heels slid on the uneven floor. She managed to stay upright, resisting the urge to feel up his upper arm muscles flexing under her fingers. As they burst through the doors, the sun's rays hit Annie's face, blinding her for a second.

Blinking rapidly, she inhaled and opened her mouth to tell him she wasn't Louise, but he got out his words first.

"It wasn't that bad, was it?"

She knitted her eyebrows. Did he think she was afraid? Or anxious about the wedding?

Squinting in a blasting sun, Annie released her grip on his arm. Then, shading her eyes, she marched toward the balustrade at the end of the platform marked by a row of Roman columns. To the right, the wide stairs led down to the park she had seen from the window of the dressing room. With her left hand firmly on the rough cold stone of the balustrade, she turned away from the sun to face the ajar chapel doors in the background and Conrad, right in front of her, with eyebrows raised like he was still waiting for an answer.

"No, no. It wasn't. Look, we need to—"

"Good! I knew you wouldn't bail on me." A wide cocky grin brightened his face, and he rested his back on the balustrade, leaning over to Annie, and wrapping his arm around her like they were close buddies celebrating a job well done. "Trust me. You wouldn't get a better deal."

What? She narrowed her eyes. *She* wouldn't get a better deal? Annie shook off his hand like it was a sleazy snake.

What was he thinking? That she was some desperate old woman who had to latch on to the first handsome guy she met?

I had better than you, Mister.

And they all were equally despicable, so no, thank you. As her experience taught her, men, especially those great-looking, were after money or control. Or both. They used women to stroke their egos as an extension of their wealth. No respect.

Annie balled her fists, took a step away from him, and gritted her teeth as she fought the urge to punch Conrad in that smug face. And to think that a moment ago, she fell for his charm. She couldn't get a better deal!? What was she, defective merchandise?

She smirked, pursing her lips in a thin hard line, then hissed, "Oh, really?"

***

"So, you think you're such a catch?" His wife's cheeks were flushed, a warm and rosy hue accentuating her anger. She jabbed Conrad straight into his chest with her index finger. "You had to buy your way into that marriage."

The blinding glare of the sun made it difficult to see Louise's face clearly. Conrad squinted and tugged at the tight knot of his tie, which constricted against his neck, making it hard for him to breathe.

That fire.

Certainly not what he expected at this wedding. He thought the most excitement he would get would be from choosing the food at the reception, as he had no clue what Maureen and Richard prepared, but he could imagine it would be a feast.

"You're underestimating me, my dear." He grinned and ran his finger against her smooth jawline. A tingling sensation of her soft skin under his touch made his heart race.

"Oh, I know your type!" She flicked his hand away and took another step back.

He caught her hand and stepped closer, only inches between their faces. She smelled of coconut and jasmine, a scent that made Conrad's head swim.

With her back against the Roman column, she had no way to go, but it felt like he was the one in danger. Who would have thought that the timid girl he had met a few weeks ago could be so fierce?

"And what type is that?"

Her hair escaped the elaborate plait, whipped by the wind. Conrad extended his hand to tuck away a loose strand, but then rested it on the smooth marble of the column behind her. She might have bitten his fingers if he touched her again.

"The I-have-money-so-I can-have-it-all type."

He chuckled. Nobody who knew him ever accused Conrad of being someone like that.

"You think a woman is just another item you can buy to add to your trophy collection?"

Her eyes could put a forest after the rain on fire, but she couldn't be more wrong than that.

"But I'm not one of them, Mister. You can't buy me."

That made him chortle. He leaned closer to her, his leg pressing against the hem of her dress, feeling the warmth emitting from her body.

"I hate to be the bearer of bad news, but you married me a moment ago." He pointed at the chapel entrance, filling up with loitering guests.

"That should have not happened." The dramatic tone of her voice made him narrow his eyebrows. "Let go of me." Louise pressed her hands against his chest, but instead of letting go, Conrad took them into his hands, pulling her even closer.

This was getting weirder by the minute, and he didn't need a scene right now.

"Stop making a scene. People are watching." He nodded toward the beaming guests. "They expect a happy couple here, so behave for a moment, and it'll be all over soon enough."

"You can bet on that!" She smirked, giving Conrad a one's over. "It will be over sooner than you think."

Conrad lowered his head, almost touching hers. "Look, I don't know what this is supposed to be, but you knew damn well that this was nothing but a financial transaction."

"Oh, really?" Her voice shook a little.

"Yes, really. We talked about this in the coffee shop not that long ago, and I asked if you were okay with this. Or maybe you forgot about that as well?"

"Well, no." She licked her lips. They looked so soft and inviting. He swallowed, feeling the rush of his blood, her scent overpowering him. How could he have missed that on the coffee date? This here, this was unexpected. Exciting but dangerous. Why would she play this game with him, though? Maybe she wasn't aware of what she did to him?

He took a step back, creating more space between them.

"But if I had a choice, you would be the last person on Earth I would have married."

The stubbornness was back, and he struggled to keep his mind on the conversation, especially so confusing.

"You had a choice. I asked." They were getting nowhere. "And why the hell did you say yes if you didn't want to?"

"Well … " She stared at him, batting her long eyelashes. That foot of distance between them wasn't enough, as with every inch of his body he ached for her, the touch of her skin, the taste of her tongue. He had to move away from her before he lost that shred of control he still had.

The crowd surged forward, and the air vibrated with the sound of their voices rising in unison.

"Kiss. Kiss. Kiss." The guests' voices blended in a jumbled mess of sound, a symphony of chaos.

A kiss?

He grinned at his wife.

"Don't you dare!" she growled at him, her eyes an emerald inferno.

Surely a game. The hell with caution. "The wedding guests demand it. My hands are tied."

Pressing fingers to her waist, Conrad pulled his wife closer, then, unable to resist, he slid his hands a little lower over the curves of her hips, which made him ache for the first night. Although, judging by the events so far, it wouldn't go the way he'd like. But they had time.

Lowering his head, Conrad pressed his lips against hers. She tried to move away, but he persisted, tasting every inch of them, circling with his tongue. Her lips, stiff at first, became soft and tender. His wife parted them a little for a split second, or maybe he had imagined it, then yanked her head away. The taste of Louise's lips lingered on Conrad's tongue for a little longer. Sweet and intoxicating.

Clapping and cheering erupted, echoing off the columns and walls of the chapel, creating a deafening roar.

"You bastard." Louise hissed into his ear and wriggled free, making him wobble and use the column as support while she broke free and stormed off toward her parents, her heels clicking against the stone floor.

Chapter 3

"Why haven't you said anything?" Annie crossed her arms, staring at her parents, who emerged from the chapel.

Her loud, angry voice made a few heads turn. Annie's father smiled at the crowd and laughed. Her mother joined, and they both cackled like she made the best joke ever.

"Darling, it's fine." Her father, Richard, in a stripy brown suit, put a hand on her shoulder and pushed her toward the stairs leading down to the park. Her mother, holding her hat down, wrapped her arm around Annie's other arm, and they whisked her away from the guests loitering near the chapel entrance.

Digging her heels into the uneven stone made no difference in slowing their descent, but as Annie wobbled on the stilettos, only the parental hands gripping her arms stopped her from tumbling down.

"I know you recognised me. I could see your face, Mother."

Her father patted Annie on the hand he was holding. "You seem flushed, honey." He looked back at the guests, who took that as a sign to follow. "Let's get you to an open space, or you might faint."

"I never—" Annie's voice turned into a high-pitched shriek when her left foot twisted under her, and she shot forward.

"Steady." Her mother, Maureen, shouted, trotting after Annie like in those comedy movies where everything happens at double speed. If Annie were the one watching the scene, it would make her cry from laughter, not horror.

Two steps later, they landed at the bottom without losing their limbs. Annie took a deep breath, steadying her racing heart and pushing down the contents of her stomach that threatened to escape.

Gusts of wind tormenting her hair lifted all the hairpins, and the veil floated into the air, then flitted toward the trees. A little girl with angelic hair giggled and sprinted after it; the girl's parents, whom Annie did not know, wobbled after her, their hands extended like they wanted to catch their daughter before she flew away with the veil.

"Now we can talk." Her father pinned Annie down with his fake smile glued on his cleanly shaved, double-chinned face.

"Talk?" Annie yanked her arms away and rubbed the red marks left by their gripping fingers. "There is nothing to talk about. We need to end this farce." She looked straight into that round smiley face. "Now."

"Slow down, darling. There is no need to rush."

Annie's father raised his manicured hand to his mouth as if sharing a secret.

"This can work for us even better. That sister of yours has brains."

A rare compliment in her father's mouth, considering he'd always seen Louise as someone merely drifting through life.

"Work for *you*. There is no *us* in all that. And don't you dare bring Louise into this! You sold her like an animal to that bastard. He's seventeen years older than her and clearly up to no good from what I could see."

Annie stepped closer to her father, invading his space. "You hear me. Seventeen years. She could have been his daughter."

"Stop being dramatic." Her mother cut into the conversation. "It wasn't supposed to last, anyway."

"Oh, really?" Annie raised her eyebrows and turned toward her mother, who was brushing off a speck from her polka-dot dress. "And what happened to what's been joined by the God should never be pulled apart by a human, Mother?"

Maureen smirked. "It was the only chance for that girl to have a proper church wedding." She put her hands together for a prayer, raising her head toward the skies. "God forgive me for wanting a good thing for my daughter in her condition."

"Her condition?" Annie chuckled. "She's gay. It's not an illness, Mother."

Maureen placed her hand to her heart, panting, with her eyes wide open.

"It's okay, my dear." Richard patted Maureen on her shoulder and pointed his index finger at Annie, narrowing his eyebrows. "Don't use such language in front of your mother."

He took a deep breath and smiled, waving at a group of passing wedding guests.

"As I said, nothing is lost yet." Richard rubbed his hands and cackled. "Who would have thought your sister had the guts to put you in her place?"

"I told you, keep her out of it. You've done enough damage. And I'm here to end this." Annie pursed her lips, glaring at him.

"I don't think so, darling. After all, it's for your sister's benefit as well as yours."

"For yours, you mean?" Annie crossed her arms. "And what exactly is this?"

He grabbed her arm, leaning over and lowering his voice as more guests gathered at the bottom of the stairs.

"You must have heard that we need the Lilac Croft cottage to unlock the inheritance."

Annie nodded, remembering her conversation with Louise.

"And the only way to bring it back to our family is through marriage. So, without it, there will be no inheritance for you or your sister."

Annie smirked. "And you want me to believe that?"

Her father put his finger to his lips and lowered his voice even more. "Let's talk about it a bit later, when we have more privacy. You won't regret it, I promise." Richard glanced around. "After all, the deed is done, so there is no rush. Nobody needs to know just yet, am I right?"

That fake double-chin smile split his face. "Just keep it as is for a little longer. It will be better that way, trust me."

Trusting her father was never a wise choice.

"Why? And for how long?"

The words left Annie's mouth before she could stop them.

"Not long." He patted her arm like she was a kid needing reassurance. She shouldn't indulge his twisted ideas. And now he would think she'd be willing to listen. Annie sighed.

"What won't take long?" An upbeat male voice next to her ear made Annie stumble to a side. Conrad grinned at her as if he didn't have a care in the world. His tie was no longer on his neck, and his shirt, unbuttoned from the top, revealed a black woven leather necklace.

"Dinner." Richard pushed his rim glasses higher on his nose. "We were just saying that dinner will be served soon, so we should head to the party tent." He gestured toward the white marquee, a stone's throw away, at the end of the sandy path.

"Sounds great. There is nothing like a wedding to whet your appetite." Conrad smacked his lips and winked at Annie.

"Don't even think about it." Her voice as hard as the ground in the middle of a draught.

Somehow, whenever that man opened his mouth, he pushed Annie's buttons. She couldn't place her finger on what exactly rattled her so much, but if she had to pick one thing, it would be that condescending smirk. He made her feel like she was his intriguing new toy to show off to his mates, and not a living, breathing person.

But what did she expect? She always sucked at choosing the right man, always mistaking a reflection in the water for the sky, and then living through the consequences. Some of them would catch up with her pretty soon, leaving her no time for games.

Conrad leaned over with that glint in his annoyingly mesmerising eyes. "Here, you lost this." He handed her the veil, brushing her skin with his fingers and sending sparks through her entire body. Annie gasped and pulled away.

What was wrong with her? Every time he touched her, her own body reacted to him like he was a delicious candy.

Before she could say anything, her father broke the awkward moment. "About that food. You need to try everything. That catering—" he placed his hand on Conrad's arm and pushed him to a side, away from Annie and her mother.

Annie massaged her temples. She really should end this right now. Her mouth opened, but she bit her tongue. Knowing her father, he'd most certainly wriggle out of this somehow—he always did. No, she needed to make it more public, in front of all the guests.

"Where is your shawl? You should cover yourself up." Mother's commanding voice made Annie shiver. It was so lovely when her mother pretended to be offended, but it never lasted long.

She looked down at her dress, dishevelled by all that tugging and pulling. She straightened the skirt and pulled down the short sleeves, as the edges had rolled up a little.

Her mother shook her head and smacked her lips. "A God-loving woman would not wear a dress like this."

"Oh, really?" Annie looked down at her cleavage, barely kept within the fabric. "I thought you picked it with all that sparkle in it?"

"Well, I did, but not for you. This dress wasn't designed for your big—" Her mother pursed her lips.

"Breasts?" Annie said it loud enough to make a few heads turn.

Maureen gasped. "A well-behaving—"

Annie strolled away before her mother could finish, carrying the veil in both hands. She stepped over the pathway edge made of pebbles and wobbled on her heels, sinking into the grassland.

A little girl in a pale blue dress with curly blonde hair, the same girl that had gone after Annie's veil, blew on the fluffy heads of dandelions covering the ground.

"Hello." Annie chirped and crouched next to the girl. Blue eyes gazed at Annie, and little fingers reached out to touch the white lace.

"Would you like to wear it?"

The eyes grew wider, and the girl's entire face lit up while she nodded.

Nope, no resemblance to any of her cousins. Maybe she was from Conrad's family?

Annie pulled the remaining pins from her hair, which fell onto her neck in a cascade of brown curls. "What's your name?"

"Natalie." An angel whispered, following Annie's hand with her eyes.

"Beautiful name. Is Conrad your uncle?"

Natalie turned her head from side to side while keeping her eyes fixed on the veil.

So, either she was the daughter of someone on the staff or Annie's parents used the wedding as an advertising opportunity for their catering and invited strangers.

Annie smiled and draped the veil on the top of Natalie's head. "Hold it here." She placed the girl's fingers on one side of the veil to hold it in place while she slid the pins in.

"You did great." Annie praised the wide-eyed Natalie after she secured the veil and stood up. "Would you like to see it?"

A vigorous nod made Annie chuckle. She rummaged through her purse before pulling out a make-up mirror and handing it to the girl.

Soon I might have a daughter like you.

Annie rested her hands on her belly while watching Natalie giggling and twirling, with the veil floating in the air.

Or a son.

***

Conrad watched his wife placing a veil on a little girl's head. When she removed pins from her plait, Louise's wavy brown hair fell like a chocolate river onto her snow-white back with a zip stretching down to the curves of her buttocks.

If he pulled on that zip from the very top of the dress, what would his fingers discover? A silky smooth lacy see-through piece or a sensible soft white cotton?

34 D.

Conrad didn't need to check to know. And certainly not a push-up. The dress properly cupped Louise's body, and there was no space left for artificial fillers.

"Is everything set for Monday?"

His father-in-law's voice brought him back. His mind went blank for a moment, and he stuttered, "Monday?"

Conrad had no idea what they had talked about and how much of the conversation, or rather the monologue, he'd lost.

"Yes, to transfer the cottage as agreed. We just talked about it, son."

"Right, right." He put his hand on Richard's arm. "I'm sorry. I was watching my beautiful wife."

"Of course, of course, my boy." Richard clasped his hands together, a gleam in his eye. "Now that you're happily married, I trust we'll soon be working on even greater business ventures together."

Conrad wasn't so sure about that. There was something off about his wife, or was it just a game to spice things up? Conrad liked himself a challenge, one that would end in the bedroom even better, but what if this wasn't a game? What if she would ditch him before the month was up?

"I'm looking forward to it." Specifically, to the part when his wife's marriage trust fund would land in Conrad's bank account.

"So, for what time on Monday shall I book the will reading?" Richard asked.

The guy knew how to close a deal, no doubt about that.

"How about you book it for Tuesday, or better yet, Wednesday?"

Richard pulled his rim glasses down, and his eyes focused on Conrad's face. "Is there a problem?"

Yeah, a big one. Your daughter seems to hate my guts.

"Not at all, but I had no chance to check with my solicitor before the wedding. You know all this preparation." Conrad raised his hands and smiled. "So, I cannot be one hundred percent sure all will be ready on Monday."

"Ah, I see your concern, but we can always rebook if things are not ready."

"Why such a rush? How about we set it for Wednesday, or better yet, the end of the week, so we don't have to rebook anything?" He beamed at Richard. "Am I right? Right?" He shook his father-in-law's hands, looking straight into those rimmed glasses. "If you'll forgive me, my lady is awaiting me, and we have a party to attend."

Conrad spun around and strode away at a quick pace. When he was only a few metres away from Louise, he slowed down before finally stopping less than a foot away. With her back to him, his wife laughed, and the chocolate river meandered on her head. Conrad swallowed and flexed his fingers. Would she mind if he touched her hair?

"Look." An angelic-faced girl pointed at him with one small finger, and his wife turned toward him.

"Geez." Louise wobbled, flailing her arms as Conrad lunged forward to catch her.

"I used to get a warmer reception," he teased, grinning at her stunned expression. "Shall we?"

His wife wrinkled her freckled nose while freeing herself from his embrace. "Shall we what?"

He pointed toward the marquee in the gardens. "The guests won't start without us, and I don't know about you, but I'm starving."

"Food, food!" The little girl cartwheeled her way toward the white tent. It made Louise giggle, softening her features. He could fall for that soft smile.

"Right, ready to get this party started?" Conrad extended his hand to hold hers, but she pulled her hand away, grabbed her skirts, lifted them in the air, and marched toward the sandy path.

Conrad exhaled, shaking his head. "Wait."

No slowing down on his account. In a few long strides, he reached her side and then reduced his pace to match her step. His hands dangled at his sides. "I don't know what game you're playing, but I'm not a monster. If you're not ready, just say it."

"Ready for what?" She looked at him, stopping abruptly, forcing Conrad to take a step back and turn on his heel to look back at her.

How could he say this without ticking her off even more? Maybe she was simply scared, and this was how she acted it out.

"Look, you might be wondering about tonight, us being husband and wife and all."

She blinked, and a slight chuckle escaped her mouth. He was right; she was afraid of him. What a fool.

"But as we only just met, I'm not going to ask you to do anything you don't want."

Her eyes and mouth opened wider with clear understanding, and then she looked down, her complexion darkening.

Good job, man. He would pat himself on the back if he could reach. Beneath that mature makeup, she was still a young woman. Maureen had mentioned Louise had little interest in boys, likely too focused on her art, so she probably didn't have much experience—if any at all.

Conrad's hand stroked her upper arm in a reassuring gesture, which she didn't shake off.

Good sign.

"Was that it? I'm sorry for being so insensitive."

Conrad extended his finger and turned her face toward him. She batted her long dark eyelashes and half smiled at him. A dimple appeared on her left cheek. She had the same expression as in the coffee shop when he had asked about men in her life.

"Finally, I recognise that innocent girl I met."

She cocked her head, biting on her lips in a way that made his blood boil. If only she knew what she was doing to him.

"I hope you're not counting on me still being a virgin?" Louise smirked, shaking off his hands like she wanted to rid herself of a nightmare, and took a step back.

Bloody hell. He chuckled, rubbing his neck. From skittish to bold in less than ten seconds.

"We all have our past. It spices up life, doesn't it?"

Conrad extended his hand to grab hers. As before, she tried to pull it away, but he was faster and held it in his. She fought to free it, but he only pulled her closer to him.

"Let go." She gasped through her clenched teeth.

"Can't do. We've got married, and people are watching." Conrad nodded his head toward a group standing in front of the marquee and waving at them. "I'm not expecting you to snog me in public, but you could at least pretend to act like my wife."

She stopped wriggling and resumed her march toward the tent. "Fine."

It struck a nerve: women and their "fine" word.

"Seriously, woman, what's wrong with you? I wasn't expecting love at first sight, but this?" Conrad waved his hand, keeping pace with his wife. "This is clearly not what I had in mind when we discussed our marriage. Last time we talked, you were up for it, but it seems you had a change of heart."

She sighed and looked at him from under those lashes. "Sorry, I might have overreacted a bit earlier. It's the nerves." A hesitant titter escaped her lips. "After all, not every day one marries a guy they never met."

Sure, he knew plenty about nerves, but not because of the wedding. Strangely, Conrad hadn't felt any wedding jitters or doubts about whether he was doing the right thing before the ceremony. If anything, he was eager to get to know Louise and possibly build something together.

Yet ever since she had spoken to him after they had left the chapel, things seemed to have gone from bad to worse at lightning speed.

Conrad swallowed and pulled on her hand, making Louise stop again and look at him. "I need to know if you'll honour your part of the deal."

Her cheeks darkened, and she averted her gaze. "My part?" Her voice was shaky and barely audible.

"Well, will you?" He was done with her so-called innocence. She wasn't that for sure.

"So, my part is to look pretty and give you pleasure in bed. And what is your part?"

He chuckled. "This is not what I asked about, although it would be nice, and I hope we'll get there."

That green in her eyes darkened so much it was almost black.

He raised his hands in a defensive gesture as she turned hers into fists. "But maybe not today. What I meant is about sticking to the financial arrangements I have made with your parents and your part in them."

"Ah, the financial arrangements." Her shoulders relaxed, and she even smiled a bit, making her face brighten up.

"Yes, and you know that cottage is not a small thing, so I need to have your word I can count on this marriage."

Louise cocked her head, and a cascade of hair fell onto one side. "Okay."

"Okay?"

Conrad stood there with his mouth open. Her recent behaviour screamed something quite the opposite. Was she for real this time, or maybe she misunderstood him?

"Yeah, I heard about that cottage. The one where my Grandma Ann—" Her voice faltered for a moment. "Where she lived as a child. So, what about it?"

Finally, they were getting somewhere.

"So, I need your word that you'll stick to your side of this financial agreement."

Louise bit on her lip. The gesture would make him want to kiss those lips if furrowed eyebrows, and a confused look in her eyes did not accompany it.

Shit.

"Your parents didn't tell you?"

She waved her hand and shrugged. "I'm sorry, I'm sure they did, but I was so occupied with all the wedding stuff that I didn't pay attention to all the details."

His wife took his hand in hers and made a step forward toward the tent, pulling him with her.

"So, what exactly about that cottage in regards to those financial arrangements?"

Her hand felt warm and soft, but he fought off an urge to caress her inner palm with his finger.

"I meant the deal we made. That cottage for your marriage trust fund, as agreed." A strong pull on his hand made him stumble, almost losing his balance.

"My marriage fund?" She gasped, breathing fast.

Great, just great.

"You didn't know?" Her eyes were wide open. It was as clear as the blue sky on a sunny day that she didn't. He had to fix this before she started screaming or, worse, crying.

"But it's all good. Your parents told me there is more for you in your grandma's inheritance."

Louise looked at him, but he doubted she heard him. Conrad put his hands on her shoulders and gazed into those absent eyes.

"I promise I'll look after you. And you'll be able to spend days doing your art or taking pictures, or whatever you want."

She was frozen in time and space. At least she wasn't screaming.

"And I'll help with the gallery. I promise you."

Her facial expression hadn't improved much. Conrad hoped she wouldn't faint.

"My marriage trust fund?"

He raked through his hair, wondering what else he could say to reassure her.

"All of it?"

Conrad nodded and exhaled. And he thought this day couldn't get any worse.

The corners of Louise's lips curled up in a polite smile that hadn't reached her eyes. "Excuse me, I need to talk to my parents."

"Now what?" He murmured to himself, kicking a pebble.

Chapter 4

Over my dead body.

Lifting her skirts a little, Annie trudged toward the marquee, her curls bobbing on her head with every step.

If only she had listened when Grandma Ann asked her to consider if Liam was the one. But she was so in love, or in hindsight, Annie was in love with her idea about Liam and the marriage. The adventures they had planned together, going to exotic places, living the high life.

And they had travelled, for four years, almost to the day. But instead of admiring the wonders of nature or experiencing the bustle of exotic cities, somehow the day would always end in a dingy casino or a bar with a slot machine. Annie had missed the signs, and when one day she had checked their savings account, half of her marriage trust fund had already been gone.

Annie's lips formed a thin white line, and a bitter taste filled her mouth. She gripped the lacy material of her dress so hard that her knuckles turned white.

There was no way she would allow Louise's trust fund to be wasted like that.

At first, Liam tried to pull the wool over Annie's eyes, explaining that the costs of travel, hotel rooms, food, and what he called attractions were high. But accounting for the missing hundred and fifty thousand pounds—even to a love-struck Annie—was impossible when they had only taken about ten trips, half of them within a hundred miles of home, staying in hostels or renting rooms through an app. It simply didn't add up.

It had taken him another year to come clean and promise to quit gambling, but one more year later, her entire trust fund was gone—along with her husband. All three hundred thousand pounds. Gone.

Annie clenched her fists, her jaw tightening even more. The story was repeating itself, this time with their parents' blessing—a man stealing a naive woman's money.

Even after Liam had left her—a broken divorcee at twenty-seven, drowning in unpaid bills and with debt collectors at her door—Annie had still loved him. Or so she had believed back then. Now, she couldn't even remember what she had liked about him. If anything at all.

That would not happen to her sister. Not on Annie's watch.

She took a deep breath. The scent of magnolia, garlic bread, and fried bacon tickled her nose. Her stomach rumbled and her feet followed her nose and stopped at the entrance to the tennis court-sized gazebo with its sides open to the blossoming magnolia trees—white, pink, and cream.

A dozen or more garden tables surrounded a small, raised decking area near the entrance. A group of musicians in white suits with cream bow ties tuned their violins and cellos. Annie rolled her eyes. A quartet—how unimaginative.

Louise, in her paint-stained denims, with brush dripping Persian blue onto a warehouse floor, swaying to an indie rock thudding through the speakers, wouldn't feel more out of place here even if she tried. What Mother called sophisticated, a majority would call plain boring. Annie shrugged. At least she wasn't paying for this.

Her gaze followed the clutter of the cutlery and the delicate clinking of china. A long buffet table filled with a variety of platters and bowls ran along the far side and made her lick her lips. Annie navigated between small groups of guests, smiling at her parents' acquaintances and relatives she had never met without stopping for a chat.

Directed by the increasing smell of bacon wafting from the middle section of the long buffet, Annie squeezed through tiny gaps around tables, avoiding the white, cream, and pale pink balloons bobbing over most of the chairs.

There was one thing her father would never refuse—a bacon roll. And there he was, bacon hanging from one side of his mouth.

Annie marched straight toward him. "You had no right!"

Her father stopped chewing and stared at her.

Maureen's polka dot dress emerged from behind a pot plant. "It's not a shouting contest, young lady. Keep your voice down." Her mother pursed her lips before picking a miniature canape from a porcelain dessert plate she held in her hand.

"You've done enough damage." Annie reduced the volume of her voice, but not the intensity. "Keep your hands off her money."

"It's an excellent investment." Richard took another bite, swallowed, and washed down with a gulp of beer from a double-bottom glass tankard. "You need to try these rolls. I bet Conrad would love to have this catering in his pubs."

Annie glanced at the table oozing with canapes, organised by their content: vegetarian on the left next to samosas and salad bowls, salmon and tuna in the centre, supported by sushi selection, and meaty ones on the right, next to sausage and bacon rolls.

Her stomach growled. She couldn't believe she could be hungry, even when she was burning with anger for her sister.

"It's her marriage fund."

Richard belched. "Excuse me." He wiped his mouth with a pink napkin. "And it needs proper investing, something neither your sister nor you are good at. If you'd let us help you invest yours, you might still have your money."

"Or you'd have it, and I'd be broken." Annie transferred a mini sponge cake onto a dessert plate and picked on its squishy surface with her fingers.

"Instead, you let that ex-husband of yours invest it in God knows what."

You have no idea.

Only Grandma Ann knew what had happened to Liam and the money. If her parents even got a sniff of the actual events, she would never hear the end of this.

"Not every investment pays back." Better they thought she sucked at investing than that she'd been used by a loser. "But don't change the topic."

Annie scooped the entire mini cake and shoved it into her mouth, letting the vanilla cream dissolve on her tongue.

"Behave." Her mother's voice, as sharp as a whip, made Annie twitch. "Use the dessert fork. It's not a fast food."

"Isn't it?" Annie smirked and licked her fingers, covered with cream. Maureen's gaze would torch someone else, but for Annie, it was a typical Sunday afternoon type of interaction. They had mended, sort of, their relationship after Annie's divorce, on Grandma Ann's plead, but it could never be called a pleasant one.

Her father smacked his lips and loaded his plate with two more rolls. "It doesn't matter now, though, since you took over Louise's place. But it's actually better this way."

"What is?"

Her father glanced around, took another gulp of his beer, and with a plate in his other hand, he strolled toward the front. He stopped at an empty table covered with white linen, surrounded by four cushioned chairs, two dressed with cream silk satchels, one for the groom and another for her, the bride.

Annie picked two more mini cakes, a couple of clementines, and a bundle of green grapes before gliding after him, with her mother's Patchouli scent close behind.

"So, why would you even consider giving so much money to a stranger? Why all of it?"

Annie ripped the satchel before sitting on the bride's chair. It made no sense. Her father was too greedy to risk the money unless he had a reason.

Richard poured himself a glass of burgundy red wine from a carafe on the table and gestured toward Annie. She covered her glass with the palm of her hand.

"It was the only way we could get the cottage."

"Do you mean The Lilac Croft? Grandma Ann's childhood home?" Annie swallowed hard. Even after nearly six months, mentioning Grandma's name was still difficult. "Conrad said the cottage was part of the deal."

Annie peeled a clementine with her fingernails, separating each section before putting it in her mouth.

"So, you know." He gulped half the glass in one go and bit into a bacon roll.

"I don't know anything. I don't understand why marriage was necessary and frankly, I don't want to know." Annie rose from her seat, but her mother's steel grip on her shoulder pushed her down.

"Wait." Maureen lowered herself onto a free chair. "Even though you had not attended my mother's funeral, God bless her soul, you must have heard about her will."

Annie nodded while her stomach twisted with sorrow. If only she had stayed in touch. If only she had not been so busy playing house and planning their future. Hers, Darren's, and their unborn …

Annie exhaled slowly, fighting to keep the tears at bay while staring at the stoned paved floor under her feet. This wasn't the place and time. And certainly not in front of her parents.

"Your grandma became the only beneficiary after my father and her husband Edward died a few years ago, but despite my pleading, she had not shared that wealth with those most in need."

Annie forced a chuckle. "By those most in need, you mean you? Please, Mother, a bit of dignity."

"After my mother's demise, God rest her soul—" Maureen continued without a single glance at Annie, who managed to put her grief aside, and shifted her focus to squashing juicy grapes with her teeth, one after another. "—an estate executor informed us there is a requirement in her will that needs to be fulfilled within six months in order for us to inherit any of her wealth."

"She screwed us all, so to speak. That old hag," Richard piped in, unfazed by his wife's stern look. "The requirement was for that cottage to be returned to the family."

Annie sniggered, imagining that moment when the estate executor had told her parents about this condition. But this still hadn't explained the wedding.

"So, why didn't you simply buy it from Conrad?" Annie licked her dry lips and reached for a jug with sparkling water resting at the centre of the table.

Her father's grim laugh made Annie raise her eyebrows. "Your grandma wasn't the only weirdo. Conrad inherited the cottage from his grandfather George who died several years ago. And in his will, he made a condition that Conrad could never sell the cottage but only gift it to his wife."

Richard clicked his tongue. "Hence the marriage." He shrugged and shoved half of the eclair into his mouth.

An eclair? How did I miss them?

"And to reciprocate with similar value, we had signed away Louise's trust fund, which Conrad will invest in Whispering Pines Country Club. A money machine if you ask me." He mumbled, licking the cream. "Win, win."

Annie grinned. Nothing was more perfect than messing with her parents' plans.

"But there is no fund, is there? And I'll break the news to Conrad about it all being fake in about—" She glanced at her white smartwatch. Five unread messages. Her heart skipped a bit."—well, very soon."

"What's the rush, darling? Why not enjoy this evening?"

Annie narrowed her eyebrows. "Cause it's wrong."

"Don't you care about your sister at all? Her future is in your hands." Her mother pulled out a cream embroidered handkerchief and brought it to her eye while blinking rapidly. "Poor girl counts on you."

Annie smirked. "Mother, we both know you wouldn't shed a tear in full make-up. Plus, Lou sent me here to pretend, remember?"

"Exactly." Her father clapped his hands. "Smart girl. She wanted you to play her part. At least for a few days. A week tops. Then you can tell him whatever you want."

"I'm not staying in this marriage for a week!" Annie shook her head. "What's the difference, anyway?"

Oh, shut up, woman.

Why did she ask that question? Now he would use it as an opportunity to make his sell.

"Oh, it's huge, my dear." Her father leaned closer, pushing his glasses up. "Once Conrad passes his cottage over to you and the will is executed, we won't need his help anymore. You can tell him that you're not a good fit or something, and nobody needs to know what actually happened."

"And you believe he would simply roll over and forget about the marriage fund you promised him? Doesn't he have a contract or something gifting him that money?"

"Of course he does. He wasn't willing to take my word for it."

Annie giggled. "What a shocker."

"But—" Richard raised a finger. "—You know the marriage fund clause. It can only be accessed after the marriage lasted for a month or there was a baby on the way. No marriage, no money."

"Are you nuts?"

A few guests sitting nearby turned their heads toward them, but Richard waved them away, beaming, and patted Annie on the shoulder. "Just a joke. We're joking."

"So, you're joking?" Annie scratched her head.

"No, of course, I'm not. It was for them." He gestured toward the other table.

"So, you really expect me to con a man out of his grandfather's cottage and leave him high and dry?"

That was rich, even for her father. Unless he was desperate. Was their business as good as they claimed? Or maybe the COVID had taken a toll, and they were broke? Annie's smartwatch vibrated with a call, so she hid her hand under the table.

"Well, it's not as bad as it sounds. This cottage is actually a burden to him, you know, as he can't sell it."

"Are you trying to convince me I would be doing him a favour?" Annie burst into laughter. "You really lost your mind."

"Don't speak like that to your father, young lady." The handkerchief was long gone.

"Not that young, Mother. Don't let that fake face fool you. I'll be thirty-five next year. Thirty. Five. Mother."

Annie's smartwatch buzzed again. She shot up from her chair. "Well, I'll leave you to your delusions. I need to use a bathroom, and then I have a reveal to make."

Before she could leave, her father caught her hand. "Annie, think about it. Not only would you have a cottage to live in, but a hefty sum from your grandma's inheritance. Without the cottage though you'll get absolutely nothing. Opportunities like this don't come often. "

His words stirred up unwanted memories. Liam had always talked about once-in-a-lifetime opportunities while taking her money to *invest*, as he'd called it—yeah, in those horses on the racetrack. She'd trusted him against her better judgment. Love made people stupid and blind.

Annie yanked her hand. "I'd rather be poor and honest than turn into you." She grabbed her skirts and leapt toward the back of the gazebo, where she hoped to find a quiet spot, as her phone would not stop ringing.

***

Conrad's fingers tapped rapidly on the side of his wineglass while he scanned the bustling wedding reception, his eyes darting from one guest to the next, searching for his bride. He caught sight of her chatting with her parents at one of the tables, her body tense and her arms crossed defensively over her chest. His heart sank.

The scent of roasted meats, freshly baked bread, and sweet pastries filled the air, creating a sensory experience that only heightened Conrad's anxiety.

How the hell was he going to convince her to play along?

From the way Louise had reacted and her current posture, the marriage fund forming part of the financial deal was like the final nudge to a boulder teetering on the edge of a steep hill. And now he had to push that boulder back up, far from the cliff's edge. He couldn't afford to let it crash down that hill, taking his livelihood with it.

Conrad sauntered over to the buffet, picking at the various dishes laid out along the long table, sampling each one from a business perspective. The delicate scent of magnolia blooms drifted through the open sides of the gazebo, mingling with the mouthwatering aroma of the food.

The warm sun shone through the trees, casting dappled light on the guests as they chatted and laughed, enjoying the food and drink, blissfully unaware of the turmoil brewing within Conrad's mind.

And what if he failed?

A sudden rush of adrenaline washed over him, making him gasp for breath. He couldn't even bear to think about it. No. Simply, no. He still had a chance. Didn't he?

"Conrad, my boy!" Richard clapped him on the shoulder, nearly knocking off his plate. "You simply must try these bacon butties! What do you think about adding them to the menu at your pubs?"

Conrad took a hearty bite, crunching on crispy bacon with no fat. The roll reminded him of sourdough bread from his grandpa's favourite bakery. Conrad licked the butter from his upper lip.

"Yeah, the butties and the pies would certainly be a great addition. Although not so sure about those tiny canapes, maybe for a special event, but not my usual type of guests."

A broad smile made Richard's face even rounder. "I knew you'd like that caterer. We can certainly send them your way and many more. The sooner you sort out the paperwork for the cottage, the sooner we can invest in that country club together, Conrad."

"Well, not that soon. Haven't you said it was a month before we could access the money from the fund? Could we speed it up somehow?"

Stuffing a mini quiche into his mouth, Richard shook his head. "Rules are rules, my boy. These steak and mushroom pies are incredible! One bite of honest working man's food."

"Without money from the fund, I can't really buy that place, can I?" Conrad tried a quiche—too dry for his taste, so he washed it down with wine.

"No, but the moment we have the inheritance, we can put the offer in for it and then finalise once the fund matures. By then, we would be ready to roll." The excitement and jolly in Richard's voice would melt the ice cap.

Conrad nodded, trying to force a smile. "About that. It seems my wife had no idea her marriage fund was part of the deal." He sipped from his half-empty glass.

Richard waved a dismissive hand as if it was of no importance. "Ah, well, you know how women are. They don't always need to know all the details."

"She seemed pretty upset, so now I'm not sure if I still have a wife."

His father-in-law chuckled. "Nonsense. She's just being dramatic. She'll come around. I'm sure." He scratched his double chin before crossing his hands on his belly. "What matters is that you keep your end of the bargain."

A gust of wind swept through the gazebo, sending a few napkins fluttering like birds. Conrad's brows furrowed, as he couldn't shake off the nagging feeling that something was off. More off than usual, as Conrad was already accustomed to Richard's door-to-door salesman style, a type who would try to sell you a snowboard in the desert.

Music, one of Vanessa Mae's creations, filled the air. A sudden false violin note reverberated in Conrad's ears, and he glanced at the musicians who continued to play, unfazed.

"I think it's my cue to find my wife so we can have our first dance." Conrad put the glass down and scanned the room, but he couldn't spot the white dress anywhere. It would be ironic if she had legged it before the first dance.

"Maureen!" Richard waved at his wife, still sitting at the table nearby. "Would you be so kind as to go and get our daughter? Conrad is getting worried."

Maureen got up from her seat with her lips pursed. "That girl, honestly. Disappearing for so long at her own wedding."

"Please, don't trouble yourself. I can go and get her." Conrad didn't need a chaperone while talking to his wife.

Richard cackled. "If you want to get on her good side, you'd rather not chase after her into the ladies."

Conrad blinked. "Oh."

What else could he say? Twiddling his thumbs, he watched Maureen disappear into the adjacent building.

Richard leaned over. "So, about the cottage ... "

Conrad's stomach twisted, and he licked his dry lips. That man was relentless, and he had no way to hide.

"How about I join you at that meeting with your solicitor, Conrad? Just in case there are any questions that need resolving."

After filling a glass with water from a crystal carafe on the buffet table, Conrad looked straight into Richard's eyes.

"Thank you for your offer, but no need. My solicitors are professionals, and if there are questions, I'm sure my wife could answer them." He took a sip. "After I convince her that her money is safe with me."

Richard didn't even blink. Instead, his eyes gleamed with a mixture of excitement and greed.

"I've got an idea. How about you take my daughter to that country club for lunch to reassure her it will be a good use of her money? Maybe even ask her if she wants to decorate it or something so she would feel more like an owner?"

It wasn't a bad idea, actually. Conrad scratched his chin. Not that he planned to use the money to buy that country club. Not only was it not for sale, but his inns desperately needed cash injection, and it was either Louise's fund or a loan from vulture capitals wanting 60% of his business in return. And that would be the end of him.

"Maybe we could hang her paintings or photographs in the main room, turning it into an art gallery."

Richard patted him on the shoulder, laughing. "I knew you'd find a way."

He forced a half smile back at his father-in-law. It still didn't answer the question of what was really going on here. Something was fishy, and his cottage was at stake.

So was his business if he pulled out now, and to save it, he would do a lot more than get married and give the cottage away. A lot more.

Chapter 5

The moment Annie reached the shaded entrance, the buzzing stopped. She leapt inside, startled by a man in his early twenties in a white uniform emerging from a side entrance carrying a round tray full of porcelain bowls filled to the brim with a variety of sauces and dressings.

An aroma of ginger and cinnamon lingered in the air for a long minute after he disappeared into the crowd. She took a few more steps into the building, intrigued by the metallic clatter, hissing, and a deep male voice singing Mamma Mia alongside the radio.

Annie peaked through a double door on the left-hand side and discovered a temporary kitchen with portable stoves full of pots with bubbling content and a row of coffee makers filling the glass pots with golden liquid.

A big man with a bushy beard wearing a white apron danced between pots, pans, and serving platters, whistling under his breath and joining with the chorus. On his next turn, he spotted Annie, and his face lightened up.

"Isn't that our beautiful bride? How can I help you, Miss?" He strolled toward her, holding a ladle dripping with gravy.

"Thank you, I'm fine. I was looking for a restroom."

He raised the ladle, pointing deeper into the building, and Annie dodged, barely avoiding a thick dollop of gravy landing on her dress.

"Oh, I'm so sorry, Miss." He took a step forward, but Annie raised her hand to stop him.

"I'm fine, so far. Thank you." She smiled and dashed away from him and deeper into the building. When she reached the ladies, a gust of fresh-scented air cooled her down. She followed that scent and, in a few steps, stood in another doorway leading to the back of the building. A refreshing smell of basil made Annie take full lungs of air and search for the herbs patch. She couldn't spot any herb garden, but less than a few metres away, a wooden bench stood with its back against an old and branchy oak tree.

With every step closer to the bench, the bustle of the party and the kitchen clatter became more muffled and distant until only the crickets remained.

Annie wrinkled her nose. The brown-painted bench was covered with fallen leaves and acorns. Instead of sitting, she simply rested her purse against it and searched for the basil scent again with her senses. Basil smelled like home. Whenever she had returned from her trips, Grandma Ann would have welcomed her with her signature tortellini with creamy bacon and basil—a dish she had always called food for the soul.

If only Annie had stayed in touch with Louise. She might have had a chance to say goodbye to Grandma Ann. Annie's shoulders sagged and tears well off in her eyes, from grief but also guilt. She had missed the funeral of the most important person in her entire life. She would never forgive herself for that. If only …

Annie blinked and brushed the wetness with her hand. She couldn't turn back the clock and she had grieved long enough over her grandma but also her miscarriage. Annie swallowed hard and shook her head, brushing off an unwanted thought. Going back to that dark place where she had spent months of her life would not change a thing.

And her life had a new purpose now. Annie traced squiggly lines on her belly with her finger. She didn't know if it was a girl or a boy, but she knew she loved that little person with all her heart and would do anything to protect that life.

Taking another deep breath, she retrieved her phone. The number that called her had no name associated with it, and it could only mean one thing. It must have been Darren.

She stared at the phone, expecting it to ring any minute now, but it stared back at her in silence and then pinged. Another message arrived. Annie tapped the notification and gasped.

There were a dozen new messages from him. He hadn't signed them, but only Darren would beg her to stop playing games and come back home, in one sentence, only to threaten she would regret she had ever left the moment he found her in the next.

He knows.

A sudden shiver ran through her and goosebumps covered her forearms while a few drops of sweat appeared on her forehead.

Annie had thought she would have at least three more days before he found out. The note he had left on the fridge had mentioned a two-week long business trip.

When she had decided to help Louise with her marriage trouble, she had banked on having those three more days to leave town and find a new home somewhere far away.

Somewhere he could never find her. Them. He could never find them.

While flipping through the messages, one made Annie's heart hammer in her chest.

Darren: "Who is he?"

How had he found out about this wedding? Annie shrunk in herself, tensed, and glanced around. A peaceful afternoon, with a light breeze on her flushed cheeks and the sun peeking through the leaves. No dark figures hiding in the shadows. She exhaled, licking her dry lips.

With trembling hands, she returned to the messages.

Darren: "I forgive you Just come back to me I miss you"

Annie smirked. That was the biggest lie one could tell. He had never missed her. He only missed the power he had over her. At first, Annie hadn't recognised it, mistaking it for protectiveness—and even cherishing it. It was so different from her ex-husband, Liam, who had only cared about his next adventure and Annie's money, which he could splurge on a new gadget or his gambling habit.

Darren, on the other hand, had always bought her expensive things and convinced her to quit her job. Well, not exactly—she hadn't had a choice after he had punched a customer to 'protect her dignity.' No one had ever stood up for her like that before. He had made her feel like a modern princess, whisking her away for weekends to watch plays in the West End or dine at posh restaurants in London.

Annie forced a grim cackle, shaking her head over her own naivety. Little by little, he had lured her into his trap and then had locked the cage, throwing the key away.

Annie straightened up, raising her chin. She wasn't in that cage anymore. She had realised her prince was an ordinary thug, and fate had given her the opportunity to escape.

And now, even though the clock started ticking again, there was still time. Darren had no clue about the wedding. Otherwise, he wouldn't be so forgiving.

But what if he could trace her phone? Annie swallowed hard and reached for a power button when her mobile rang—an unknown number.

It could be him. It would be him. She wiped her sweaty palms against her dress, leaving a darker smudge.

She couldn't avoid him forever. With a shaking finger, she accepted the call and uttered a faint, "Hello?"

"How is the ex-bride doing?" Louise's chirpy voice washed over Annie, and she felt dizzy. Without thinking, she pressed her hand on the rough bark with a cushy moss as she worried her legs might give way.

After a few deep breaths, the dizziness subsided. "Where are you?"

"Oh, you wouldn't believe it. It's the most magnificent place on Earth. And so peaceful, and nobody frowns at me and Meggie holding hands or embracing each other. They simply mind their own business."

Annie smiled, imagining Louise and her girlfriend wading in the shallow waters with sandals in hand and squinting in the warm sun.

"I'm so happy for you, sis."

"But enough about me. How was the wedding? Has Mother made a scene?"

Annie chuckled, remembering the horror on her mother's face. "It was close, but no. Father talked her out of it."

"Of course he did. What about Conrad? It must have been a shock. I feel a bit sorry for him."

"Oh, don't be. That smug man told me I couldn't find a better deal. Can you believe that? He thinks he owns me." Annie's weakness was a thing of the past, her eyes ablaze.

Louise laughed wholeheartedly. "Oh, Annie, don't be so hard on him. Poor bloke didn't know what hit him. Put yourself in his shoes. After all, you ditched him at the altar."

"No, I didn't. And he had the nerve to tell me we could take it slow." Annie waved her hand and whimpered in pain when her palm hit a poky branch.

"What happened?"

"Nothing. I just grazed my skin." Annie licked the drop of blood from the wound.

"To take it slow? What do you mean? I don't understand?"

"You know, the whole marital intimacy thing."

"How come you even talked about it? When?"

"After we left the church, and then he ambushed me, and the guests cheered and demanded a kiss. And I told him, don't you dare, but he wouldn't listen, would he?"

"Slow down, Annie. What are you saying?"

"That bastard snogged me! Said we can't disappoint the guests." Annie huffed.

"What!" Louise gasped. "But you're not married!"

"But we are."

A thud followed by a rattling noise came from the receiver.

"Lou? You there?"

"Just dropped my phone. Say it again. You are what?"

"We got married. Accidentally."

A longer silence on the other end. "How on earth does one get married accidentally?"

"Well." The sound of approaching footsteps made Annie look toward the entrance. A figure in a polka dot dress strolled toward the bench. "Need to go. Mother's coming. Love you."

Annie ended the call and slid the phone into her purse before her mother reached her.

"Here you are, gossiping on the phone while your guests wait."

"It was a voicemail from work. I had to check it." She wasn't in the mood for another lecture; besides, Mother had no idea Louise had flown away on her well-deserved holiday with Meggie.

"Oh really, are you in a habit of talking on your phone when nobody is listening?"

"I had to confirm my password to access the voicemail. But what are *you* doing here?" The sooner Annie changed the topic, the better. "Have you got lost on the way to the bathroom?"

"I never get lost. Your husband is worried about you, and the quartet started playing."

"So?" It was time to get back, but Annie would never pass the opportunity to rattle her mother.

"Do I have to spell out everything to you?" Maureen narrowed her brows. "It's time for your first dance. What would it look like if you missed it?" She pressed her hands against her chest.

Annie sighed and grabbed her purse, then marched toward the building entrance. "Indeed, what would people say?"

The sooner she ended this, the better. There was no way to tell when Darren would find out about this wedding, but that he would, Annie was certain of it.

A sudden gust of wind twirled the leaves under her feet and sent chills down her spine. And she'd better be as far away from here as possible by then.

But where could she go? Without money, and a place to stay? And with a baby on the way, who would hire her? Annie took a few deep breaths, glancing at her mother gliding with her head held high a few steps ahead.

Asking her parents for the loan was probably out of the question right now. Annie shivered. Not that she would ever want to do that.

Unless I played along.

If she played along, she wouldn't have to ask them for anything. As her father had said, there would be an inheritance for Annie, maybe enough to rent something and live for a year without worrying.

But how could she look in the mirror if she had done such a thing to another person?

She raised her eyes to the blue sky, praying silently to a deity she had never believed in, to help her, because what other choice did she have?

***

As the last notes of Sam Smith's "Stay With Me" filled the air, Conrad swayed gently to the music, his palms lightly pressed against the lacy fabric on Louise's lower back. Her body felt delicate in his arms, and he sensed an underlying sadness within her.

Conrad could feel the heaviness of her hands wrapped around his neck like she was a wreck survivor, and he was a drifting piece of wood on open waters. She let out a soft sigh, her eyes gazing into the distance, her forehead creased as if she had abandoned all hope of being rescued.

These emotions and protectiveness he was feeling seemed strange even to him. Not that long ago, she had been shouting at him and calling him names, and all he had cared about was surviving the day, somehow. Now, she seemed so vulnerable and fragile that he would do anything to see that fierceness in her eyes again.

Trying to lift the mood, Conrad joked, "You know, most people get cold feet *before* they say 'I do,' not after."

But there was no retort, just a faint smile that never reached her eyes. He pulled her closer, wrapping his arms around her, one a bit lower than the other, feeling the warmth of her skin beneath the dress. A spark of desire kindled within him, but he shook his head to dispel the feeling. This wasn't that kind of intimacy.

She's not into you.

Of course, she wasn't. Although, he had not imagined her lips giving in earlier. During that first kiss, it had shocked him. Conrad had expected a peck, but instead, he had met those full, welcoming lips.

And then later, despite reacting with anger afterwards, he could swear she had enjoyed their snog. Both times, Louise had acted like she fancied him.

It's your imagination, mate. Shut it off.

What if it wasn't? He caressed her back with his fingers, risking a slap—his jaws tightened, expecting it any second now. Instead, she leaned closer, brushing her hips against his and making his blood boil. Conrad looked at his wife's face, expecting to meet her eyes, but found Louise gazing in the distance, her eyelids half closed, like she was in a trance, not even aware of her surroundings.

Bloody hell.

Her body did things to him without her even noticing. That was bad. Pretty bad. He needed to cool off and find a way to keep her—well, convince her to stay. And maybe with time, her mind would catch up with her body, and maybe he would stand a chance. Just maybe.

Conrad inhaled through his nose and counted to three to clear his mind.

The physical aspect wasn't important at the moment. As much as Conrad enjoyed this dance, it wouldn't last forever, and his only chance was to convince Louise to give this marriage a go. Almost against his will, Conrad loosened his grip, shifting his hands higher and creating a bit of space between their bodies, then glanced around at the smiling faces of their guests. They looked like they expected something. But what?

Say something, man.

"Your father wants me to sign the paperwork on Monday so you can get on with that inheritance." Despite trying, he couldn't hide a hint of bitterness in his voice.

"I bet he does." She laughed. A hollow kind of laughter.

"I saw you talking to your parents earlier. Was it about the deal?" Conrad looked at her, genuinely curious.

His wife nodded but remained silent. Her hands slid down over to his shoulders, loosening her hold.

Speak, woman.

Conrad gently brushed her cheek with his fingertips to make her look up at him. "And what do you think?"

She clicked her tongue. "From a strictly business point of view, it's a sound idea and beneficial for both sides."

But?

He waited. His wife swallowed, parted her lips to speak, and then closed them again without a word. It was like trying to squeeze juice from a dry lemon.

"And from your personal point of view? How do *you* feel about it?"

"Since when do you care about my feelings?" Her tone was more curious than hostile.

"Since you became my wife, for better or for worse." He chuckled, but his eyes searched hers intently.

His wife blinked, and her gaze became focused. "I need to tell you something." She stopped halfway through the turn and took a small step back, her hands falling to her sides. "Actually, everyone needs to hear this."

She raised her hand, cutting the song short.

"Could you please take your seats?" Her voice was loud and clear, like the evening air.

"Good idea. I have something to say as well." Conrad took her warm hand and pulled her gently toward the centre of the stage with a microphone.

Holding her delicate, small hand in his callused one made him feel for a second like they were an item. While he waited for the chatter and laughter to subside, a longing awoke in him for something solid and real.

When Conrad gazed at the gathered faces, he realised that there was nobody here he truly cared about, no family to speak of—just two business associates and Colton, his faithful driver, who was probably the closest to a family member he could get.

A memory of his grandpa's warm presence by the fireplace filled Conrad's mind. He recalled the evenings they had spent together when Grandpa George had told him about the love of his life, Louise's grandmother Ann. They had never got together, but his grandpa had loved her all the same.

Conrad knew his grandfather had wanted to give the cottage back to Louise's grandmother, but she had been married, and it hadn't seemed right. He remembered his grandpa's words on his deathbed like it had been yesterday.

"This cottage is full of memories. I wish for you to keep it or gift it to the love of your life. Never sell it, my boy."

Funny how things turned out. Work was always the love of Conrad's life—his chain of inns, now in peril. He loved the cottage, but there was no other way. As long as he made Louise stay. At least for a few days. So, he could show his wife how good her life would be with him.

The clinking of a spoon tapping at a glass captured Conrad's attention. A hush fell over the guests as they turned their faces toward the couple on the stage. His wife retrieved the microphone from its stand and cleared her throat.

A sudden thought crossed Conrad's mind, and he leaned over to his wife. "If you don't mind, I'd like to say something first."

She nodded with her eyebrows raised, and Conrad took the microphone off her hand.

"Thank you all for joining us here on this wonderful day. As most of you know, my wife and I haven't had the chance to get to know each other yet."

Guests murmured and nodded. Conrad raised his wife's hand to his lips and placed a gentle kiss before continuing.

"To remedy this, I'd like to take my beautiful wife for a honeymoon where we could get to know each other better, sharing great food and drinks while taking in the local sights."

With a hopeful glint in his eyes, he asked, "What do you think,

Louise?"

Surprise flitted across her face as she glanced at her parents. He followed her gaze, noting their alarmed expressions. This wasn't part of their plan, but it would buy him some time. He needed to ensure she would honour her end of the bargain.

Uncertainty clouded her eyes, and she shook her head ever so slightly.

"We deserve a bit of a holiday, a week maybe?"

He almost pleaded, and the guests joined him, chanting, "Do it. Do it. Do it."

She bit her lip, glancing at her parents again, who were shaking their heads so vigorously that Conrad worried they might spin away.

"We could go anywhere you wanted, to an exotic location or hide somewhere where nobody could bother us? Not even your parents." He took both her hands in his. "Please," he whispered so only she could hear him.

A gasp escaped Louise's mouth, and she glanced up at the sky with a bright smile on her face before focusing her gaze back on him. "Of course! This is exactly what I ... we need!"

While the crowd cheered and whistled, her father shouted. "Excellent idea! We'll organise something for you, and you can go even for a month in a week or two!"

That wasn't what Conrad wanted.

"How about now?" He laughed, his eyes focused on the emeralds sparkling again.

"Now?" she asked, her voice a mix of disbelief and excitement.

"Yes, why don't we leave now?" The thrill of spontaneity rushed through him.

A mischievous twinkle appeared in her eyes, and dimples graced her cheeks.

"Actually, why not? Let's go!" She creased her forehead. "But where?"

Good question. He hadn't expected her to say yes, and now he wasn't sure where to take her. An exotic beach? A mountaintop retreat? He knew nothing about this girl. But he knew they had to leave before her parents could change her mind.

"No idea, but we'll figure it out." Conrad waved at Colton and grabbed his wife's hand, pulling her toward the gazebo's exit.

The sun was setting, casting a golden glow over the marquee as they hurried through the rows of tables. A warm breeze ruffled their clothes and carried the scent of magnolia and the night stocks. Balloons bobbed around them as if cheering them on, and the quartet struck up a lively tune in celebration.

Chapter 6

Annie scuttled along as fast as she could, her red stilettos clicking against the paved path leading toward the road, and her heart pounding loud in her chest. Conrad tugged on her arm, propelling her forward toward the limousine.

I must be crazy.

Who in their right mind would agree to a honeymoon with a stranger without even knowing where they were going? Especially someone like Conrad, clearly up to no good. Annie chuckled lightly. It was genius. If she didn't know where she'd be spending the next few days, Darren wouldn't be able to find her, either.

Her prayers had been answered! She'd been given the time she needed.

I'll tell him when we get there.

Wherever it was. Much better than here, near her parents' house and Louise's apartment. Annie would bet their addresses would be where Darren would start looking for her. The wind blew at Annie's back, urging her to run faster, swirling around her bare ankles while her feet wobbled on the uneven surface of the paving slabs.

Out of the corner of her eye, she caught sight of her parents in the fading sunlight, their faces etched with worry as they trailed behind. Annie nearly reached the car when her heel caught in a crack in the sidewalk, and she winced at the sudden jolt of pain.

Conrad caught her before she could fall—his arms a protective net.

"Are you okay?" he asked with concern flashing in his eyes.

Annie whimpered, unable to put any pressure on the throbbing ankle. "I can't run in these shoes."

"No worries."

Conrad bent down and lifted her in one smooth motion, without even a hint of struggle, like she was a newborn baby, not a mature woman. Holding her close to his chest, he carried Annie toward the awaiting limo.

A delicate scent of wood shavings and coffee beans made Annie want to close her eyes and lay her head on his muscular shoulder.

Oh, wow.

Annie smirked and stiffened in Conrad's arms, keeping her head away from his devious body.

That was quick even for you. Not so long ago, you wanted absolutely nothing to do with him and now you want to stay in his arms forever?

Annie glanced at Conrad's face, unsure if the conversation took place in her head or if she said it out loud.

His gaze was fixed on a man in a chauffeur uniform that stood next to the opened side door. A moment later, Conrad lowered Annie onto a plush seat, his fingers briefly touching her calves, making her gasp from the sensation, while he positioned her legs on the sofa.

Before Annie could pretend she didn't like it, Conrad shut the door and plunged his body onto the other end of the sofa with a deep sigh of relief.

"Are you comfortable?"

Maureen and Richard banged on the metallic exterior of the car, looking frantic, so instead of answering Conrad, Annie lowered the window.

Her father bent down and stuck his head through the open window frame. "What's the rush? Where are you going?"

Conrad's grin deepened, creating wrinkles around his eyes—something Annie found oddly comforting. "My wife deserves the best honeymoon, but it's a surprise. We'll be in touch once we reach our destination. Thank you for the party, and goodbye."

He waved at them as Annie raised the window inch by inch, forcing her father to withdraw his head.

Conrad leaned toward the front of the limousine, where the driver had already started the engine. "Let's go, Colton."

The car pulled away, leaving Maureen and Richard in the middle of the gravel road.

Colton, the driver, wearing a suit, driving gloves and a chauffeur's cap, glanced into the rearview mirror.

"Where to, Mr Conrad?"

Conrad rattled off an address in a cryptic manner so Annie couldn't quite make out the details. She looked around. The posh interior, complete with a minibar, plush seating, and dim, romantic lighting, made her yearn for such a comfortable life.

A life with no worries about where to stay the night, about the next meal, and about the jerks harassing bar staff after a couple of pints. This idea of an untroubled life had made her fall for Darren in the first place. And made her blind to his other side, the cruel and manipulative person he had turned out to be. Or probably had always been. Annie bit on her nail.

So lucky I managed to escape.

Such a coincidence that the wedding invitation had arrived exactly on the first day of his so-called business trip. And that he had left her on her own, thinking that as ill as she had been, she would simply stay put.

"A penny for your thoughts?"

Annie blinked, noticing Conrad's blue eyes checking her out without even an attempt at hiding it.

"You think I'm so cheap that to share my thoughts for a penny?" She puffed. "Where are we going?"

"Well—" He raised a finger, as if making a point, and opened the minibar. "How about we have a toast first? Then we can discuss where we're going." He reached for a bottle of champagne and nodded toward Annie in an inviting gesture, but she shook her head. "I can't drink on an empty stomach, and I'm not really a fan of champagne." "An empty stomach?" His eyebrows shot up, accompanied by a wide grin. "I saw you eating at the party." Annie rolled her eyes. "A *reasonably* empty stomach. I only had a piece of cake and a few grapes. That's all I've eaten today." *And I spent most of yesterday throwing up.* Two days with barely any food, but he didn't need to know that—or why.

A light chuckle escaped Conrad's mouth. "Fair enough."

He retrieved a bottle of Perrier water and filled the champagne flutes halfway through, placing one of them in her hand.

"Let's have a toast to our happy future and an enjoyable honeymoon."

They clinked their glasses of sparkling water, making the bubbles rise. Annie took a sip, her mind racing with thoughts, a bile of guilt coming up from her stomach to her throat.

A happy future together?

No, she couldn't let him believe there would be a happily ever after. That was just wrong, no matter what her father had tried to make her believe. Turning the glass in her hands, she cleared her throat.

"I wish there was a happy future for us, but unfortunately, that's not on the cards."

Conrad raised his hands. "Oh, come on. Give us a chance." He leaned closer, emanating that wood dust and coffee scent, a scent of hard work and safety. "Let's spend some time together before making any rushed decisions."

Annie found herself drawn to his eyes, which were full of intensity and attention.

"I wish it was that easy."

"Then what is it? Is it about the deal?" he asked, his eyes searching hers.

Annie hesitated, knowing she had to tell him she wasn't Louise and that there would be no deal. She bit on her lip, trying to find the right words.

Before she could speak, her phone rang, making her roll her eyes. "I bet it's my mother."

"You'd better take this, or they'll send a search party."

Annie chuckled and pulled out the phone from her purse. When she glanced at the screen, she noticed her sister's name.

"Mother, we only just left. I'm in the car with Conrad, so I'll call you later."

Louise paused for a second, then played along. "Sure, honey. I was worried since you didn't answer my texts. Talk to you later."

Annie hung up and checked the message from her sister.

Lou: "He was at my place asking for you. Paul, our doorman, left me a message that Darren would be back later. Be careful xx"

Annie gasped and gulped down her drink, her heart pounding like the frantic wings of a caged bird.

Conrad noticed her reaction. "What is it?"

She swallowed hard, uncertain of what to do or say. Darren was closer than she thought. Like a trapped animal, she tensed and shrunk into herself, expecting an attack. Her eyes darted from side to side, looking for a way out.

When she shifted in her seat, a pain shot through her leg.

"Ouch. My ankle."

Annie extended her hand to touch it, but couldn't quite reach her foot without moving in her seat again.

"Your ankle? Let me see it."

Annie blushed, "No, it's fine."

Conrad removed his suit jacket and tossed it onto the seat next to him before bending down to examine her ankle. When he lifted the bottom of the dress enough to see, he whistled.

"Definitely not fine. Nice shoes, by the way. Not what I'd expect with a white dress. You need to take them off, though, as very soon you won't be able to. And we need to get you an ice pack to reduce the swelling."

He lifted his head. "Colton, could you stop at the nearest grocery store or a petrol station, please?"

"Right away, sir. I believe there's a Tesco Express, not a mile from here."

"Excellent." Conrad looked at Annie with concern in his eyes while rolling up the sleeves of his shirt, uncovering muscular and tan forearms. "I need to remove your shoes. It may hurt a little."

"But I have no other shoes. In fact, I don't have any clothes or anything." Annie's voice reached a high pitch. "I wasn't planning on travelling anywhere after the wedding. My change of clothes is still at the venue."

Tears welled in her eyes as she struggled to breathe. Not only because of the pain, but also because Darren had finally tracked her down, and she had nowhere to go.

"If I may," Colton interjected, his soothing voice calming her down like Aloe Vera on a sunburn. "Your suitcase is in the car boot, ma'am. We packed it right after the ceremony, ready to go back to Mr Conrad's house in Bath for the night, as planned."

"Your house in Bath?" Annie blinked the wetness from her eyes, sniffling, and looked down at Conrad.

He nodded while unstrapping her shoe, his fingers working with precision, gently pulling it free—his chiselled hands like unfinished sculptures against the smooth curves of her calf and foot. The pain subsided, replaced by a tingling warmth that seemed to seep beneath the surface of her skin, stirring feelings long dormant.

Annie's cheeks darkened, and she tore her gaze away, needing a distraction before she did something stupid, like moan or massage his neck.

"But we've left Bath, haven't we?" she blurted, her voice sharper than she intended.

"Yes, we have." He made a face. "But I'm not going to tell you where we're going. It's a surprise, remember?"

The limo pulled over at a petrol station with a Tesco Express store.

"I'll go and get that ice." Conrad opened the door and stepped out. Then he turned around, bending slightly to meet her gaze. "Do you want anything to eat or drink?"

Her stomach growled audibly at the mention of food. She tried to laugh it off but gave up. "Actually, I'm starving. Maybe a sandwich or a wrap? Ham, chicken, or cheese. And a drink."

Annie's eyes opened wider, and she licked her lips. "What I'd really love is a burger or a hot dog, but I doubt they have any of that."

Conrad chuckled, his laugh deep and rich.

"What?" she asked, narrowing her eyes.

He shook his head, still grinning. "Nothing. Just imagining you in that white dress, biting into a burger."

He winked at her and strode away, not letting Annie have the last word. She shook her head, half amused, half irritated.

Not that she came up with any retort, anyway. The moment he disappeared, Annie checked her swollen ankle. It hurt under her touch. When she attempted to put pressure on her foot, a sharp pain shot up her leg, and she bit her lip to stifle a cry.

"Are you okay, ma'am?" Worried eyes looked at her in the rearview mirror.

"I'm fine—" Annie hesitated before adding, "Colton? May I call you Colton?"

"Yes, ma'am." His tone was polite but kind, carrying a warmth that made her relax a fraction.

Annie shifted in her seat, wincing as she tried to find a position that didn't aggravate her ankle.

"It's just this damn ankle. I can't stand on it."

"Don't worry, ma'am. No walking necessary tonight."

Her brow furrowed. No walking, huh?

Maybe the driver would share more on the destination. He must have understood Conrad's directions, as he had not asked for clarification.

"Speaking of which, where are we going?" Annie watched the man's brows furrow.

"Sorry, ma'am. Mr Conrad didn't want me to say." His voice was warm and apologetic.

Well, it was worth a shot. Annie leaned back, drawing complex shapes in the misted window with her finger. "But maybe you could give me some clues. Is it far?"

"No, ma'am." Colton glanced at the sat nav. "About half an hour's drive."

Her lips pressed into a thin line. "It must be one of his pubs, then." She didn't sound thrilled by the prospect.

"No, ma'am."

She raised an eyebrow at his quick response. Colton touched the air-con controls and increased the airflow while reducing the temperature. The mist dissolved.

"It's clearly not in Bath, since we left it behind. Is it in the countryside?"

Colton offered a comforting smile. "I've already said too much, ma'am. And Mr Conrad is coming back."

Annie sank back into the plush leather seat, frustrated but unwilling to push the kind driver any further. Instead, she turned her gaze to the landscape outside the window. The sun was sinking lower now, casting the rolling hills and scattered cottages in a golden glow that made the entire world feel softer and quieter. Peaceful. Yet inside, her thoughts churned.

Her fingers brushed her lap as she considered the situation. *Where is he taking me?* The unknown unsettled her, and a faint knot of anxiety tightened in her chest. She didn't like being out of control—not anymore. But at the same time, a flicker of excitement sparked deep down. A part of her, one she hadn't acknowledged in years, wanted to believe this was something good. Something unexpected and maybe even … thoughtful.

Before she could overthink it, the car door opened, and Conrad returned, a plastic bag in hand.

"Here—a Caesar wrap and an orange juice for the lady." Conrad handed food to Annie before crouching down to wrap a cold compress around her ankle. The sudden cold against her feverish skin made her jump, but the pain started to dissipate.

"Painkillers?" He extended his palm with tablets that she accepted and swallowed, washing them down with the juice. After helping her with the seat belt, Conrad motioned for Colton to drive.

"Let's get going. We can sort a proper dinner and everything else once we get there."

"Get where?" she pressed, her voice tinged with both curiosity and suspicion.

Conrad's lips curled into a mischievous grin, but he said nothing. Unbelievable.

Annie rolled her eyes and leaned back in her seat, torn between annoyance and intrigue. The landscape outside blurred as the limo rolled forward, but her thoughts stayed sharp.

What is he planning?

Part of her hated not knowing, the vulnerability of being in someone else's hands. But another part, one she wasn't sure she trusted, whispered that maybe—just maybe—it was still okay to let someone else take the lead sometimes.

The wrap in her hands sat forgotten as her mind wandered, wondering what the next half hour would bring.

***

Annie watched the scenery pass by as the limo drove deeper into the countryside, her mind a whirlwind of thoughts while she dangled her shoes on her fingertips. Her injured ankle rested on the seat with an ice pack on top—a constant reminder of her predicament.

How did he find Lou's address?

Annie couldn't recall if she had ever shared it with Darren. Probably not. Not that she had any reservations about him knowing—well, not till recently anyway. He had never been interested in her family. Worse, he was the reason her relationship with Louise had suffered, sulking for hours every time Annie had made so much as a call.

At first, she had tried to talk to her sister when he hadn't been around, but one time he had caught her, and it had ended in weeks of silent treatment, with Annie begging him to forgive her.

How could she be so malleable? At what point had she lost herself so completely that the only thing she had cared about was his approval? And love. And that had only been offered when she had behaved exactly as Darren expected her to.

Since the escape, Annie had felt like she could breathe again. And now … Now he was closing in.

Leather creaked when Conrad shifted in his place.

"A devil and a saint," he muttered.

"What?" Annie's attention snapped back to the present.

Conrad pointed at the red stilettos she held by the straps. "Those shoes. One minute, they're an elegant accessory, and the next, a twisted ankle's worst enemy." He smiled, and she couldn't help but return it.

Annie turned the shoe in her hand, running her finger over the polished, shiny surface that caught the sunlight streaming through the window. Conrad was so right. The shoes that made her feel so powerful and bold had this time led to her fall. Quite literally. However, her ankle hurt a bit less, thanks to the combined efforts of the ice pack and painkillers.

The limousine slowed as the road turned into a gravel path. Conrad leaned closer, his bare, tan forearm brushing against her pale skin, and pressed the button to open the window. "We're almost there."

The smell of freshly cut grass, spring blossom, and hot rubber tingled Annie's nose. "Where?"

She peered out the opened car window, her eyes widening as she took in the picturesque scene while they zoomed by.

Tall lilac trees lined the driveway, their sweet fragrance wafting through the air now, overpowering all other scents, their leaves rustling in the wind. The cobblestone path led to a charming cottage surrounded by blooming flowers, with wisteria climbing the sandy brick walls, bathed in the golden hues of the setting sun.

Her breath caught in her throat. "Is this what I think it is?"

As the limo came to a stop in front of the house and the driver opened the door, Conrad dashed to help her out. In just her stockings, which provided little protection for her injured ankle, Annie leaned on him and Colton for support and opened her eyes wider to take in the enchanting place—a sanctuary hidden from the world.

She couldn't help but feel drawn to the building, the green wooden shutters and thatched roof exuding warmth and charm. She had seen photos of this cottage in her grandmother's albums, but she had never expected it to be so well-preserved and inviting.

"Is this the Lilac Croft, the old, dishevelled and rundown cottage, according to my parents?"

Conrad laughed. "Is this what they said?"

Annie nodded. "You could fool *me*!" She scoffed, more at herself for having believed her parents instead of Grandma Ann, who had always cherished this place, saying how magical it was.

With a jingle of keys, Conrad unlocked the front door. He put his arm around her waist, placed her arm around his neck, and almost carried Annie inside, while Colton stayed behind.

The warm, inviting living room beckoned with its crackling fireplace, exposed wooden beams, and lilac branches in a tall vase on a side table. The immaculate condition of the cottage—from the polished wooden floors to the carefully renovated door frames—left Annie standing there with her mouth open, like a little child in a candy shop.

"Did your grandfather live here before he passed away?"

Conrad nodded, leading her down a hallway to a bedroom, the wooden floor creaking under their steps. As he opened the door, Annie could feel the lingering presence of another woman.

She glanced at Conrad, her curiosity piqued. "Was this your grandmother's room?"

A nostalgic smile played across Conrad's lips. "It was. A long time ago. But it looked different then."

As Annie lowered herself into a wooden chair by the window, Conrad loomed over her, his arms dangling at his sides, his thigh brushing against her hip. She averted her gaze, unsure of what to say, and the awkward silence stretched between them.

"You okay?"

She nodded without lifting her eyes, suddenly realising that this was it. She was here, in his house, with this man, alone. Well, with Colton too, but he didn't seem to actually live here.

She cleared her throat. "I need a minute."

Conrad shifted from one leg to the other, increasing the distance between them. "Take your time. I'm going to get changed and help Colton unload the car." He strolled toward the door and left the room.

So, what now?

Louise's place was out of the question. But even if Annie could stay there, she couldn't walk, not without someone's help, anyway.

"Here's a crutch to help you move around, ma'am." Colton stood in the doorway with Louise's battered leather suitcase and a shiny red crutch matching Annie's shoes.

"Thank you, Colton." Annie beckoned him to come inside, and he placed the suitcase on the wooden double bed, handing her the crutch.

"Do you need any help unpacking, ma'am?"

"No, I'll manage on my own, and please, call me A—" She blinked. That was close. "—ahem, using my name."

"Certainly, ma'am." She raised her eyebrows. "I mean, Ms Louise. Is there anything else I can do for you?"

Annie shook her head. "I could use some time alone if you don't mind."

"Of course. Just let me know if you need anything."

Once the sound of Colton's steps faded, Annie hobbled to the bed with her crutch and unzipped her suitcase, assessing its contents—there wasn't much inside. Louise had packed for an overnight stay, not a honeymoon in the cottage.

All of Annie's clothes and possessions were in her sister's apartment, except for a pair of joggers, a hoodie, and trainers she had worn when she sneaked into the dressing room in the morning. That suitcase had been already there, along with the wedding gown and accessories, so Annie had simply shoved her casual clothes inside alongside Louise's clothes.

She rummaged through, looking for something casual enough for an evening in, avoiding her own crumpled clothes. After finding a pale blue shirt and loose grey trousers, Annie unzipped her dress and pulled it over her head, leaving on her skimpy white lace underwear. As delicately as possible, she rolled off her stockings without touching her ankle and pulled on the trousers, leaving her feet bare. Sitting on the bed, she fastened all but the last button of her shirt and glanced around the room.

Her gaze landed on a rustic wooden wardrobe, then a matching dressing table with a tall, cushioned chair. Light, flowery curtains hung on both sides of a double window hidden behind white voile dancing in the breeze. The attention to detail gave the room a feminine touch Annie found comforting.

She limped toward a wall adorned with framed pictures, her eyes drawn to a familiar image. It was a photo of her grandmother as a child and a boy holding her bicycle. The same photograph she had seen at her grandmother's house. Beside it, another image caught Annie's attention—her grandmother as a young woman, her smile radiant and full of life.

The sound of a lawn mower in the distance drifted in through the open window, mingling with the scent of lilac and the soft chirping of birds. Annie closed her eyes for a moment and took a deep breath, the idyllic scene offering a temporary relief from her troubles.

As Annie opened her eyes again, she noticed a small inscription at the bottom of the second picture. It read, "To George, Always Yours."

***

His wife stood by the window, supported by the crutch, sunlight streaming through and casting a warm glow on her loose shirt and casual trousers. Her curly hair cascaded down her back, giving her an innocent, youthful look. She seemed so thin, almost fragile, as she traced her grandma's face in the picture. Conrad couldn't help but feel a sudden urge to protect her.

He approached her quietly, and when he was just behind her, he spoke softly. "Beautiful pictures, aren't they?"

Startled, his wife nearly lost her balance, but Conrad caught her just in time and helped her into a nearby chair.

"I don't understand," she stammered. "This is my grandma, isn't it?"

Conrad leaned against the wall, raking through his hair. "Indeed."

"But how?"

"That's a long story." He motioned toward the door. "Shall we order some food, and I can tell you all about it?"

She nodded and, holding on to her crutch, started hobbling toward the door.

"Would you like some help?"

His wife turned her head to glance at him, a question in her eyes. He pointed at the crutch, took a step forward and extended his hand to wrap it around his wife's waist, but a vigorous shake of her head made him stop.

"No, I'm good, but thanks." A small smile brought out a bunch of freckles on her face that he hadn't noticed before.

She trudged to the living room with Conrad following close by, ready to scoop her if she wobbled. With a sigh of relief, Louise lowered herself onto his favourite three-seater sofa. The weathered leather creaked under the pressure of her body. After securing the crutch against the arm of the sofa, she stretched her legs and sunk deeper into the cushions.

Conrad grabbed his tablet and flopped down beside her. The scent of coconut made him lick his lips in anticipation, as if she were a dessert he had craved for days. And maybe she was.

He cleared his throat, hoping his thoughts were not showing. "What do you feel like eating?"

"Pizza." Her eyes sparkled like precious stones. "I'd like vegetarian with ham. What about you?"

"That's an interesting combo." He chuckled. "I'll go for something hot and spicy."

Swiping and tapping on the food delivery app, he composed their order in seconds.

"What about Colton?"

He looked up, confused. "Colton?"

"Yes, shouldn't we ask him what he wants for dinner?" Louise tilted her head.

Conrad waved his hand. "Ah, no, he already left to return the limousine and go home to his family."

"Oh." She shifted on the sofa and crossed her arms.

"Are you cold? I can bring you a blanket?"

His wife shook her head and averted her gaze.

Not cold then. Maybe she was scared? Alone with a stranger. He had to make her feel at ease. Somehow.

"Food will be here in about forty minutes." Conrad jumped up and headed to the side cabinet, which held bottles and glasses.

"What would you like? Baileys?" He lifted the chocolate-coloured bottle and showed it to her. Louise shook her head, bending a little, dragged a cushioned stool closer, and lifted her leg onto it.

Moron. He should have thought about that. Returning the Baileys to the cabinet, he shifted bottles around.

"How about wine? Red or white?" He held a bottle of each in his hands, waiting for a decision.

"I prefer red, but not today. So much has happened." She massaged her temples. "But if you have some juice or sparkling water that would be great."

"Sure." After putting the bottles down, Conrad strode to the kitchen area and rummaged through the cupboards. No juice. Not that he expected to find any, but Colton might have stocked some up.

Instead, he filled a bottle with filtered water and attached it to the soda stream machine. The water in the bottle fizzed when he pressed the button, then he transferred it to a tumbler with a thick bottom.

From a fruit bowl, Conrad selected a sunny yellow lemon and decorated the glass with a slice.

In a few steps, he returned to the sofa when his tablet pinged and flashed a notification that their pizzas were on the way.

"Here you go." He handed her the glass. "Do you mind if I have a beer?"

His wife shook her head again while taking a sip of water. Not so talkative anymore.

After a quick trip back to the fridge for a bottle of Punk IPA, Conrad finally collapsed on the sofa, an arm's distance away from his wife. They still had about half an hour before the food would arrive.

As they sat in silence, he could feel the tension in the room growing, like a thickening jelly, trapping them in the awkwardness.

"So." Conrad smacked his lips, not sure what to say next.

His wife shifted in her spot and turned toward him with a curious look on her face. "So, what is that long story?"

Conrad forgot all about it. What an idiot.

"As you know, this cottage used to belong to your family, and your grandma had spent her childhood here."

She nodded, while he took a sip of cold liquid from his bottle.

"What you might not know is that our families knew each other, and my grandpa was a frequent visitor whenever his own father met with your grandma's father."

"The boy on the bike." She clasped her hands.

"Exactly." Conrad smiled, mesmerised by the childlike wonder in her eyes.

"So, what about that other photo?" Her curious voice nudged him back.

"Well, let's not get ahead of ourselves. So, they were childhood friends until the day her dad, your great-grandfather, lost the cottage to my great-granddad at the gambling table."

Her eyes widened as she gasped.

"You didn't know?" That was weird. Conrad rose from his seat and walked to the bookshelf in the room's corner with his grandpa's photos and documents. He picked up a folder and carried it back to the sofa.

"Check this out." He retrieved a laminated document signed by her great-grandfather William transferring cottage ownership to Conrad's family. While he handed it over to his wife, the doorbell rang.

"Our food is here." He opened the door and accepted the steaming boxes. Pepperoni and oregano filled the air. "Plates and forks? Or boxes and—"

"Box is fine." She waved a hand holding the document. "This is … Wow. I had no idea."

Conrad pushed the side table toward Louise and placed the pizza boxes on it while shifting the document folder to the side.

"So, what happened next?" His wife shoved half of a slice into her mouth like she hadn't eaten for days.

A woman after my own heart.

He could count on one hand the women he knew who enjoyed eating openly, as most either were constantly on a diet or never ate in public. Conrad bent a slice in half from his box and chewed on it.

After swallowing the piece, he washed it down with his beer.

"Well, as you can imagine, the families were no longer friendly, and the kids were not allowed to hang out together anymore." He pointed with another pizza slice in hand in Louise's direction. "Your family moved to Bath, and it would have been the end of the story if—" Conrad swallowed another bite. "—my grandfather George hadn't bumped into your Grandma Ann in the shop when he was in town. One thing led to another, the old friendship rekindled, and they started seeing each other."

"No way." A shock in her voice made him pause. Conrad smiled. He had reacted the same way when his grandpa had told him the story for the first time.

"Oh yes. In secret, of course, as their families were still sworn enemies. As you may imagine, the friendship turned into love."

Louise wiped her mouth and hands with a napkin, her box of pizza half empty.

"But my grandma never mentioned your grandpa. And also, she was married to my grandfather Edward. So, what happened?"

"Well, life happened. Her parents chose your grandpa Edward as a suitable husband, and your Grandma Ann had no say in it."

Conrad paused with a slice hanging from his fingers, thinking about their own arranged marriage. Maybe his wife loved someone else, but her parents had made her marry him instead. The thought gnawed at him, sending a pang of jealousy through his chest, followed quickly by a wave of guilt. He had no right to her heart—not yet anyway. Still, the idea of her longing for someone else left him feeling unexpectedly disappointed. Not everyone was married to their work, and she would certainly have her pick if she wanted.

So, what if there was somebody? Would she meet with him in secret or remain unhappy for the rest of her life? How could he live with himself if that was the truth?

"And this was the end?"

Louise's question pulled him back to the story, pushing his worries about his wife's potential lover aside. For another day.

"Not exactly." He wiped his mouth with the back of his hand and gulped the rest of his beer. "Even though my grandpa George got married and had kids, he never stopped loving your grandma."

Conrad looked toward the window, remembering the smell of cigars and the old-style armchair that had stood there, near the window, his grandpa's reading and napping spot.

"Grandpa George told me once that she was the love of his life. And he knew the cottage was precious to her, so he offered it to her."

"When?" His wife held her breath, covering her open mouth.

"Several years ago, after my grandma died. They met in Bath and sat on the same bench they used to sit on in their youth. But your grandma refused to accept it."

Louise leaned forward, her shoulders tensed, like someone watching a film who was afraid of what was coming but couldn't live without knowing.

"See, it happened when your grandpa was still alive, and she believed that wouldn't be appropriate."

"Inappropriate." Louise shook her head. "What a love story."

His wife's gaze wandered over to the open window and she stared at something, but Conrad would bet that she was there on that bench with her grandma.

He reached out and picked a small box from a shelf above his head. After retrieving a soft green leather pouch from it, he took Louise's hand and emptied the content of the pouch onto her palm. An old key fell out with engraving on its head: "To Ann, the love of my life."

Louise stared at her hand with eyes matching the colour of that pouch.

"My grandfather hoped that one day he could make things right, and this cottage meant more to him than anything. It reminded him of the love of his life, and that's why I cannot ever sell it."

Conrad moved closer to his wife, the jasmine scent of her hair intoxicating.

"So sad." She turned the key in her fingers while her eyes focused on his. "And that's why you're gifting it to me?"

A question hung in the air as their eyes met, and their hands brushed against each other.

"I might be your wife, but I'm certainly not the love of your life." A twinkle in her eyes and the warmth emanating from her made his heart race.

Wistfully, he said. "Not yet, but one day, hopefully."

He leaned closer, losing himself in her eyes. Tracing her chin with his fingers, he stroked her hip with his other hand, feeling the heat emanating from her body.

The softness of her skin and the enlarged pupils reminded him of the kiss earlier, back at the church. Every muscle in his body ached for her. This was real. Neither of them could deny the magnetic pull between them.

"Admit it, you're starting to find my charm irresistible," he said in a deep tone of voice. His wife jolted back.

"What?" Her eyes flared, but not with the kind of fire he'd hoped for.

"I don't know what you're thinking but I'm not part of your fan club."

Conrad groaned. "I was joking." Was he? He could swear she wanted him as much as he wanted her. It was all going so well.

Louise huffed, grabbed her crutch and limped back to her bedroom, slamming the door behind her.

Staring at the polished oak door, he wondered if he should follow and apologise again or let her sleep her irritation away. The anger in her eyes and her flushed cheeks made her look incredibly attractive, but somehow, he knew that if he mentioned this to her, she might bite his head off.

He sighed and decided to take a cold shower to clear his head.

As he stripped down to his boxers, he couldn't shake the image of her fiery, flushed face and glimmering eyes. He needed to find a way to break through her defences, to make her see that they could have a future together.

As he strolled past Louise's room, she opened the door and gasped. "You must be kidding me!"

Before he could utter a word, Louise slammed the door shut, causing small pieces of plaster to fall from the ceiling.

Shit.

He knocked on the door. "It's not what you think." What a stupid thing to say. "I'm just heading for a shower." No response. "I'm sorry. I didn't mean to scare you."

***

Annie lay on the bed, mortified by the unexpected encounter with Conrad in his boxers.

"The nerve!"

What was he thinking? That the sight of his naked body would make her weak in her knees? Seriously? She had met men with enormous egos, but this one would easily take the first place if there was a contest.

Her heart raced, and she tried to focus on the soothing sounds of the crickets chirping and the distant barking of a dog.

After a few moments, she heard the shower turn off, followed by the sound of his footsteps retreating down the hall.

So, he took a shower after all.

A weight lifted from her chest, and she giggled like that little girl chasing her veil.

"He was on his way to the shower." She snorted. Not so ladylike. What were the odds?

An image of the encounter appeared in her mind, his hairless, muscled chest so close to her fingers. It wasn't what she would expect from the businessman sitting behind the desk all day.

Her swollen ankle throbbed, but she wouldn't dare look for an ice pack now. What if she bumped into him? Rummaging through the contents of her suitcase, hoping for some soothing balm, Annie picked out the sound of light steps outside her room, followed by the thud of a door being shut.

The house had grown quiet, except for the rhythmic sound of wood being chopped outside. Between the steady thuds, she could hear a voice, though the words were inaudible. Straining to listen, Annie hobbled toward the open window.

"What an idiot." Swoosh. Chop. "Moron." Chop. Thunk. "Really, man?" Creak. Clunk.

Annie chortled, shaking her head. He wasn't such a narcissist after all. If only she could see him right now, channelling all that energy into splintering wood.

Seizing the opportunity, Annie grabbed her sister's overnight bag and limped to the bathroom, locking the door behind her.

The hot water washed away her uneasiness and worry as she let her thoughts wander, the tiny droplets massaging her tense muscles. As she dried off and wrapped herself in a fluffy towel, she examined her sister's lacy nightgown—too daring to wear in Conrad's presence. Why did Louise pack it instead of a sensible cotton PJ?

A blush crept up Annie's cheeks, and she splashed cold water onto her face. An image of Conrad's toned muscles flashed in her mind, surprising her with a sudden desire she hadn't felt in a long time. She bit her lip, remembering that kiss after the wedding ceremony, and his powerful arms when he had carried her to the limo.

When his hand touched her thigh on the sofa, the only thing she could think of was his lips on hers. If he hadn't opened his stupid mouth, who knows what would have happened?

Annie hadn't been with a man since … Memories of Darren invaded her thoughts, and she shuddered, rubbing her arms for comfort. Then massaged her belly. It would work this time. She wouldn't be able to live through *this* again. This. No, she couldn't go there. Blinking fast, she pressed her hands against her ears, pushing the memory of her miscarriage back into the box she had kept it in. As long as she stayed away from Darren, all would be fine.

"Fine." She took a few shallow breaths. "All will be fine. I promise you." Taking a few more, slower and deeper breaths, Annie unclenched her jaw and glanced around at the tiled walls. After checking a few cupboards, she found a thick white bathrobe, only a size too big.

Who was she?

Annie stroked the fluffy fabric, wondering if Conrad brought many women to his cottage. She rummaged through cabinets, looking for clues and signs of other women, but found nothing else.

A sigh of relief escaped her mouth, and she shook her head.

And what if he did?

It was his right. They weren't a couple, not really.

Somehow, thinking about Conrad pulled Annie back into the present, with all its endless possibilities, rather than trapping her in the past that she couldn't change.

Annie cleared a steamed-up mirror with a sleeve. Her own face, without make-up, stared back. Older. Annie lifted the skin around her eyes in a futile attempt to remove wrinkles. The moment she let go, they were back. Not the face of a twenty-seven-year-old, for sure. But why would it be? She wasn't Louise.

With a sigh, she slipped into the silky, lace-trimmed nightgown. The fabric was soft to the touch, but the gown was too short for her comfort. Shivering, she wrapped the robe around her like a warm blanket and cracked open the bathroom door.

No sounds apart from a fridge whirring and a clock ticking in the distance. With her sister's bag in one hand, Annie limped to the kitchen and retrieved a fresh ice pack from the fridge. With floorboards creaking beneath her feet, she returned to her room.

As Annie nestled into the bed, the silky nightgown cold against her skin, she wrapped the robe around her like a protective shield. With her back against the pillows and legs resting on the duvet, she carefully applied the ice pack to her ankle, wincing as the coldness seeped into her skin, numbing the pain.

The sound of wood chopping had stopped as the wind picked up and ruffled the voile. Annie re-read the text from her sister about Darren visiting her apartment, and her hands trembled. So close, too close.

He had been charming, even loving, convincing her she didn't need her family, and that he was all she needed.

Darren's soothing voice echoed in her head, promising love and devotion.

And she had believed him until she had overheard him using the same soothing voice on the phone saying, "Teach that geezer a lesson. The hospital is fine as long as he lives. He owes me. And tell him his wife and kiddo are next."

That had hit her like a ton of bricks. What else hadn't she known about him? Darren had always described himself as a businessman, frequently travelling and attending meetings in far-off cities, but she had never truly known what his business entailed. He had kept her in the dark, brushing off her questions with charming smiles and condescending reassurances about how she didn't need to worry her pretty little head with unnecessary details. At that moment, when she had overheard him, Annie had realised those trips might have involved more than simple deals and networking.

And now he'd found her sister's place. The wind outside intensified, rattling the windowpanes and mirroring the horror brewing within her.

Annie's gaze drifted to her grandmother's photo on the nightstand. How wonderful it must feel to be loved so deeply by someone.

"But not by this one, you blew it already," she whispered into the shadows, only brightened by the moonlight. Even if she told Conrad the truth about her now, he would never forgive her. Besides, he wasn't such a catch himself. Even if her own body kept betraying her.

She had never felt such chemistry with Darren. Not even at the beginning. He had won her with his chivalry and kindness, or what he had made her believe. Annie bit on her nail, remembering Darren's pleasant smile. Wolf in disguise. She knew better now.

"What if he finds me?" Her heart pounded fast, her breathing shallow.

But he wouldn't know about the cottage, would he? Nobody knew except for her and Conrad. And Colton. But that man had already gained Annie's trust. She was safe here. For now.

The raindrops splashed at the windowsill like a series from a machine gun.

Chapter 7

Sitting in a swivelling office chair, Conrad sipped his morning coffee, the bitterness invigorating him as he stared at the final notice letter. The rising sun cast a muted glow through the mist that hung over the orchard behind the cottage. The distant shriek of a bird echoed through the quiet morning.

He glanced at the wall, covered in photos of happy memories at each of his inns, wondering how many he'd have to sell to stay afloat. How many people would he have to let go? He had already cut back their hours to keep everyone employed, but the bank's deadline loomed, and the pressure was mounting.

Massaging his neck, Conrad shifted his gaze to the bundle of cream-textured papers on his desk. The rough finish made his heart bleed. Giving away the cottage to save the love of his life—his pubs—was a necessity. But would it be enough? Would Louise keep her end of the bargain? After last night's encounter, there was no way of telling if she would.

The alternative was even worse. Those venture capitalist vultures would provide the money, but with a 60% stake, they would make the decisions. It would no longer be his business, and he knew they would expect him to reduce the costs, which to them would mean firing even more people.

For him, this wasn't a solution. These people were like family; heck, he had grown up with some of them. There must be a way to make Louise stay for long enough. A month was what he needed. Long thirty days.

The faint whine of an electric car and the sound of a door shutting outside signalled Colton's arrival. 9 a.m. Conrad sprung up to his feet, and in two strides, he exited his study. Closing the door behind him, he strolled through a short corridor, decorated with nothing but a few black and white photographs of his grandparents, and entered the kitchen.

The aroma of freshly ground coffee beans and cinnamon reached Conrad's nose even before his eyes spotted a plate of warm croissants, pastries, and bread rolls from the local bakery.

Colton, wearing a casual jacket and jeans, folded a paper bag. "Figured a sweet breakfast wouldn't hurt." He gestured to the spread. "How's the lady?"

Conrad shook his head, recounting the previous night's awkward moments. "After last night, I doubt any pastry in the world would make it better."

"Last night?" Colton placed a white mug under the coffee machine spout and pressed the button.

Conrad ruffled his hair and shook his head. "You don't want to know."

Colton raised his eyebrows, but Conrad only waved his hand.

"So, what's the plan?" his driver asked.

Conrad opened his mouth to answer when his wife appeared in the doorway, her hair tousled and her eyes dreamy. She walked with care, favouring her injured ankle. Seeing her like this, Conrad's heart skipped a beat. If he could wake up to that sight every morning, he'd be a lucky man.

"Good morning, how's your ankle?"

"Better, thanks. The ice helped." She stopped in front of him with her moist lips slightly apart.

The perfect makeup from yesterday had vanished, revealing a face sprinkled with freckles that stood out against her paler skin. Her natural beauty was striking, with her features sharper and a quiet confidence radiating from her half smile. Conrad found himself drawn to this unguarded version of her—real and effortlessly captivating.

"So, will I get one, or will you just stand here?"

Blinking, Conrad looked around for something to do and grabbed a dessert plate. "Do you fancy a pastry? Or, I could make you eggs?" He opened the fridge, where only a jar of marmalade, leftover pizza, and a box of eggs awaited.

Colton intervened. "I'll get it, Ms Louise. How strong do you like it?"

"One shot, please."

She settled into a wooden chair with a blue cushion and reached for a chocolate twist—no mention of last night's events. Like nothing ever happened. It worked for him.

Colton handed Louise a cup of coffee. "Milk?"

She nodded, and his driver poured whole milk from a canister that stood on the counter next to the coffee machine. Conrad shook his head in amazement. What would he do without Colton? He thought of everything and was always there to help. More like a father than an employee. Well, he had started working for the family two years before Conrad had been born and had been the only constant presence in Conrad's entire life.

Conrad would sell his kidney before he would let the old man go. Well, maybe not his kidney, but he would certainly do anything in his power to ensure his faithful assistant kept his job.

The sun was finally breaking through the morning mist, casting a hopeful circle of light in the middle of the room.

"So, what's the plan for today, Mr Conrad?" His chauffeur straightened his cap.

"Good question." Conrad bit into a crunchy croissant, the almond custard melting in his mouth. "Well, normally on Sunday, we'd visit the inns, check on things, and speak with the guys on the floor."

Licking the custard off his lips, he squinted, looking at his wife holding a bread roll in her slim fingers and covering it with a thick layer of butter. A woman who could enjoy little pleasures in life—definitely a kindred spirit. If only he could make her see the potential in their marriage.

A gold band shimmered on her finger. She was still wearing the ring.

Good sign.

Conrad touched his finger, where he wore his own band of cold, polished metal.

"We could grab brunch at one of them if you're up for it, Louise." He gestured at her ankle. "I'd like to introduce you to the staff since you're the owner now, too."

She glanced at him, her eyes betraying a flicker of uncertainty.

"And then maybe we could have a chat about going away for our honeymoon if you're still interested?" Conrad suggested, trying to ease her apprehension.

Her eyes widened. "I don't have any change of clothes."

"We could swing by your apartment." She gasped, and Conrad creased his forehead. What was wrong with that question? "Or maybe you fancy something new?"

A glint of interest appeared in her eyes, and she tilted her head. "What do you mean?"

"New life, new wardrobe," Conrad laughed. "Bath has great shops. And we definitely need to do some grocery shopping on the way back."

His wife bit on her lip and took another sip of the coffee. "Alright then. I'm going to get ready." She slid off her chair. "Would we return here afterwards or stay in your house in Bath?" she asked.

An empty posh mansion in Bath. A house he had bought as Elisabeth had wanted to be close to where life was happening, as she liked to say. But Elisabeth was long gone, dropping him like an old hat out of fashion. He had never liked that house. Most of it belonged to the bank anyway, especially with him constantly falling behind on the payments.

"Where would you prefer?"

"Here? I like this place."

You and me both.

He nodded and grinned when a faint smile appeared on her face before she retreated to her room.

Colton scratched his chin. "Taking her to the inns. Is that wise?" He leaned toward Conrad and lowered his voice, concern in his tone. "What if someone mentions the trouble? What if she finds out her money isn't for the new desirable location but to rescue a debt-ridden business teetering on the brink of collapse?"

Conrad shrugged. "Let's hope she won't."

***

The Tesla hummed along the country road, flanked by vibrant green fields. Colton focused on the road, navigated through twists and turns, tapping the steering wheel to a catchy indie tune playing on the radio.

The morning mist had cleared, and the sun broke through the clouds, casting dancing shadows on the windshield. A fresh scent of damp earth and wildflowers floated in through the open windows.

Conrad cleared his throat, breaking the silence. "About last night … I'm sorry I startled you. I didn't expect you to leave the room at the same time."

His wife waved her hand, smiling, her dimples appearing. "It's alright. I overreacted. You caught me off guard."

"No, no, it's my fault." He rubbed his neck. "I'm not used to having guests."

"Guests?" Louise raised an eyebrow with a playful smirk. "We're married now, remember?"

"Right, right, we're family now," Conrad stuttered. "But you know what I mean."

His wife leaned in, a teasing glint in her eye. "I'm sure there must have been women in your life before?"

"There might have been." His tone was light, and a mischievous smile played on his lips. "But none quite like you." Conrad took her hand and bowed dramatically, placing a gentle kiss on her knuckles. She chuckled, and the scent of her perfume—citrus and jasmine—drifted up to him, both intoxicating and soothing.

Louise cocked her head. "Well, I did find a white bathrobe in the bathroom and some women's running clothes in the closet. So, at least one woman treated this place as her home."

Conrad shifted uneasily in his seat, the leather creaking under him. "If I didn't know any better, I'd say you're jealous."

"If I didn't know any better, I'd say you're avoiding the answer," she countered, squinting at him.

She was right. Conrad didn't want to talk about it. Besides, it was never a good idea to discuss an ex with any woman, as they all preferred to believe they were the one.

"So?" she asked, her eyebrows raised playfully.

"So what?"

"Are you going to tell me about her?"

"Just after you tell me about your last bloke." Conrad grinned.

A shadow crossed Louise's face, and her voice lowered. "What do you know about my ex-boyfriend?"

"Nothing, absolutely nothing." Conrad raised his hands in surrender. "It was just a joke. A bad one, apparently. Let's change the subject."

Eager to steer the conversation elsewhere, Conrad handed his wife a small box wrapped in decorative paper. "Here, I got you something."

She turned the box over in her hands. "What is it?"

"Open it up."

She carefully unwrapped the gift to reveal an old-fashioned Leica 35 mm film camera. Her forehead creased as she ran her fingers over the worn metal casing.

"I thought you might like it." His voice tinged with uncertainty. "The film's already loaded, and there are a few extra rolls in the box in case you run out."

He could have sold it on eBay and earned a decent coin, but it had seemed like an ideal gift for an amateur photographer. At least, it had seemed so at the time, but not so much now, as her expression stayed puzzled.

"Bad choice?"

"Oh, no." A dimpled smile lit up her face as she looked up at him. "It's perfect, but you shouldn't have." She cradled the camera as if it were a fragile treasure.

"Anything for my wife." A wide grin cracked his face. "But full disclosure, it's not new. It belonged to my father. I thought you two would have a lot in common."

"Would have?" Louise's smile faded, her brows furrowing with concern.

Conrad's expression turned sombre. "Yes, my parents died in an accident."

His wife gasped, covering her mouth. "I'm so sorry, I didn't know."

"It's okay." Conrad touched her hand gently. "It was almost thirty years ago."

"Thirty years?" Her eyes opened in shock. "You were only sixteen …"

Conrad nodded. "Fifteen to be exact. I thought your parents told you."

"No, they didn't." Louise shook her head and looked down at the camera in her hands. "They didn't tell me much about anything," she added with bitterness in her voice.

When she lifted her head, a shadow seemed to hang over her features, casting her once radiant smile into the depths of melancholy.

"I'm truly sorry, it must have been horrible." The corners of her lips turned upward in a half smile. "And thank you for the camera. It's a real gem."

The intimacy of the moment hung between them as their fingers brushed against one another. Louise leaned in, her emerald eyes captivating him. The scent of her perfume heightened his senses, and his heart raced. Holding his breath, Conrad moved closer to her, feeling a sensation he hadn't experienced in a long time.

Then her lips brushed his cheek, and she stroked his shoulder in a reassuring gesture before pulling away.

Idiot. What did you expect? She pities you.

***

The Tesla pulled to a stop in an unnamed alleyway near the Kennet and Avon Canal, the back of an old building looming ahead. Conrad flashed a boyish grin at Annie.

What is he up to now? Annie's curiosity was tinged with scepticism.

"This is my favourite pub, but don't tell the others," he said, helping her out of the car. "It was my first purchase when I inherited the chain."

Annie stepped out, taking in the sight of the unimpressive building. The weathered sign for The Canal Inn hung crookedly from a stone wall covered in moss and ivy.

This is his favourite?

The place seemed more like a forgotten relic than a beloved destination. It was a stark contrast to the picturesque countryside inn they had visited earlier, which had exuded a welcoming warmth.

If I passed this on my own, I'd probably keep walking.

"Well, that'll probably change once you use my marriage fund to purchase that country club. My parents couldn't stop raving about it."

Conrad's eyes seemed to grow heavier. "Yes, it's amazing," he sighed and shook his head as if it was causing him a headache. "But until then, let me present to you the jewel in my crown."

He playfully nudged her toward the side of the building, and as they rounded the corner, Annie's mouth fell open in awe. Simple wooden tables shaded by garlands of spring flowers and awnings sat next to the canal, where swans and ducklings glided through the calm waters.

Conrad grinned at her reaction. "How about we have that brunch here before going clothes shopping?"

She nodded, still taking in the charming scene. They stepped inside the pub, which resembled the cosy interior of a narrow boat. Conrad led her to the bar to meet the staff.

He draped an arm around her shoulder. "Everyone, I'd like you to meet my wife, Louise." The staff clapped and smiled warmly, offering their congratulations on the marriage.

Annie blushed, feeling a mixture of embarrassment and pride. But mostly embarrassment. "It's nice to meet you all."

Conrad glanced outside and took her hand. "Let's eat outdoors, shall we?"

She nodded, and he looked back at one of the crew members. "Bring us two specials, please."

"Of course, Mr Brenman," a young lad replied, already bustling away to prepare their order.

Annie started to object, but Conrad pulled her hand and guided her outside to a table near the family of ducklings.

She tugged on his sleeve. "Wait, what did you order?"

"Don't worry. You'll love it." He flashed a smile at her. "Only the best for my wife." He pulled out a chair and gestured for her to sit.

Annie furrowed her eyebrows. "I like to choose my meals."

Conrad waved his hand dismissively, brushing off her concern. "This is your first time here, so I want you to have the best experience. You won't regret it, trust me."

Her jaw tightened. *This isn't about the meal but about you deciding for me.*

Annie felt the tension build, but before she could voice her thoughts, he pointed at the canal lock. "Look, it's opening!"

While she watched the lock gates ajar, Conrad's phone vibrated, catching his attention. He looked apologetically at her.

"Sorry, Lou, I have to take this call. It won't take long, I promise." He got up from his chair, grabbing the phone.

Annie waved him off with a reassuring smile. "No problem. Go ahead, I'll be here enjoying the view."

He flashed her a grateful smile before striding toward the building and out of her sight.

A narrowboat navigated into the lock and gently pulled to one side, leaving a space for a dinghy. Annie was waiting for the water to lift the boats when a waitress arrived with their food. The smell of a sizzling steak and rosemary made her mouth water. She stared at an enormous plate filled to the brim with a 12-inch piece of meat, rosemary fries, and a double portion of mixed salad.

Annie had to admit it was a superb choice, and she wouldn't pick any better. The server placed a bucket with napkins and cutlery in the middle of the table and set a glass of red wine in front of her.

"I'm sorry, I'd prefer sparkling water, please."

"Not a problem," the waitress replied with a warm smile. "Anything for the woman who saved the pub. We were really worried, but Mr Brenman said it'll all be okay now."

Saved the pub?

Annie scratched her chin as the server walked away, leaving her with more questions than answers.

The sun peeked through the clouds, casting a warm glow on the water, and a gentle breeze rustled the ducklings' feathers, carrying the mingling scents of blossoming flowers and her delicious meal. Everything looked perfect—almost too perfect, like a scene crafted to hide something lurking beneath the surface.

Her gaze drifted back to Conrad. His face appeared tense as he spoke on the phone, but the moment he noticed her watching, his expression softened into a smile.

How much of this is real? The tranquillity of the scene only seemed to emphasise the tension coiled inside her, a sense that she was missing a crucial piece of the puzzle.

"What have I got myself into?" she murmured as an unexpected shiver ran down her spine.

***

Annie trotted behind Conrad as they navigated the bustling streets of the shopping centre, sunlight dappling the pavement and a light breeze carrying the scents of vanilla, cinnamon, and curry. He seemed to know exactly where he was going, confidently weaving through the Sunday crowd, dodging pedestrians and outdoor coffee shop tables.

"Conrad, slow down!" Her voice was muffled by a child's scream and the pneumatic noise of a bus door opening. She tugged on his hand, her cheeks flushed from keeping up with his pace.

"Can't keep up?" he asked with a glint in his eyes.

"My ankle still hurts, you know."

He gasped and stopped. "So sorry. Totally forgot as you seem to be doing so well."

To be fair, her ankle seemed to have healed well. It looked like the ice pack had done its job, but he didn't need to know that.

"Besides, I thought we came here to shop, not run a marathon!" Her words got stressed by a rattling trolley on the cobblestones.

Conrad reduced his pace to a snail, his eyes scanning the surroundings. "Almost there."

"Where?" she uttered, still out of breath.

His grin widened, but he said nothing.

She caught a glimpse of an art coffee place as they zoomed by. "Can you at least give me a hint about where we're going?"

"Trust me. You'll love it."

Annie's forehead creased, scanning the area filled with typical high street boutiques. Where on earth was he taking her? They had already passed an entrance to the shopping mall with all the usual brands she loved to shop for, and it seemed the street had nothing but art, coffee, and solicitors' offices to offer.

Suddenly, he turned on his heel and led her into a small, inconspicuous shop tucked next to a modern gallery. As they entered, plush carpets, armchairs, and a reception desk greeted them. A round, bald man wearing an old-fashioned waistcoat and bow tie rushed to them.

"Welcome, welcome. Come inside. We've been expecting you." A toothy smile spread across his clean-shaven, shiny face. "How are you today, Mr Brenman?" He bowed to Conrad before turning to Annie. "Mrs Brenman? My name is Robert Klatz, and I'll be your personal shopper today."

He gestured toward the interior side door and followed them into a room lined with mirrors, changing rooms, and additional seating. Two young, tall, and slim women—looking as though they had stepped straight out of a fashion catalogue—stood waiting, tape measures in hand.

While Annie scanned her surroundings, the women began taking her measurements, and Mr Klatz poured tea for everyone. She glanced at Conrad, who seemed to enjoy the spectacle.

"Milk?" Mr Klatz offered her a delicate china cup, which she gripped with both hands, anxious about dropping it. She nodded, and he topped up her tea with milk from an equally delicate jug. As she sipped her drink, the assistants finished taking her measurements—including her feet—and presented the scribbled results to Annie: size 8-10, regular length, and shoe size 4. When she nodded, both women swiftly departed through another door.

"What's going on? Where did they go?"

As much as she enjoyed surprises, this one felt like something out of *Alice in Wonderland*. There was something about Mr Klatz that reminded her of the rabbit.

"They'll be back, relax." Conrad took her arm and guided her to a velvety burgundy armchair beside a tall mahogany side table. She placed her cup down and lowered herself into the cushioned seat, running her fingers over the silky-smooth fabric. It was so soft and elegant—clearly worth a fortune, but not her style.

The women returned, pushing trolleys laden with clothes and boxes of shoes, ranging from casual, cosy outfits to elegant evening gowns in every style and colour.

Mr Klatz squinted at Annie.

"Would you be a dear and turn around for me, please?"

Sounding like a jovial uncle, Mr Klatz straightened his bow tie, watching her twirl like a little girl. With a thankful nod, he began selecting pieces from the casual rack.

"Try these on first, my dear. Soft fabrics for a cosy evening by the fireplace or a leisurely stroll in the countryside."

Still dazed, Annie let the man nudge her toward the changing room, where he offloaded the hangers on the rail and closed the curtain behind him.

As if an invisible puppet master were manipulating her arms and hands, Annie tried on one outfit after another. For a man, he had an impeccable eye. The clothes hugged her body like a second skin, accentuating her slim waist while leaving enough space for her hips. She glanced at her reflection. The colours complemented her natural complexion, now that she had already ditched Louise's makeup.

That morning, the smell of fresh coffee had lured her out of her room before she had fully woken up. Her brain had still been sluggish, and she had forgotten about the makeup—or the lack of it. By the time she remembered the need for her disguise, it had already been too late. Conrad had seen her. For a long moment, she had been certain he had seen through the charade, as he had stared at her without blinking.

As the tension reached an unbearable level, she had made that stupid joke about not being served a coffee, and Colton had stepped in while Conrad had offered breakfast. For some odd reason, neither of them had commented about her face looking so different and, frankly, older. So, now she could be herself, at least in the way she looked.

Of all the clothes she had tried on, Annie especially loved a jumper in shades of orange that made her eyes shimmer. Paired with warm brown leggings, it made a perfect outfit for a cosy evening indoors.

A gasp escaped her mouth when she checked the price tag. She could get several jumpers for that price in her usual shopping places.

"Do you need help, Mrs Brenman? A different size, perhaps?" A female voice asked.

"I'm fine, thank you. They fit pretty well."

Too well. Annie checked the price again, stroking the soft fabric, and glanced at her reflection in the mirror. It looked great. With a heavy sigh, she took it off. There was no point shopping here, not with these prices, even if the fabric was as fluffy as a teddy bear.

When she emerged with clothes hanging off her arm, Mr Klatz and his assistants waited with two dozen more for her to try on. Not only did she not need that many, but she certainly had no money to pay for even one piece, let alone all of them.

"Thank you for all of this. Those are lovely clothes, but I really don't need any of them."

Conrad raised his eyebrows. "I thought you said you needed some clothes?" He gestured toward the pile in her arms.

She leaned toward him. "I did, but not here."

"Why? Don't you like these?"

"Have you seen the price tags?" Her voice was merely a whisper.

Conrad smirked. "Of course, sweetheart. Why do you think I brought you here?" He gave a bow. "Consider it a gift from your loving husband."

Was he mocking her? That she thought these clothes were too expensive? But they were. Who would want to spend a week's salary on a jumper? Even if it complimented her eyes so well.

He turned toward Mr Klatz. "My wife said you picked well, Mr Klatz. We'll take all of these." One of the ladies freed Annie's arms, and before she could object, Conrad selected a few more evening dresses from the gown rack and placed them in her arms. "Try these as well."

Annie took a deep breath as the room seemed closing on her. "I appreciate the gesture, but it's too much."

He dismissed her with a wave of a hand, adding a few more to her load.

A bitter taste filled her mouth. Even if it wasn't her money, she could still remember how a lavish lifestyle had drained her resources in the blink of an eye when she had let her ex-husband Liam splash it on anything he had laid his eyes on.

"Thank you, but no. I'm not a princess or a character from Pretty Woman." She pursed her lips.

"Fine." Conrad rolled his eyes as if she were the one making things awkward. "But at least take a dress for our dinner tonight. We're going to an exquisite restaurant."

Annie glanced at the red dress he pointed to, her heart softening. It was beautiful and would go perfectly with her wedding shoes.

She sucked air through her teeth. He was rich, wasn't he? He could afford this. It was tempting to accept the gift, but she couldn't shake the feeling that it was all part of his game to get his hands on her marriage fund—or rather, Louise's.

Her eyebrows knitted together, she pushed back. "I'll take the sweater, leggings, and a set of underwear. That's it." Annie reached for her card— she would find a way to return them later.

Conrad brushed her hand with the card aside. "Put it on my tab, please, Mr Klatz." He reached for that red dress. "And we'll take this one too. Darling, I can't take you to that restaurant in leggings and your shirt."

Annie's face flushed with anger. She pointed at the dress, her finger shaking. "Do what you want, but I won't wear that dress, and I'm not going to that restaurant either!"

She stormed toward the shop exit, refusing to be treated like a possession. This was worse than anything she had gone through with Darren. What was wrong with men?

For Liam, she had been nothing but an ATM. Darren had disguised his obsession with controlling her—and her every thought—behind fake protectiveness. And now this. She had no name for it. A peacock showing off his feathers? Did he want her to clap or bow to him? Or what? Annie couldn't stop shaking. Her hands had formed tight fists, her nails digging into the soft tissue of her palms.

The moment she stepped outside, she bumped into Colton.

"I'm so sorry, Ms Louise. I didn't see you coming out."

His sincerity hushed that barrage of thoughts. He was an innocent bystander and, so far, had been nothing but helpful. She shook her head. "No, it's my fault. I didn't look."

She started breathing through her nose, trying to calm herself.

"Did you enjoy your shopping experience, Ms Louise?"

Annie clenched her teeth. "You have no idea," she replied, her voice dripping with sarcasm. Then, inspiration struck.

"Colton, could you drive me back to the cottage, please? Conrad has some important business to finish here, and he said he'll catch up with us later."

Colton hesitated for a moment, but then nodded in agreement, offering her his arm—at least one real gentleman with no hidden agenda.

Chapter 8

Conrad stepped out of the shop, arms laden with bags of expensive clothes, hoping Louise would have calmed down by now. She wasn't there. He raised his eyebrows and scanned the colourful crowd, but he couldn't spot her hazelnut hair anywhere. She had simply vanished—along with the Tesla that Colton was supposed to bring over.

Struggling to balance the stiff glossy paper bags in one hand, he fished his phone out of his pocket. After a few clumsy attempts, he tapped the car number, and Colton picked up almost immediately.

"Mr Conrad, I'm on the way to the cottage with Ms Louise. She said you made other travel arrangements."

"Did she now?" Conrad clicked his tongue.

"Isn't that so? Would you like me to come back and pick you up, sir?"

"No, it's fine. Things didn't go as planned, but I'll make my way back."

"Are you sure?" Conrad could hear the concern in his assistant's voice.

He exhaled in an attempt to make his voice sound reassuring. "Absolutely. Don't worry about it."

"Have a great evening, sir."

"You too, Colton. Have a great time with your family."

Conrad shook his head, shifted the bags in his arms, and marched to the taxi rank. An old-style black cab waited, and he climbed into the backseat. The cracked grey faux leather groaned beneath him, and the scent of sandalwood and green apple air freshener filled the cab. He barked his address at the driver, making it clear he wasn't in the mood for chitchat.

As the taxi cruised through the countryside, with the windows partly open and the plush dice bobbing from the rearview mirror, Conrad brooded over Louise's behaviour. Why was he trying so hard when she kept rejecting him? What would he need to do to woo her enough to stay? Would that even be worth it?

The contents of the bags on his lap could easily cover a month's salary, yet she'd acted as if his efforts were insignificant and beneath her. It seemed pointless. Why was he going to such lengths, pushing himself deeper into debt, when she was too stubborn to see him as an ally?

When the taxi arrived at the cottage, Conrad paid the £100 fare, his teeth clenched with anger swelling within him as he stepped out. Using his elbow and knee for support, he opened the cottage door and stumbled inside, making enough noise to wake a bear from hibernation. Instead of luring her out, his entrance was met by the sound of Louise's bedroom door slamming shut.

Pursing his lips, Conrad dropped the bags on the coffee table and stormed over to her room.

Banging on the door, he shouted, "Why the hell did you ditch me in Bath? I was trying to buy you clothes. Is this how you show gratitude?"

"Gratitude?" Her voice was loud and clear. "You were treating me like a doll! Like I was your property, deciding what I should wear and eat without asking what I wanted. I'm not a puppet!"

"I was trying to make you feel special." His voice faltered. Didn't she see that? How hard he was trying?

"I certainly didn't feel that way. How many women have you sent to Mr Klatz before whisking them off to a fancy dinner? I bet you choose the same bloody restaurant each time, don't you?"

That struck a chord. It *was* the best restaurant in town. Obviously, he had been there once or twice. With women.

"I was trying to do something nice for you. But I got a barrage of insults, instead."

He clenched his fists and stormed off to his study, shutting the door behind him with a bang.

Inside, he buried his head in his hands, taking a few deep breaths, but his jaw remained clenched so tightly it hurt.

"A big mistake." He rubbed his temples to ease the tension building there.

Maybe it would be better to end it all. He might have to sell his soul to the vultures, but he'd manage. Some people would lose their jobs, but what could he do? He had tried, and he had failed. No one could blame him for not putting up with a woman from hell.

An email notification pinged on his phone—a supplier asking when they would get paid. Conrad felt the walls closing in on him. He burst out of his study and through the living room, shouting toward her closed door, "I'm leaving. Don't wait up!"

A sting came straight back: "I never planned to!"

He slammed the door behind him—the sound echoing through the cool evening air. *So much for having the last word.*

A gust of chilly wind hit him, cooling his head. What now?

A tantalising aroma of steak drifted through the breeze, a reminder of the dinner they'd missed.

He scoffed. "She can handle her own food."

As Conrad marched through the quiet streets, his footsteps echoed on the cobblestones, and his pace relaxed the farther he got from the cottage. The ten-minute walk made his anger simmer away as he pictured himself enjoying a few pints of cold beer, far from the tension awaiting back at home.

The Swan pub came into view, its entrance adorned with twinkling fairy lights. A solitary car sat in the small car park, a testament to the pub's laid-back atmosphere. Conrad had never understood how the place stayed in business with so few customers, but tonight, he didn't care.

Nothing would take the edge off better than a few pints and a lighthearted conversation with the locals.

"And she can do what she wants." Conrad puffed, shaking his head. "Let's see how well it works out for you, Little Miss Independent."

***

Annie cracked open the door, straining her ears for any sound of Conrad's presence. All she could hear was a dog barking in the distance and the gentle rustling of leaves in the light breeze. Perhaps he really had left the house, as he'd said. She pulled her packed suitcase into the living room, its wheels rattling across the floor.

Her gaze fell on the olive-green paper bags on the coffee table, and she couldn't resist taking a peek. In two strides, she reached the table and nudged the stiff bag open. Inside was the sweater she had chosen. Its cosy fabric under her fingers, along with the scent of wood smoke drifting through the windows, reminded her of a summer evening by the campfire. She pushed the jumper aside to check the rest of the bags, and the rich red of a dress appeared. Annie smirked and put the bags down. She wouldn't take charity from that guy.

Scanning the room for a pen and paper, she noticed a small blackboard beside the kitchen counter. Her fingers gripped the chalk, feeling it crumble slightly as she wrote, "It's over. Don't look for me."

Satisfied with her last words, she grabbed the suitcase's rough plastic handle and rolled it across the polished floor toward the door.

She paused and turned to take in the cottage with its rustic charm, inhaling the fresh air drifting through the open windows. For a fleeting moment, Annie imagined raising a child here, away from the city's noise, surrounded by the orchard and breathing in the lilac-scented air. She shook her head, banishing the thought, and pulled out her mobile phone to call a cab.

Just as she was about to dial, her phone lit up with several missed calls from her father. Before she could decide what to do about them, it rang again. Annie rolled her eyes. She wasn't in the mood to talk to her parents, but rejecting his call would certainly offend him—and somehow, she couldn't quite bring herself to do it. Besides, she couldn't avoid him forever. With a sigh, she answered, and his voice immediately shattered the serenity of the place.

"Why haven't you called us? Hold on, I'm putting you on speaker. Did you convince Conrad to sign the paperwork?"

Annie clenched her jaw, her fingers digging into her palm. "I haven't, and I'm not planning to. He's a pathetic excuse for a human being. How can you expect me to be with such a man even for a second longer? I'm done with this whole charade. Forget about it."

Her father's voice remained calm. "Darling, slow down and think before making any rash decisions."

Her mother chimed in, "Would you rather live with that rude man than a respected gentleman like Conrad?"

Annie's stomach twisted in fear as her grip on the phone tightened.

"What man?"

"The awful man who barged into our house earlier today, demanding to see you." Her father's tone suggested he blamed Annie for the unexpected visit.

Annie swallowed hard, leaning against the wall by the door for support as a wave of dizziness washed over her.

"Did you tell him where to find me?"

"Of course not!" her mother snapped. "But if you want, you can call him yourself." She rattled off the number Annie knew all too well. Darren. He had found them.

Annie bit her lip, tasting blood. "What did you tell him about me?"

"Nothing, other than that you don't live here and to bugger off. But enough about that man. You could do so much better with Conrad."

"You can't expect me to stay in this fake marriage!" Annie's face grew hot.

"You don't have to—not for long. Just postpone your departure, darling." Her father's jovial tone made her cringe. "Once the cottage is transferred, you can tell him you've changed your mind and walk away. Everyone wins."

"Except for Conrad," Annie pointed out.

"Well, we'd be doing him a favour, really. He couldn't get rid of that cottage anyway, and we'd just be taking the problem off his hands." Her father chuckled. "And he's got his inns. He's not a poor man. He'll get over it."

Her father was right. Judging by the way Conrad had splashed cash around town today, he wouldn't be that much worse off. But what about her? Could she live with herself if she did such a thing? Annie would never go through with it if it were just about her. But what about her baby? What mother wouldn't do everything to ensure her child had a safe place to call home?

***

The door to the dimly lit pub squeaked as Conrad stepped inside, announcing his arrival. The Swan, a local favourite, had an eclectic mix of rustic charm and industrial design, with wooden beams and stone floors juxtaposed against metal accents and exposed pipework.

He breathed in the familiar scent of a pub—stale beer, a hint of fried food, and the faint trace of decades of spilled alcohol. This place had the soul of a hardworking man, reminding Conrad of how his life used to be.

Magic Radio played feel-good '80s tunes—not too loud, but enough to muffle conversations. As he took a seat, the bar stool scraped against the stone floor with a metallic screech that made him cringe.

"Conrad! Long time no see, mate." Tony, the bartender, greeted him, pulling a squeaky pump and pouring a pint of Punk IPA. The beer swooshed into the glass, its bitter aroma filling the air.

"Cheers, Tony." Conrad took a sip of the refreshing beer and grabbed a handful of wasabi peanuts from a bowl, enjoying the heat that made his eyes water.

"Shouldn't you be on your honeymoon or something? I heard you got married." Tony wiped down the counter.

Conrad raised an eyebrow. "News travels fast around here."

Tony chuckled. "You know how it is. So, who's the lucky lady? Never seen you bring anyone here before."

"It's an arranged marriage." Conrad shrugged and took another swig of his beer.

"Oh?" Tony shuffled some bottles around. "Sounds ... interesting."

"You have no idea." Conrad sighed, raking a hand through his hair. "She's the most ungrateful and insufferable woman I've ever met."

Tony refilled Conrad's glass. "Really?" Then he raised his index finger. "Be back in a moment." He strode to the end of the bar to serve another customer.

Conrad played with a round coaster, sliding it back and forth on the counter. The pub's warm, strategic lighting and muffled music created a cosy environment that seemed to encourage honesty.

"So?" Tony refilled the peanut bowl.

"You won't believe it, man." Conrad shook his head in disbelief. "She's been nothing but trouble since the wedding. And today, just a day after we got married, she ditched me in Bath."

"No way!" Tony raised his eyebrows. "What for?"

"I was trying to treat her, you know." Conrad sighed. "Took her to an expensive boutique, bought her clothes, planned a fancy dinner ... and she just flipped. Said she'd never wear the red dress I picked out for her and refused to go to the restaurant I booked."

"That's odd," Tony mused. "Why would she do that?"

Conrad shook his head. "Who knows? She muttered something about making her own choices and not being anyone's puppet. But I was just trying to be nice and make her feel special."

Tony leaned in, his eyes twinkling with amusement. "So, you like her, huh?"

"What? No!" Conrad waved his hand dismissively. "I just told you she's the last woman on Earth I'd want to spend my life with."

Tony raised an eyebrow. "If you didn't like her, you wouldn't go to so much trouble to please her."

Conrad huffed, taking a swig of his beer. "I only just met her."

Tony chuckled, shaking his head. "You always liked feisty girls. Remember Nicky?"

They both cackled, and Conrad grinned. "Oh, yeah. She was something else. Hot as the surface of the sun."

Tony lined up the coasters. "So, what are you gonna do about your wife, then? Divorce her?"

"I can't. I need her money, and I need her help to get it." Conrad's mood darkened, and he stared into his pint glass.

"Ah!" Tony tilted his head. "I knew there was an ulterior motive. Does she know about it?"

Tapping his fingers on the counter, Conrad nodded. "She knows about the money. It was part of the arrangement."

The bartender scratched his chin. "Well, you just said you're getting *her* money. I bet she's not thrilled about that."

Conrad shrugged. "Well, it's a trade. She's getting a cottage for it."

Tony's eyes widened in surprise. "George's cottage?"

"Yeah."

The bartender froze with a glass in his hand. "Your cottage?"

Conrad nodded again.

"Your home?"

"Yes, my home." The bitterness of the words lingered on his tongue.

"Damn, man."

Chapter 9

The mobile phone vibrated on the oak bedside table. Once. Twice. Annie sighed and sat up in bed. She checked her phone and tensed as a message from Darren appeared.

Darren: "You can't hide forever. And when I find you, you'll regret not replying to me"

She blocked his number again, but it felt like a lost cause—he used a new number every time she blocked one. Despair washed over her as she gazed out the window at the sunlit orchard. Birds chirped as if there were no troubles in the world, and the breeze carried the rejuvenating scent of morning dew, with hints of lilac and freshly cut grass.

The suitcase lay open in the room's corner, its contents strewn about like the remnants of Annie's hope. Returning to her sister's place or her parents' home was out of the question now. He knew about them, and Annie was certain he would have his guys watching. Fortunately, she didn't need to worry about her family's safety. Lou was safely away, and if it came down to a showdown between her mother and any thug, Annie would bet on her mother. Besides, he wouldn't hurt them; he only wanted Annie.

She faced two choices: run away and start a new life, with no money to speak of and no job, cutting all ties with her family, no matter how thin and strained they were, or stay here for a while. It was fake, but safe. And as her father said, if Conrad signed off on the cottage, she would get more of the inheritance money and could leave this infuriating man and build the future for her kid.

And help them con him out of the promised money?

She shrugged.

It wasn't his, to begin with.

It was Lou's, and he shouldn't have bet on using her money for his own benefit. Bloody men, they wanted to have it all.

Her parents had no right to gift Louise's money. They would have to come up with an alternative. That was on them and not on Annie. And she would tell them to make it right by him. With the catering healthy income and the money from the inheritance, they could surely cut a new deal and get Conrad off her back.

Resolved, Annie now needed to mend fences with Conrad. A memory of last night's argument, ending with a slammed door, flashed through her mind. Had he even returned yet? Annie gasped, covering her mouth. Had she wiped that message off the chalkboard? If not, it would be hard to explain. She hurried out of her room to check.

The message on the blackboard mocked her. She glanced around, but the house was quiet. Wetting a strip of kitchen towel, she quickly wiped it clean. With any luck, Conrad hadn't seen it when he had returned yesterday.

Relieved, Annie returned to her room, slipped into her bathrobe, and grabbed her toiletry bag for the bathroom. Just as she tiptoed down the hallway, the door to Conrad's room creaked open, revealing him in his boxer shorts, hair tousled and eyes puffy.

They both froze.

Annie clutched her bag to her chest. "I can wait." She wanted to comment on his dishevelled appearance, but remembered she needed to make amends, not fan the flames.

"I can wait," she repeated, turning to retreat to her bedroom.

"No, no. Please. I'll go after you," he rasped, closing his door without waiting for her response.

Annie shrugged and headed to the bathroom. A quick shower invigorated her, washing away her worries with hot, steamy water. Her hair felt bouncy after drying it with a towel, though she regretted not buying a hairdryer the day before.

As she walked past his door on the way back, Annie gave it a quick knock and called, "All yours," before hurrying back to her room. She closed her door just as his opened.

Yesterday's clothes lay in a heap. She held them in her hands, missing that fresh laundry scent. Deciding against them, still in her bathrobe, she peeked out of her room. With the sound of running water in the bathroom, she dashed to the dining room, grabbed the shopping bags, and returned in a few strides.

The leggings had a smooth finish and hugged her legs snugly, while the sweater enveloped her in warmth and softness. They seemed to infuse her with strength, as if whispering, "This is the beginning of something better, a better life." She knew it wasn't her life, but at that very moment, she needed to believe it was.

The water ceased, and she heard the door open and then shut. Annie left her room and entered the kitchen. She opened the fridge, its emptiness mirroring her own stomach—only a box of Lurpak, a bag of coffee beans, half a pint of milk, and a lone lemon that rolled out and fell to the floor. She picked it up and placed it in the fridge drawer. There were no eggs.

Hunger gnawed at her insides. She had only eaten a piece of cold pizza last night. The bread bin contained out-of-date, but not yet mouldy bread. Rummaging through the cupboards, she discovered a tin of Heinz beans.

"Beans on toast it is, then," she murmured, pushing two slices of bread into a toaster. As she searched for a can opener, Conrad appeared in the doorway.

"Morning." His voice was still hoarse.

Annie glanced at him, dressed in jeans and a white polo shirt accentuating his tan arms.

"Morning." She sounded as cheerful as she could manage under the circumstances. "How do you like your coffee?"

"Black." Annie turned toward the coffee machine, but he added, "You don't need to make me one."

"It's no trouble." She waved her hand. "And you look like you need one. Besides, I'm making breakfast." Annie placed the mug under the spout and pressed the double cup button. The machine whirred, and hot liquid squirted down.

"You look lovely in those clothes. Great choice." He stood right beside her. A slight scent of an exotic cologne stirred her senses.

"Thanks." She smiled.

Annie wanted to say something about last night, but her voice caught in her throat. She was worried he might ask her to leave, that things were not working out. She bit her nail, her eyes flicking to his face for any sign of what he might be thinking.

***

The aroma of freshly brewed coffee and toasted bread wafted through the kitchen as Conrad braced himself for the conversation that lay ahead. He still couldn't gauge whether his wife was angry or simply indifferent. The clatter of plates and cutlery punctuated the silence, but Conrad decided to break the ice.

"Look, I'm sorry about yesterday," he began, rubbing the back of his neck. "I didn't mean to offend you. I wanted you to feel like a princess, you know. Isn't that every woman's dream—to be looked after like that?"

Louise smirked, buttering the toast. "I'm not a princess and never wanted to be one. I've always been more interested in what I could achieve myself than being handed everything on a silver plate."

She glanced up at him, her eyes softening. "How many slices of toast do you want?"

Conrad shook his head. "You don't have to do that for me."

Louise rolled her eyes. "I'm already making them for myself, so it's no trouble."

"Alright, two would be great," he said as he opened the fridge.

Shit.

He'd forgotten the grocery shopping. Milk for his wife's coffee and a forgotten half-empty marmalade jar were the only things he could contribute to breakfast.

Handing her plates as she needed them, he placed the salt and pepper shakers on the dining table, returning for her coffee mug as she carried the full plates to the table. They worked together like a well-oiled machine, their movements fluid and in sync.

Louise sighed, taking a seat at the table. "I'm sorry, too. I should've told you I didn't like what you were doing instead of yelling and stealing your ride."

"Oh yeah, you had poor old Colton wrapped around your finger." Conrad chuckled. "But seriously, tell me what I should've done differently."

Louise took a sip of her coffee. "I would've preferred if you'd just asked for my opinion yesterday."

Conrad furrowed his brow. "But I thought you wanted to go shopping, and we agreed to have dinner later."

"Yeah, but you decided for me what I was going to wear and where to buy my clothes," she pointed out, her tone light but firm.

"But Mr Klatz could get you anything you wanted," Conrad defended himself.

Louise shook her head. "I didn't want it like that, because I like roaming around my favourite shops. I enjoy the experience."

"You enjoy the experience?"

She nodded, taking a small bite of her toast.

My worst nightmare.

Even thinking about crowded shops on a Sunday afternoon sent shivers down his spine, like walking through a maze of mirrors, each reflection a sea of bodies, endlessly multiplying and closing in.

"I always preferred having my measurements taken and then ordering a week's worth of fitting clothes."

"Well, I hate fuss like that." Louise took a sip of her coffee and nudged the leaflets neatly stacked at the corner of the table—no doubt brought by Colton.

"So, what's the plan for today?" she asked, pushing the brochures around, none of them catching her attention. "It's Monday, isn't it? I think my parents mentioned you planned to meet with the solicitor about the paperwork?"

"Oh, well, that can wait."

Until I know your intentions.

"So?" Louise cocked her head, her eyes focused on his.

"Well ... "

Now it got tricky. In the past, he would have played the surprise card and whisked her away to some exotic, expensive location. But his gut told him that wouldn't be well received under the circumstances. He had no other ideas about how to impress her enough to win her cooperation.

Conrad leaned back in his chair, his voice softening. "You tell me. I meant it when I said I wanted you to feel special. So, tell me—what would make you happy? Going away for a week, somewhere warm or cold, maybe? And how's your ankle?"

"My ankle is much better, thanks. And no, not away. I like it here. Plus, I don't have my passport."

That killed the idea of getting closer under the tropical sun. Not that Conrad could afford to fly anywhere, but sometimes investments like that were necessary for future gains.

"So, what would you like to do then?"

Louise stroked the sleeve of her sweater—the one Conrad had brought back from the shop yesterday. Was now a good time to point out that *he* had been the one to buy it? He scratched his chin. Maybe later.

Conrad shifted in his chair, which screeched on the wooden floor, breaking the lengthening silence.

"Well, I still don't have enough clothes." She gestured to her outfit. "Thank you for bringing them back. They're lovely."

Conrad nodded, hiding a smile. A point for him.

"And I noticed a shopping mall with my favourite brands on the way to Mr Klatz's place."

Nooo! Conrad swallowed, bracing himself internally for the horrific experience. But nothing worthwhile came easy.

"So, you'd like to go shopping in Bath, but your way. Am I right?"

A wide smile brightened her face, her eyes sparkling as dimples appeared on her cheeks. The entire room seemed to light up.

"Absolutely." She reached out and touched his arm. "Thank you for listening." The warmth of her touch travelled along Conrad's spine, sparking a cascade of tingles.

"Okay, I'll let Colton know our plans." He reached for his phone to call his assistant.

"Do you always make Colton drive you everywhere?" Her surprise seemed genuine, without a hint of sarcasm.

It was a good question. But since the only presentable car was Colton's Tesla, there wasn't much of a choice for getting out and about.

"Well, he was coming here anyway, to pick up the—" Conrad waved his hand, searching for inspiration around the room. "Books, yes, for the accountant. Month's end and whatnot."

Without giving her a chance to react to his rambling, Conrad speed-dialled Colton while carrying his mug to the coffee machine for a refill.

"Good morning, Colton. I hope you won't mind, but my wife would like to go shopping in Bath today."

"Beg pardon, but with you, sir?"

Conrad chuckled. "Yes, with me. I know. But she wants to go to a shopping mall this time." The coffee machine whirred and sputtered as if sensing Conrad's unspoken emotions.

"Oh, I see. I'll be on my way then. I should arrive within half an hour."

"That's fantastic, thank you."

"My pleasure, sir."

After ending the call and grabbing his full mug, Conrad strolled back to Louise. "He'll be here in thirty minutes. Would you like another coffee?"

She shook her head, so he sat down. Turning the mug in his hands, he took a deep breath.

Better sooner than later.

"About that arrangement … you know, your marriage fund?" Conrad let the question hang while he sipped his coffee in silence.

Louise tilted her head but said nothing.

There was no backing out now. "At the wedding, you acted like you weren't aware of that part of the deal?" The silence grew louder as Conrad finished his coffee, waiting for his wife to open up.

And it paid off.

"I was simply confused." She got up from her chair and began collecting the plates, as if this was the end of the conversation.

"That's good." Conrad forced a chuckle. "You got me real worried."

A half-smile appeared on her face, but it didn't reach her eyes, and she rushed to the kitchen. Fishy. Conrad grabbed the salt and pepper shakers and followed her.

"So, that marriage fund thing … it's kind of sexist, don't you think?"

That got a reaction; her cheeks reddened.

"Yeah, it looks that way, doesn't it? I guess my grandma was old-fashioned when it came to tradition."

Conrad stood with his mouth open. What did her grandma have to do with this? Another puzzle to solve? "Your grandma?"

"They didn't tell you?" Louise smiled—a genuine smile this time, with tiny wrinkles radiating from her eyes in a burst of diverging lines.

"It was a tradition in my family for generations, and my grandma wanted us—" She cleared her throat. "Me, to have it. In her eyes, it was a sign of partnership." Louise used her hands to emphasise her point. "That a woman would bring to the marriage as much as, or maybe even more than, the man. You know."

"Well." Conrad shrugged. "I don't know."

It was a strange way of putting it. To him, it sounded like telling a guy that marrying this woman came with a hefty paycheck. Wasn't that like a bargain?

"Me and you both. I loved my grandma, but this—" She practically spat out the word, pointing at some imaginary stack of money. "I find it the most chauvinistic way of putting a value on a woman."

Conrad exhaled and chuckled. "Oh my God. I'm so glad you said that. That's exactly what I thought." Or close enough, anyway. At least they agreed on something.

"Ironic, isn't it?" Her chuckle was more sombre.

Conrad shifted from one foot to the other. He was clearly missing something. "What is?"

"That you think this way, yet the only reason we got married was that money." She scoffed, crossing her arms.

"Oh, come on. Not only." He raised his hands in a defensive gesture. "The reason *you* entered this marriage was to get the cottage." Conrad pointed at the meticulously polished floors—his cleaner was a wonder woman as the floors stayed shiny after days of use.

Louise opened her mouth, to argue the point no doubt, but the bell rang, and Colton entered, bringing in the smell of damp earth.

Chapter 10

The heavy aroma of exotic, fruity, and floral perfumes mixed with a hint of sweat invaded Conrad's nostrils, tickling his throat. Sweat he could handle—especially as sweet as this—but the scent of spices scratched at the back of his throat.

Conrad picked up yet another pair of sunglasses from the display and tried them on. Elvis style. Definitely not for him.

A metallic click-clack caught his attention, and Conrad turned around. Through his tinted lenses, the shop looked like a dimly lit factory, full of clothes, racks, and shelves stacked to the ceiling. Louise was methodically shifting hangers with shirts back and forth like a robot. Click. Clack. Click. Clack.

Every five or six pieces, she'd pick a hanger, examine the item, and then add it to the growing pile on her other arm, already burdened with its load.

"Have you found anything interesting yet?" He removed the glasses, letting the sparkling light from myriads of spotlights back in.

"Not really, there's not much of a selection here." She sucked in air through her teeth without breaking her rhythm.

What? By Conrad's count, she'd already been to the fitting room three times, each time with at least ten pieces. And she still hadn't found anything? At this rate, they'd be here until tomorrow.

"Maybe I can help? What are you looking for?" He lifted the colourful bags from the other four shops they'd visited earlier and marched to the rack beside Louise.

"Nah, thanks. I'll just try these—" She raised her arm, loaded with a variety of tops and trousers. "And then I think I'm done with this place."

THE BIG DAY DECEIT

Finally.

Conrad exhaled in relief, hiding a wide smile. "Okay, take your time. I'll be here."

His wife smiled and nodded at him before turning on her heel and waltzing toward an empty fitting room.

This was the last one. Soon, the torture would be over. How could anyone put themselves through this voluntarily? He stroked the sleeve of a soft blouse, only to catch a disapproving glare from a woman walking by, who narrowed her eyes as if he were some kind of pervert.

He yanked his hand back—no more touching—and gestured toward the fitting rooms. "My wife … "

The woman disappeared into another part of the shop without a second glance. If he lingered here much longer, someone might call security. A rack with belts stood a few steps away. At least nobody would scoff at him for checking them out.

Conrad strolled over and picked up a brown leather belt with a traditional brass buckle.

"Oh, excuse me." A short woman, with makeup that would make a clown jealous, brushed her chest in a low-cut top against his shoulder, reaching to a shelf on the other side. Conrad took a step back, only to bump into another rack.

"Don't you mind me," she purred, flashing extremely white teeth that probably glowed in the dark. "I'm looking for something pretty for the evening."

"Ah."

What else could he say? This definitely wasn't a woman with whom he wanted to have a chit-chat in a women's clothing store—or anywhere else, for that matter. She had that predatory look about her.

"Would you be a dear and help me reach that skirt?" Her hand brushed against Conrad's chest before pointing upward.

How did she get so close, so fast?

"Of course, ma'am. The blue one?"

If he didn't help her, she'd probably chase him around the entire shop.

"Yes, and the orange one as well."

Conrad reached for the skirts, feeling the heat of her body uncomfortably close.

No freaking way.

"Here." He handed the clothes to her and retreated toward the tills. "I need to help my wife."

"What a shame ... "

Not for him. Gasping for air, he scanned the shop for signs of Louise. If she was still in the fitting room, he would have to—Conrad spotted her, waiting in line at the third till. With a sigh of relief, he slowed down and joined her in the queue.

"You must have found something then?" Craning his neck, he looked at the clothes in her hands. Not a pile, just a pair of jeans. "What happened to all those shirts?"

"Not good." She shook her head and then clicked her tongue. "I looked for you when I left the fitting room, but you were busy helping another customer. You looked ... cosy."

Was she jealous?

She sounded jealous.

"Oh no, you got it wrong. She was a predator who wanted to eat me for lunch." He shook his head in mock horror, which made Louise burst out laughing, her face lighting up with a playful expression.

Stop staring, you moron.

A beep of a card reader later, his wife handed him another bag and marched toward the shop exit. With an almost wistful smile, Conrad waltzed after her, silently vowing never to enter this shop again.

Outside, the sun was high in the sky, making Conrad squint in the sudden brightness. A gust of wind carried the smell of cinnamon and freshly baked bread, causing his stomach to gurgle in unison with nearby pigeons. His eyes followed his nose, and he spotted an Auntie Ann's Pretzels cart in the middle of the square. Conrad nudged Louise in the direction of the gorgeous smells of tasty treats and freedom.

"Oh, you're right. Let's go to Marks next."

No, no, no. Conrad shook his head slightly. He'd only now spotted the big Marks & Spencer sign on the corner building behind the cart.

The shop they'd just left was supposed to be the last one. There was no way he could bear another minute in any clothing store.

And the Auntie Ann's Pretzels stand was luring him in with an invisible thread of sweet vanilla and cinnamon.

"Sorry, Lou, but I had a miscall from my accountant. I need to call him back."

"Oh?" An indecision painted on her face.

The last thing he wanted was for her to wait around while he faked a call.

"Go ahead, I'll join you after I'm done." Nudging her lightly toward the M&S entrance, Conrad pulled out his phone from his pocket.

As soon as she entered the massive building, Conrad stashed his phone away and sidestepped over to the pretzel cart. After ordering two portions of cinnamon sticks to go, he collapsed onto a wooden bench with a clear view of the store entrance.

Good thing he'd let Colton go. The poor man would have probably read a whole novel while waiting.

Judging by the last visit, Conrad figured he had at least an hour.

He bit into a warm, chewy cinnamon stick.

"Ooh, that's good."

A taste of pure joy. And sweet. Too sweet. Conrad wiped sugar from his lips, scanning the South Gate Street for a coffee place sign.

He stood up, torn between the blue and purple coffee shop signs in the distance, weighing his chances of getting stuck in a queue, when a familiar figure appeared at the M&S entrance.

No way.

Barely ten minutes had passed since they'd parted. Spreading the cinnamon all over his jeans, Conrad patted his pockets, searching for his phone. Not there. Where the hell had he stashed his mobile? Any second now, she'd spot him sitting here.

Watching her without blinking, Conrad checked his jacket and sensed the sleek shape of his phone. Before he could pull it out, though, Louise glanced over her shoulder, then hurried off toward the side street, as if someone were chasing her.

Conrad hung all the bags on his arm, holding leftover sticks in his hand, and rushed after his wife.

What if she stole something?

Conrad chuckled. That would be the highlight of the day. And then he could come to the rescue and bail her out, like a proper hero. But if she had taken something, must've been small—she wasn't carrying anything extra. Yet she kept glancing back, staying close to the grocery stalls lining New Orchard Street, like she wanted to blend in. Not a chance. On a

Monday morning, the locals were at work and tourists at the Cathedral square or visiting the Roman Baths—certainly not here.

Conrad raised his eyebrows and sped up to close the distance between them, watching the path from the shop to Louise, expecting guards or someone else to follow her, but nobody emerged.

Just as he came within earshot, Louise turned back toward the M&S entrance, unaware of him. One more step and Conrad tapped her shoulder. His wife froze and turned around so slowly that he thought the time had stopped. The moment her eyes landed on Conrad's face, her shoulders relaxed, and a sigh of relief escaped her mouth.

"You scared me."

She didn't look scared. Not of him, anyway.

"That was quick. I thought you needed more stuff?"

"Oh, I just needed a bit of fresh air." Louise pulled one bag from his hand and resumed her walk down New Orchard Street, away from the shops.

"So, are you done for today?"

As he caught up with her, she nudged him slightly to squeeze between him and a vegetable stall, barely glancing at the produce.

What on Earth?

Conrad narrowed his eyebrows. "What happened back there?"

"What do you mean?" The innocent surprise in her voice would probably fool him on any other day, but what he had experienced wasn't normal.

Leaning toward her ear, he whispered, "Did you nick something?"

A hearty laughter and a genuine amusement on his wife's face was a clear sign he was way off. What then?

Louise lunged for the shadows and collapsed on a wooden bench with a metal curvy back toward the shops, facing the row of trees with juicy green leaves and the bicycle stand, with a lonely, dilapidated bike attached.

Conrad sat down next to her, grinning as if he'd won the lottery—actually, leaving that shopping spree was better than winning—and taking full lungs of exhaust fumes from the speeding away motorcycle on its way to deliver food.

"So, seriously. What was that all about?"

Louise grimaced, massaging her ankle. "I spotted my ex, Liam. The last thing I wanted was a chit-chat with him and his new wife."

"His wife?"

That must've been awkward. If he bumped into Elisabeth with a new dude, he probably wouldn't be as calm as Louise.

"Yeah, and his kid."

She seemed lost in thought. Did she still have feelings for him? Was she imagining it could have been their kid?

"You mean a baby? It couldn't be that long since you were together. Still getting married, and having a baby, that seems fast."

Was he her first? Or only? Was he a reason she had agreed to marry a stranger for money?

"Oh no, it was ages ago." She smiled, though her eyes remained focused on something in the distance, and she kept turning the wedding band on her finger.

Conrad touched his own ring, wondering if it meant anything—the fact she still wore hers.

"It couldn't be that long ago. Unless it was a puppy love? Was he your first?"

Conrad sucked the air. Stupid question. Too early.

Louise raised an eyebrow, a playful smile parting her full lips. "Jealous?"

"Of course not. Just checking if I need to send a few thugs after him with a strong message to stay away or—" The smile faded, and her face turned ashen. "I was joking." He raised his hands in surrender.

"Yeah, I know." She shook her head. "It's not you. It simply reminded me of something I'd rather forget."

He should probe deeper. A caring husband should know stuff about his wife that causes the blood to drain from her face. She seemed so fragile right now. Conrad touched her shoulder and cleared his throat.

But he wasn't a loving husband. They barely knew each other. What if she told him to mind his own business and get cross with him?

Louise gasped and opened her eyes wider.

What now?

"Are those Auntie's Ann's?" She yanked the last cinnamon stick from his hand and shoved it into her mouth before he could object.

"Don't give me that look. You had most of the pack already." She mumbled with her mouth full. "You could've asked me if I wanted some when you knew you would be buying. But no. You didn't think of me or my needs. All that talk about wanting to make me happy was just that. Talk."

A second pack he had bought for her rested in his palm, under the jacket. Conrad would enjoy that. Should he let her talk more, or would she be upset that he let her dig a deeper hole for herself? Yeah, knowing women, she would turn it around and he would be the villain.

Looking straight into those shimmering eyes, he placed the bag full of cinnamon sticks in her gesticulating hand. The warmth and softness of her skin made him want to hold on to her for longer.

"What?" She pulled her hand toward her face, breaking the link between them, and looked inside the bag like she was expecting to find a snake.

"You were saying?" He couldn't help the smug grin—making a woman speechless. Little pleasures in life.

"Well...thank you."

Louise lifted one stick into her mouth in a manner he found seductive—while she would simply call eating—and bit into the dough, licking her lips after each bite.

Pigeons. Twats on bicycles.

Conrad needed something to distract him from those tasty lisps or he would end up kissing her and probably get smacked for it.

Pigs.

How could he miss this earlier? There was a pig covered in colourful mosaic just next to the bicycle stand. "Look." He extended his finger toward the unusual animal sculpture.

"No, listen." Louise froze with her finger near her ear and mouth lightly open. A melody drifted from between the buildings, making Conrad chuckle—a live concert.

"I know exactly what it is. Want to check it out?"

She brushed off crumbs from her lap and folded the empty bag in her hands. "Absolutely."

The swarm of pigeons landed next to their feet and attacked the sweet leftover.

"Come on." Avoiding the birds, he led his wife toward the end of the street and to the left, into Henry Street—not the most vibrant of places and it would be quicker to go back through the shopping centre, but he couldn't risk her being attracted to another shiny window display. Or bumping into her ex. The last thing he wanted was for her to rekindle some old puppy love.

***

The pull on her hand was firm and commanding, and Annie obediently followed as Conrad led her away from the encounter with Liam. Her ex-husband's calls after her still echoed in her ears. At first, his voice had carried a surprise, then uncertainty when she had ignored him and retreated as quickly as she could. When she'd felt that tap on her shoulder, her mind had gone blank. How would she explain to Conrad that not only had she been married before but also that her ex-husband had a habit of calling her by a different name?

Annie wiped a bead of sweat from her forehead and exhaled with relief. That was so damn close. She would bet that if Liam had been alone, she wouldn't escape with such ease. But with his wife and child by his side, he must've decided against chasing after his ex-wife.

A boy. Who would have thought? Back when they were married, Liam had been dead set against kids. "Screaming monsters," he'd called them. That was one of the many differences between him and Darren—or so she'd believed. When Darren painted a picture-perfect life, complete with two children—a boy and a girl, of course—Annie had thought she'd struck gold finding a decent family man.

"Family, my ass," she muttered, glancing around at the looming tall, sand-coloured facades of a powerful city that had weathered generations.

"What?" The hand holding hers pulled Annie toward the narrow street opening on the left-hand side.

"Oh, nothing." The last thing she wanted was for this man to dig into her past. Not him, and not yet. Too raw.

The melody she'd heard earlier seemed to have faded away. Annie squinted, straining to hear it, but all she caught was the sigh of a distant bus pulling away from a stop.

"Wait, where are we going?"

The street they entered was so narrow Annie could almost touch both sides if she stretched her arms. Blue doors and flower pots turned this otherwise plain alley into a dance of colours.

Conrad slowed to a stroll. "You said you wanted a closer look."

"Yeah, but we seem to be moving away from the sound." Annie gazed at the soft shadows enveloping the surrounding buildings, and then her eyes shot up to the sunnier tops. Not even a small cloud, and yet no sun would reach down here.

"I found us a different route. Trust me."

Annie cocked her head. *Trust him?* A soft chuckle escaped her mouth, but she said nothing. Besides, that firm grip of his hand weirdly reassured her that he knew what he was doing, even though her head seemed sceptical of such a ridiculous idea as to trust a man. Any man.

The shadows deepened as they stepped under a passage formed by adjoining buildings—like the width of the street that kept them apart was too much for them. Even those massive, strong buildings needed another one for support.

A few steps later, Annie raised her hand to shade her eyes. Trusting a man was bad enough, but following him blindly into a fast road was plain stupid. The hum of buses, the squawk of seagulls, and the overbearing smell of burning rubber and asphalt halted her.

Annie cringed. "Are you sure we're in the right place?"

Conrad chuckled. "Patience."

Without warning, he pulled her toward the left and into a colourful crowd of people rambling in every possible direction.

Great. She barely avoided a woman walking backwards—her camera pointing at something Annie couldn't even see. A bicycle whizzed past Annie with a loud ring, making her turn on her heel, only to be turned back by the pull of Conrad's hand sweeping her into another narrow street.

The city noise faded, and among those ancient walls, she caught the faint strains of that melody again.

"It's back. I can hear it." She beamed at Conrad, quickening her pace.

"Told you." The smug smile on his face made her stick her tongue out at him. Not lady-like. Not at all.

Conrad laughed. A good kind of laughter. One that she could fall in love with.

Wow, woman!

Where had *that* come from? Annie shivered and shook her head. Not a freaking chance.

That little street spat them out onto a square with an oak tree in the centre and an inviting sign of a restaurant garden. The smell of bacon reached her nose, and her stomach rumbled. Must be lunchtime.

"Could we stop for a bite? I'm getting peckish?"

"Sure, I know the perfect place—right where that music's coming from."

The moment he said it, Annie picked on the passionate thrill of the violin and the beginning to—"Is it the Roxanne? I mean—" Annie turned her head to hear better and almost tripped over an uneven paving slate of the alleyway. Only a quick grip of his hands kept Annie upright.

"Yeah." That lazy, seductive voice vibrated right next to her ear, raising hairs on her forearms. "El Tango de Roxanne from Moulin Rouge."

His lips were so close, the moistness on them inviting her to taste them, his hands holding her tight, his hips radiating heat, his …

No.

"Shall we go?" She took a step to the side, breaking the spell.

"Sure." Was there a disappointment in his voice? Or was she imagining it?

Keeping her eyes on the ground to avoid any more uneven slabs, Annie followed Conrad to the edge of a grand square filled with benches, pigeons, and lots of people, but no violin source. The music seemed to come from across the square, and she could hear the body-shattering lyrics: "Jealousy. Anger. Betrayal."

Annie picked up the pace, practically running. She had to be there for the chorus. Startling a feeding pigeon and barely dodging a boy on a tricycle with the rhythmic thud of Conrad's feet behind her, she reached a narrow passage leading to a smaller square in front of the Gothic cathedral.

Her eyes widened as she took in the scene: five couples in motion, red skirts twirling, black and red sequins shimmering in the sun, boots stomping to the tempo set by the violin. Annie halted, transfixed, watching the spectacle unfolding in front of her. And then she lost her balance when a body rammed into her from behind. Conrad held onto Annie and brought her up before she hit the pavement.

"Ouch. You could've warned me you were going to stop like that." He massaged his jaw while standing a step behind Annie.

"Shh." She waved him off like a buzzing fly, her gaze locked on the passionate dancers, as she sang with the lead: "Roxanne … "

Annie's voice was quiet. In the staccato of boots, the singer's voice, and the violin, nobody could hear her.

Except for Conrad.

"I like your voice." His rasping whisper tickled her ear and caused a tingling sensation in her stomach. Her cheeks darkened, and she stopped singing.

"Don't stop." His hot breath as he spoke, raised the hairs on Annie's neck.

Conrad's hands touched her shoulders, then lazily slid down her crossed arms, his chest brushing against her back, the heat from his thighs radiating toward her hips. Finally, his fingers reached Annie's wrists. She could sense the rough skin of his hands when he covered her soft palms, the firm grip suggesting a hidden strength.

The sudden tug made her turn around and only then did Annie realise it wasn't a seduction technique—which was totally working, by the way—but a dance.

"No, I can't." Her voice muffled as the sudden move pushed her face into his chest.

"Oh, but you must." Conrad chuckled, placing her into a firm tango frame, and guiding her as though he were born on the stage.

Annie had no choice but to follow.

"Where did you learn this?" she uttered, breathless.

"A school prom dance if you can believe it."

"No way." A giggle escaped her throat and died out a second later from a surprise when Conrad pivoted her body with a mastery, she wouldn't have expected from a man running a chain of pubs. Her body responded instinctively, pivoting, shifting, and turning, in perfect synchronisation with the mesmerising music. Nothing else mattered at that moment.

A small cry escaped her lips as the song ended, like a life cut short by a knife. The crowd erupted in applause, clapping and whistling. She would've joined, but her hands were still locked with Conrad's, their faces inches apart. Her heart pounded, either from the joyous labour of the dance or maybe from the proximity to the man who seemed to have more hidden talents than she would've given him credit for.

"For a person who can't dance, you did pretty well," he said in a rasping tone, still catching his breath, as he leaned forward. "You were amazing."

She blushed and batted her eyelashes, feeling like an emotional teenager unused to compliments. Whom she had been the last time she had danced—in that ballroom class Grandma Ann had signed Annie up for. A long time ago.

"So ... " His eyes met hers, intense, searching. His hands on her back now, not in a tango frame anymore. She could feel the heat on her skin through the fabric of her blouse where his fingers touched her.

No, she shouldn't.

But he was so close. His lips, his breath on her cheek. Annie swallowed and, as if pushing through a drying concrete, she managed to increase the distance between their faces, only an inch but enough for Conrad to blink and step back, his hands falling to his sides. He pointed toward the dancers with a slight smile.

A new, much more mellow melody began, and the singer cuddled the microphone in his hands, ready for the next song.

"Shall we grab a bite at the café over there?"

Only now did Annie notice the outdoor garden of a little restaurant tucked behind the colourful dancers waltzing across the square.

Annie nodded. "Sounds good." Her own voice betraying the emotions still swirling inside her. Her last dance partner had two left feet and pimples, and she'd always dreamed of muscular arms whisking her away.

Despite the thick crowd, Conrad somehow created a path for them. Annie followed him like a marionette, with her eyes glued to the show and her mind still recalling the passion of the dance.

"Here?" His voice pulled Annie out of her dream and made her focus on a small table in the corner, under a canopy supported by the wooden beams, with a grand view of the cathedral and the live concert.

"Perfect." Annie beamed at him. She wouldn't have picked any better.

Conrad pulled out a chair for Annie and planted the multiple shopping bags she'd forgotten about on two other chairs. "I'll go grab the menus. What would you like to drink?"

"Orange juice would be great. I'm quite thirsty."

Conrad nodded, lightly touching her shoulder, before heading to the café entrance. Annie lowered herself into a rustic wooden chair, taking full lungs of wildflower-infused air from the vase on the table. As she let the breeze play with her curls, she scanned the colourful bags, recalling the contents of each and every one.

This had turned out to be a fantastic day. Maybe she'd spent a bit too much on the clothes, but Annie couldn't remember the last time she'd enjoyed shopping like that. Darren had rarely let her go shopping at all, always insisting on ordering online, even if it meant returning half the order.

And if, by an odd chance, they visited a mall, and she spent more than five minutes in a store, he'd sulk for the rest of the day, reminding her for a week of how much he'd "suffered" for her. After a few incidents like that, she'd stopped even glancing at clothing stores.

Annie exhaled with relief. Today, though … today had been different. Even though she could see Conrad had been bored out of his mind, she had fun, as she hadn't tried to please a man. For once, it was about her.

She stretched her neck. And actually, he hadn't made it about him. Not once.

***

The charcoal smoke from the BBQ made Conrad cough, his eyes watering. He turned the burgers with the tongs and took a sip from a cold beer bottle standing next to an aluminium tray filled with halloumi slices, waiting to be grilled.

The clatter of cutlery made Conrad turn toward the raised patio, where Colton laid the outdoor table surrounded by an old sofa with cushions and a couple of camping chairs, far more practical for eating than the loungers that usually took up this space.

"Dinner in ten!" Conrad shouted toward the open patio door. Whistling a tune under his breath, he shifted the chicken and pepper skewers to a higher rack on the BBQ to make room for the cheese.

Colton appeared beside him with an empty plate ready to transfer the burgers.

"Looks like you had a good day today, sir."

"Oh." Conrad chuckled. "I was never so bored in my life." He turned to his friend. "Can you believe she spent over an hour just trying on tops?" He shook his head. "A long freaking hour. And she only bought one in the end!"

Colton laughed, handing him the plate. "I suppose she enjoyed it, though?"

"Seems like it, but I still don't know if she's planning to stay or leave. She kept avoiding the topic."

Conrad flipped the halloumi slices, which were getting brown on the edges. His whistling returned.

"Hmm." Colton raised an eyebrow. "From what I can see, sir, it couldn't have been all that bad. If you don't mind me saying so, you seem ... happy."

Conrad beamed. "Well, there was this band. You know, that *Roxanne* group?"

"The live band playing in the square, you mean?"

"That's the one." Conrad gestured with the tongs, giving the burger one final poke. The juice sizzled, releasing a mouthwatering aroma. "I think it's ready."

Colton held the plate while Conrad stacked the burgers and skewers neatly.

"We heard the music from a distance, and when I saw her face light up, I thought it might save me from another hour of shopping."

"Sounds like it did." Colton chuckled.

"It was more than that. Well ... " Conrad paused, as a memory surfaced—their dance, the almost-kiss.

"Well?"

"She sang. We danced."

"I beg your pardon? You danced, sir?" The surprise in Colton's voice made Conrad laugh wholeheartedly.

"I know, I know. It was in the moment. I couldn't resist."

"Forgive an old man, sir, but it sounds like you showed off again?" A hint of disapproval in his friend's voice made Conrad ponder it. Then he shook his head, but Colton wasn't anywhere near to see it. Conrad's gaze followed the sound of Colton's footsteps drifting away.

"It wasn't like that! I mean. If anyone showed off, it was her."

"Oh?" Colton's voice was barely audible as he reached the patio and placed the food in the centre of the table.

Conrad hung the tongs on the BBQ and with the halloumi tray in one gloved hand, he lunged toward the patio.

"If only you'd seen her dancing. Man. It was mesmerising."

"A woman of many talents, it seems, our Ms Louise." Colton centred the bread basket and lined up all the sauces he must have brought earlier. "So, you admit you had a good time in the end, sir?"

"Well, it wasn't half bad." A bright grin was a clear sign it was better than that. Much better.

After placing the cheese on the table, Conrad sank into one of the chairs, his smile fading.

"But that was just one day." He pulled off the oven glove and rubbed his neck. "Well, two, if we count yesterday's total disaster of a day." He exhaled heavily. "I have no idea what to do next."

"What are you talking about?" His wife's voice caught him off guard.

He looked up, startled. Louise stood there, her face framed by loose waves held back by sunglasses perched on her forehead. In a hoodie and a pair of leggings that hugged her perfectly shaped legs, she looked like she had always lived here. So at home.

A sudden pang of longing hit Conrad right in his stomach. Something he hadn't felt for a long time since … well, since Elisabeth.

"About tomorrow."

And how to make you stay.

"Tomorrow?" Louise slid into the corner of the sofa and reached for a bottle of sparkling water.

"Allow me, Ms Louise." Colton opened the bottle and filled a tall glass almost to the brim. Then he indicated toward Conrad, who shook his head and tilted the beer bottle over his mouth. A few last drops.

Conrad jumped up from his chair and strode toward the house.

"I'm going to grab a beer. Do we need anything else?" he asked, with his hand on the door frame.

"I think we're good, sir." Colton gestured to the table oozing with food while his wife sipped her water from the glass like it was an expensive champagne, watching something in the distance.

Inside, the house felt cooler, darker, all his financial troubles lurking in every corner. And the solution to all of it was sitting outside, probably already tucking into a burger. Conrad opened the fridge and grabbed two slim, cold bottles. If only he knew how to make her stay.

Tell her the truth, a small voice nagged in his head, but he dismissed it with a grim expression. That was the worst advice. The only way to get more money was to appear as if one had plenty already. No, the only way to make it work was to show her what a splendid life she could have.

Conrad twisted the cap and took a swig of a cold refreshing liquid before stepping out onto the sunny patio.

"There you are, Mr Conrad. Would you like one of each?" Colton held an empty plate, ready to serve.

"Colton, please, sit down and enjoy. You're not at work." He gently took the plate from his mentor's hands and transferred two burgers and two skewers onto it, topping up with a dollop of coleslaw.

Louise shifted in her seat. "So, what's your story, Colton?"

"My story, Ms Louise?" Colton picked a slice of bread and covered it with a thin layer of butter from an open tub.

"Yes. How did you end up working for Conrad?"

"Oh, that's a long story, and it goes back to Mr Conrad's—God rest his soul—father."

Colton arranged a slice of halloumi and one chicken skewer on the left side of his plate, then filled the rest with the Greek salad Conrad hadn't noticed before.

"Sounds interesting, and we've got time." Louise curled up her legs on the sofa and brought her plate to her chest, nibbling on a burger.

"Well, it all started with my mother. She used to work for Ms Alice."

"My grandmother," Conrad offered, seeing the confusion on his wife's face.

She nodded, and Colton continued. "When I turned sixteen, Sir George offered me a place as his personal assistant." The older man smiled at the memory. "I had no experience, but what I lacked in skills, I made up for in eagerness and loyalty."

"And two years later, a screaming baby was born, and Colton became a nanny." Conrad made a bow to his wife and grinned, then looked at his oldest friend, remembering how annoying he had been as a child and in his teenage years, but Colton never had lost his cool.

"Oh really? So, you've known Conrad since he was a baby? I bet you have some stories." The amusement in his wife's voice made Conrad chuckle. Oh yes, there were many stories, but knowing Colton, she would not get a word from the old man about any of them.

"Well, I was barely an adult myself back then, Ms Louise, and some of those stories would incriminate me as much as your husband, so if you'll forgive me, I'd rather not talk about them." The older man straightened up in his chair, looking rather uncomfortable. Conrad was ready to step in and change the subject, but his wife seemed to have picked up on this as well.

"So, you knew Conrad's Grandpa George pretty well, then?"

Colton visibly relaxed. "Yes, I did."

"How about my Grandma Ann?"

Colton smiled and looked at Louise. "I never had the pleasure, Ms Louise, but I heard only great things about her. And of course, I learned about their story when it couldn't harm anyone anymore—two broken hearts."

He pressed a hand to his chest. "When I met my wife, I knew she was the one. I can't imagine what it'd be like to be separated from her and never reunited."

"Ah, yes. Conrad mentioned you have a wife." Louise placed her empty plate on the table. "Any kids?"

Colton's gaze wandered off before he answered. "Sadly, no. We tried but God didn't bless us with any." His old friend glanced at his watch, swallowing hard, likely hiding a tear or two. "Oh dear. I had no idea it was so late. Please forgive an old man for taking so much of your time." He stood up, brushing crumbs off his trousers.

Conrad jumped up from his chair and stood next to his mentor. "Don't be silly, Colton. You know you're always welcome and I promised your wife we'd look after you while she was away at her sister's."

"I'm with Conrad." Louise rose from her seat and touched Colton's shoulder. "You're always welcome. How long is she away for?"

"Oh, only a few days. And thank you, Ms Louise, it means a lot."

He started collating empty plates, but Conrad placed a hand on his shoulder, stopping him. "Please don't. We've got this. Like I said, you're not at work."

Colton looked like he wanted to say something, but Conrad held onto his arm and gently guided him away from the table. "You've helped enough, my friend. Thank you."

"Well, I'll be going then." Colton picked up a hat from the nearby chair and placed it on his head, draped his jacket over his arm. "Good night, Ms Louise. It was a pleasure."

"The pleasure was mine." Her voice sounded so soft and warm that it sent chills through Conrad's body.

He watched Colton stroll toward the side gate and then disappear onto the street. The hum of the Tesla a moment later made Conrad realise he was now alone with his beautiful wife, without the slightest idea of what to do next.

"So?" He collapsed back into his chair and took a sip, searching his mind for a conversation topic.

"So." His wife sat on the edge of the sofa. "You mentioned something about tomorrow."

Idiot.

Now he remembered. He was supposed to come up with a plan for tomorrow.

"Right, yes, tomorrow. How about … "

Think, man, think.

A screeching seagull broke the silence. *Odd.*

"The seaside?"

He hadn't meant to say that out loud, but it was actually a good idea—a few days at the seaside, ice cream, romantic walks, sunsets.

"What would you say about a couple of days on the Isle of Wight?"

She bit on her lip in a way that made him want to taste those lips again. Although it clearly wasn't a good sign.

Too much? Maybe she was worried about intimacy and staying in the same room together.

"I need to check out a pub down there," he quickly added. "One that's for sale."

She stopped biting her lip and cocked her head instead. It was working.

"So, I thought we could go together, and while I was doing business, you might want to take some photos with your new camera. Maybe paint a little?"

"Paint?" Her confusion was obvious.

"Oh right, you've got no supplies, but we could get you some—unless you don't want to go?"

She waved her hand. "No, no. It sounds like a great idea. Let's just focus on the photos this time. It'll give me an opportunity to get used to the camera."

"So, it's settled." Conrad took a full lung of air.

That wasn't so hard, was it?

Now, he had to make a call in the morning to invite himself to one of two pubs in the area under the pretence of scouting the opportunities. Luckily, he knew a few owners down there.

Now what?

Should he ask about her intentions? What if he spooked her?

Louise yawned and stood up. "I think I'll call it a night. It was quite a full-on day."

She reached for the plates that Colton had left, prompting Conrad to spring up from his chair.

"Don't worry about it. I can clean it up."

He touched her hand, but she shook her head and lifted the dishes. "You cooked, so it's the least I can do."

Conrad opened his mouth to object, but she had already disappeared inside the house. With a shrug, he loaded his arms with the bread basket and remaining salad bowls, following her inside.

When he reached the sink, his wife was already on her way back to the patio. If he recalled correctly, there wasn't much left out there. Conrad opened the dishwasher, scraped the leftover food from the plates into the bin, and stacked them neatly in the machine.

A minute later, a light breeze brought her scent, so he turned and barely avoided a collision with Louise, who stood right next to him.

"Gosh, you scared me. I didn't know you were that close."

She handed him the remaining plates with leftover burgers and a lone pepper—nothing left of the chicken skewers. Their hands brushed for a split second, reminding Conrad of that dance and passion earlier in the day.

They stood so close he could see her breasts rising fast in shallow breathing. Her lips glistened in the dim light, and her long lashes cast shadows over those emerald green eyes as she looked at him. And then she yawned and laughed, breaking his trance.

"I'm knackered. What time do you want to leave tomorrow?"

"Oh, sometime after breakfast. But no rush."

She nodded, touching his shoulder for a brief moment before dancing away toward her room.

The urge to follow her was strong. And stupid. Conrad rushed outside, reaching the BBQ in a few long strides. Using a metal brush, he scrubbed the leftovers from the grill, focusing on the task rather than the woman inside the house.

This was getting out of hand. Conrad was nowhere near securing his funds. He needed a cool head, yet it seemed impossible around her. This was not what he had expected. Not at all.

A femme fatale.

Life had taught him to stay clear of that kind. They would suck you dry. But he had no choice here.

Still, he had to admit that when she wasn't accusing him of being a bastard, she was actually an excellent companion.

"Just keep it cool, man. Keep it cool."

***

Annie closed the door behind her and marched toward the open windows with the energy of a three-year-old. A scraping sound made her listen for clues.

A chuckle escaped her as she caught Conrad's voice, muttering curses under his breath. She shut the window, silencing both the scraping noise and the chirping of birds outside.

"Good." Conrad wouldn't hear her either.

Annie climbed onto the bed, plumped the cushions, and arranged them behind her back before picking up the phone from the nightstand. No new notifications. She should have felt relieved, but her tense shoulders and neck suggested otherwise. Darren. Even without a new text from him, Annie could feel him circling, getting closer.

Her hand stroked her belly in a protective gesture. No, she wouldn't let this baby be harmed like—

Tears welled in her eyes, and she blinked them away. Thinking about the past wouldn't help the future. She took a few deep breaths, rolling her head from side to side to relax her neck muscles. Once she trusted her voice, Annie tapped the video call button on her phone.

A tanned face framed by joyful copper curls, adorned with a vivid orange flower, appeared on the screen with a wide grin. All of Annie's worries drifted away at the sight of pure joy on her sister's face.

"Someone's having a great time." Annie tutted, unable to hold back a smile.

Louise's grin widened, even though it seemed impossible. The view shifted, showing the lounger she rested on, a side table adorned with colourful cocktails in fancy glasses—complete with mandatory umbrellas. The view blurred for a second before zooming in on Louise's hand.

A ring. A fiery dragon winked at Annie with its amber eye. Annie shrieked. Any other woman seeing this dragon ring might have questioned her partner's taste, but this ring was *so* Louise.

"Oh my God, Lou! It's perfect. When did this happen?"

"I know, right?" The amber eye blinked, reflecting the evening sun's rays. "It was waiting on a pillow for me when I woke up today."

"And you didn't tell me earlier!" Annie jumped up from the bed, unable to sit still.

"I thought about it, but we had a full-on day with the volcano tour, and the signal was patchy."

Annie paced around the room, brimming with energy. "This is so amazing, Lou. I'm so happy for you—and for Meggie!"

The camera panned back to the cocktails, then to another lounger, where Meggie reclined with effortless ease. Annie had only met her once, but the impression lingered—this was a woman of quiet strength and unwavering confidence. Her straightforward demeanour and warm, steady gaze had instantly earned Annie's admiration, but it was the gentle way Meggie's hand rested on Louise's arm as if anchoring her, that truly spoke volumes.

"Hi Meg, congratulations."

"Thank you." Meggie waved, her smile stretching from ear to ear.

The scenery changed, showing the sun setting over the ocean, and then circled back to Louise's face.

"So, when's the big day? Have you thought of a date yet?"

Annie stopped pacing, watching as a slight crease formed on her sister's forehead.

"Not sure. I'm still trying to get over the shock, you know." Louise's giggle filled the air. "And I'll need to tell Mother."

"Oh my. Yes. She'll probably have a heart attack or simply pretend it hasn't happened."

Annie wandered to the window.

"Do you think she'll come to the wedding?" The light tone was underpinned by uncertainty.

Annie lifted the voile. No sight of Conrad or anything else apart from the sun setting over the orchard, bathing the trees in oranges and reds. So calm and serene.

"Annie? Are you there?" Her sister's concerned voice jolted her back.

"Oh, yes, sorry. Got lost for a moment." Annie turned, so the sunset framed her head in the phone's camera. "Check this out. And yeah, I'm sure she'll come if only to complain about how horrible everything is."

A relieved chuckle escaped Louise's mouth, and Annie smiled. She'd forgotten how easy it was to lift her sister's spirits. How much she looked up and trusted Annie. The same way Annie had always trusted Grandma Ann. Her rock.

"I wish Grandma Ann was here to see you right now." Annie strolled over to the wall of family photos and flipped the camera on her phone so Louise could see them, too. "She would be so delighted you followed your heart."

"Yes, she would be." A nostalgic tone in her sister's voice resonated with Annie. "But enough about me. Something tells me you're still at the cottage. Have you told him yet?"

Annie flipped the camera back and settled into a nearby chair. "No, I haven't. Because Darren—" She swallowed, suddenly remembering the danger. "He's close. He paid Mother a visit."

"Oh no, Annie! What are you going to do?"

"I don't know." Annie rubbed her neck. "But at least you're safe."

Louise shook her head. "But you're not. He could show up at your door any minute now."

The panic in her sister's voice made Annie's heart race. With a few deep breaths, she slowed it down. "I'll be fine. We're going away."

"Away?"

"Yes, Conrad suggested a trip to the Isle of Wight for a couple of days."

"Okay." Louise scratched her chin. "But what about after that?"

Annie shrugged. Good question. One she had no actual answer for. But only a few hours ago, she could feel Darren's vile breath on her neck, and now there was an escape—if only for a few days.

"That buys me some time. Maybe he'll give up. Or maybe I'll find a job at some bad and breakfast on the Isle of Wight and stay there. Far from his reach."

"That's actually not a bad idea. With your experience, any B&B owner would be lucky to have you." Louise's voice sounded calmer and more certain now, quite the opposite of the turmoil in Annie's head.

She might have had the experience. After all, she had managed a busy pub for quite a few years before COVID, but she couldn't exactly offer any references without Darren getting a sniff of her location. And with the baby on the way ...

"But you should tell him."

"Tell who?" Why on earth would Louise insist she got in touch with Darren? This was the last thing she wanted.

"Conrad, of course. I love you, sis, but it's not right. Regardless of what you think about him."

Conrad. Her fake husband. Her ticket away from the abusive past and terrible memories.

"I know. I just need to find a way to tell him the truth."

And to convince him to still give me that cottage.

Footsteps echoed outside her room, followed by a soft knock on the door. Annie pressed the end button without saying goodbye to Louise.

"Everything okay in there?" His deep voice sounded close, like there were no walls between them.

How long had he been standing there?

"I'm fine, thanks."

"I thought I heard voices."

What should she say? Not the truth, that's for sure. Did he hear anything in particular? All of it?

"I was just getting ready for bed when my father called to check on the situation, but I told him I was tired."

"Oh, okay." A hint of apprehension in his voice. Annie swallowed hard—he bought the lie this time. "Good night, then."

"Good night." She tiptoed to the bed, changed into her nightie, and listened to his footsteps fade away, followed by the faint sound of his door clicking shut.

Only then did she release the breath she'd been holding. She typed a reply to the question mark text from Louise.

Me: *Sorry, Conrad was outside the door*

Lou: *Ah, no worries then*
Me: *Once again, so thrilled for you, sis*
Lou: *Thanks. Enjoy the Isle of Wight. Text me when you can xx*
Me: *Sure xx*

Annie plugged in her phone and lay on her back under the comfort of the duvet. Louise was right—she had to come clean. She'd never been good at lying. Besides, this wasn't the life she wanted to live. But her baby needed her. And needed a safe place to grow up.

What could she offer Conrad to make him keep his end of the bargain after such a deception? Her father would say it was good for his business and that Conrad would be a reasonable man. But if someone had done this to her, she'd refuse the deal, no matter what they offered in return.

Was Conrad more like her or like her father?

A couple of days ago, she'd been certain he and her parents were made of the same cloth.

But now ... she wasn't so sure anymore.

Chapter 11

Conrad finished reading a message from Colton, who was on his way to pick them up and drive them to Southsea. Having a car on the island might come in handy, but what could be more memorable than a hovercraft ride? Besides, the hotel he'd booked was close to the local bars and the beach, so the car would probably be more of a nuisance than a help.

The rattling of wheels on the floor caught his attention, and he looked up.

"Oh dear. We're only going for a couple of nights, not a month-long holiday." He laughed, eyeing Louise's suitcase.

She shrugged and wheeled it closer to the door. "This is all I have anyway. No point in splitting it up."

Was that a subtle hint he should finalise this deal and stop stalling so she could retrieve her things from home? Conrad shivered. Until he knew exactly where she stood, he wasn't going to step foot in the lions' den. Her father gave him the creeps.

"Aren't we going yet?" She stood by the door, with her hand gripping the handle, clearly waiting for him to lead the way.

"Oh, no. Sorry. Not yet. Colton's on his way, but he has to make a pit stop first so, at least half an hour or more."

"Colton? Is he driving us to the Isle of Wight?" Her eyebrows shoot up.

Conrad chuckled. "No, just to the port. We're taking a ho ... ferry." Better to keep it as a surprise for later.

He wandered over to the kitchen area and opened the cupboard. "Would you like a cup of tea or coffee while we wait?"

"Tea, please." His wife let go of the handle and sauntered toward the breakfast table, then turned on her heel and continued toward the bathroom. "Be right back."

While the kettle boiled, Conrad placed tea bags in two colour-coordinated mugs—black and white, with Yin and Yang symbols. His mind wandered, playing out scenarios for the trip. Should he start the big conversation on the hovercraft, where she couldn't simply escape to her room? But what if that made her feel trapped and scared of him? Maybe an evening meal at some picturesque location by the sea would be better?

"So, what's the story behind that bathrobe?"

He dropped a spoonful of sugar onto the counter, crystals spreading everywhere. "Gee, woman."

"Sorry." His wife stood less than a foot away from him, holding the white piece of a gourmet in her hands.

Scooping the sugar with a cloth, Conrad ignored her question, hoping she'd forget about it.

"So, what's the story?"

Not a chance.

"You seem awfully interested in that bathrobe." He winked. "Are you jealous?"

She rolled her eyes. "I'm not jealous. I just want to know what happened. We both have our share of experiences that affect us, and it's part of getting to know each other."

Conrad sighed. "The bathrobe is just a reminder of something I should have learned years ago. Sugar?"

"No, thanks." She shook her head, and then her eyes twinkled with interest. "So, what happened?"

"It's a long and very old story." Conrad picked up the mugs and walked over to the sofa in the living room.

She followed him, still with the bathrobe in her hands. "We're not going anywhere until Colton gets here. I've got time."

After placing the mugs on the coasters, he collapsed on the sofa and raised his hands in surrender. "Fine."

His wife placed the bathrobe on the back of the chair before nestling herself in the other corner of the sofa, with her legs curled up. Then she looked at him with eyes wide open, like a kid waiting for a bedtime story. There was no more stalling.

"I was engaged once, to my first love. I was young—about your age." He glanced at Louise, who raised an eyebrow in response.

"Maybe a little younger. And she was much older, wiser." He took a sip of tea, sinking deeper into the sofa. "My grandfather insisted on a prenup because I was supposed to take over the family business soon. But my fiancée didn't want to sign it. Grandpa warned me that if I married her without the prenup, I'd be cut off from the family business."

"Wow, that's harsh." Her concern seemed genuine, and she moved closer, like she wanted to hear better, their arms almost touching.

Conrad shrugged. "I was ready to build my own future. As long as I was with her, you know?" He glanced at his wife, catching her gaze. It stirred that longing in him again. A sip of tea helped.

"But she wasn't having it. She was upset that I'd even considered the prenup and broke off the engagement." A bitter chuckle escaped him. "I blamed my grandpa for years."

"I'm so sorry to hear that." His wife brushed his arm with her fingers.

Yeah, I was too. It was the biggest lesson life had taught him—about women.

"One day, a police officer came to our house, asking if we'd heard from my ex-fiancé. Turns out she was wanted as a con artist who posed as a bride."

Louise gasped, covering her mouth.

"It wasn't her first scam. She'd done it a few times—marrying wealthy men, then vanishing with half their fortunes. In a twisted way, I got lucky, thanks to my grandpa. But at the time, it didn't feel that way, as I deeply loved her."

She looked at him, her eyes filled with empathy. "So, that's why you never got married?"

"Pretty much. There were other women in my life, but I always had this nagging doubt of whether it was for real or not."

Her gaze drifted to the bathrobe. "So, why keep that after all these years?"

"It's not hers." Conrad paused, choosing his words carefully. "It belonged to … someone else." He shrugged, trying to play it off, but the image of Elisabeth's face flashed through his mind, sharp and uninvited. That wound was still too fresh, too complicated to share. "I kept it as a reminder that things aren't always what they seem."

She wrapped a strand of hair around her finger, its rich colour shimmering in the sunlight streaming through the living room windows.

"After such experience, I'm surprised you agreed to our marriage. It's about as fake as it gets."

She had a point.

"You'd think so, but at least it's not built on false assumptions, right?"

She furrowed her eyebrows, biting her full lip. "What do you mean?"

Conrad leaned closer to Louise, looking into her eyes and feeling the warmth radiating from her body, the scent of jasmine and lilac mingling together. "We're not pretending to be in love."

Though he wouldn't mind if that changed. Wouldn't mind at all.

Their eyes locked, and the air grew thick with tension. Just then, his phone buzzed, making them both jump and pull away.

He checked the notification bar. Not a text. The phone rang again, displaying a number belonging to Sophie, the bartender at The White Horse.

Odd. Every staff member had his direct number, but he could count on one hand the times they'd called him directly—and it was never good news.

Conrad's heart pumped faster. "Hello?"

"Mr Brenman, I don't know what to do," Sophie blurted out in a high-pitched, trembling voice. His stomach clenched.

"Slow down, Sophie. What happened?"

A warm hand touched his shoulder, and Louise looked at him, a question in her eyes. He waved her off, waiting for his bartender to reveal the catastrophe. There must have been a disaster, he was sure of it. For a polite young Sophie to call him and not even say hello, that said a lot.

"Nobody is here." Conrad could clearly hear a voice in the background, so it wasn't about a quiet day in the pub. "Donna and Bobby are in the hospital with food poisoning. Jackie's away on her holiday, so she can't come in, and that temp that was supposed to cover for her didn't show up."

"Food poisoning?" His voice came out louder than expected. He couldn't sit still any longer. Pacing around the living room like a caged tiger, he fired off questions like a machine gun. "How are they? Were any guests affected? Do we know what food caused this?"

His mind flashed with nightmare headlines: "The White Horse

responsible for Hospitalising Guests." He shook the image off and pressed the phone to his ear.

"No, no, sir. They were on a date night in that new fancy restaurant last night—that's where it happened. Salmonella. But they're okay."

Conrad exhaled and staggered back to the sofa as the room started spinning.

"So, none of our guests were affected then. Good." And then it hit him. "Oh my God, Sophie. You're on your own, and it's The Hikers Club."

"Yes, sir."

Droplets of sweat appeared on his forehead. Thirty-plus people for lunch, plus the regular Tuesday quiz crowd.

"I don't know what to do," she cried out and started sobbing.

He didn't know either. His mind raced. A glass of water appeared in front of his eyes, held by his wife. Conrad accepted and gulped it in one go. A few drops spilt on his T-shirt.

"I'll be there in half an hour and will try to get some help." Conrad took a deep breath, slowing down his pumping heart, and used his most reassuring voice. "Everything will be fine. Thank you so much for calling it in. You're a star."

He hung up and hid his head in his hands.

"That bad?" Louise's light touch and warm voice made him look.

"You have no idea." Conrad shook his head, trying to clear his mind, searching for options.

"I think I do. I used to work at the bar."

He blinked. "You did?"

"Yeah, summer job." His wife marched toward the door, where she grabbed her abandoned suitcase.

Oh shit.

"I'm sorry. The trip ... "

She simply waved him off. "Don't worry about it." She pulled the suitcase and rolled it deeper into the house. "You're short three people?"

"Yeah. At least. With two at the bar and two on the floor, it's usually challenging on Tuesdays in The White Horse."

"So, you're going?" Her voice sounded distant. Conrad looked up and saw her suitcase disappearing into Grandma Ann's room.

"Of course. I promise I'll make it up to you." But where the heck would he find more staff on such short notice? Maybe he could pull someone from another pub?

"Call Colton." Her voice came muffled through the door, followed by a thud that made him jump up from the sofa and dash toward the bedroom.

"What was that? Are you hurt?"

She reappeared, now dressed in jeans and a T-shirt, her hair pulled into a ponytail. "I'm fine. It was my suitcase—I dropped it."

Conrad exhaled, and his heart slowed down. He had enough of disasters for one day.

"Call Colton and tell him about the change of plans. He can meet us there. Let's go."

"What? Where?"

Colton? Change of plans? This was all too confusing, and he had no time for charades. He could almost hear the crowd in the unmanned pub.

"You and Colton on the floor, me and Sophie manning the bar. Four." She held up four fingers, as if he might need the visual aid.

He just stared at her, struggling to process what she was saying.

Louise shook her head and took the phone from his hand, pressing his thumb to unlock it.

"Colton? Mrs Brenman here. Sorry to bother you, but we have an emergency situation at The White Horse—" She looked at him with a question in her eyes, and Conrad's head bobbed up and down as if someone else were pulling the strings. "—Yes, The White Horse. We have a staff shortage, and we need your help."

Conrad stretched his neck as he regained control over his muscles and brain.

She said we. He smiled, catching the murmur of his driver's voice, followed by his wife's crisp and clear, "Thank you. We'll meet you there."

Without slowing down, she grabbed his hand and pulled him toward the door. "He'll meet us at the pub. Get the keys."

***

Annie wiped down the bar and stacked coasters together, making space for new orders. Sophie was pouring pints of Doom Bar from the tap for a group of local lads. Annie scanned the room for the next customer, but for the moment, everyone nursed a drink.

At the far end of the pub, a group of tourists ploughed through their lunch at a long wooden table, nestled beneath low, exposed beams. Only a few of the guests were visible from Annie's angle, as the rest were tucked away in a cosy alcove. Most had opted for soft drinks, with only a couple choosing a light beer. This lot wasn't here to stay but on their bus tour to see all the white horses of Wiltshire. They were in for a treat, with the oldest one located a mile away on the Salisbury Plain. Annie had seen it as a kid, the giant chalk figure etched into the hillside. It had left an impression—like a direct link to a distant past.

She glanced around the rustic pub, with its wonky cushioned wooden chairs, the long, polished tables, the old fireplace, and the walls covered with framed pictures of the old days. The place looked oddly familiar. She might have even stopped here for lunch back then.

"My, my. If this isn't a lucky coincidence, I don't know what is."

Annie turned to see a woman at the bar in a teal blouse with a brown scarf that matched her short red hair. The woman took a small sip of her white wine, then nodded toward the window. Annie's eyes followed her gaze.

Framed by the bay window stood Conrad, talking to a tall, slim woman with blonde hair cascading down her back. The highlights shimmered as she turned her head.

"Look at our Elisabeth and Conrad." The redhead clicked her tongue. "I'd challenge anyone who says they're not meant for each other."

"It's an absolute nonsense, Linda." Sophie shook her head, taking a sheepish glance at Annie. "Mr Brenman is married now."

"Oh, do tell?" Linda's eyes lit up as she leaned forward on her bar stool.

Annie gave Sophie a quick, subtle squeeze on the hand and a tiny shake of her head, reminding her she wanted to stay anonymous.

"They got married just last week. But we were short-staffed today, so he came to the rescue."

"As he always does, doesn't he? A golden boy, our Conrad, isn't he?"

She clasped her hands together and focused her gaze on Annie. "And you are?"

Sophie's face turned pink, and she shuffled on her feet. Annie knew there was no sidestepping this question—gossipers like Linda were relentless. Better to bite the bullet.

"I'm Mr Brenman's wife's sister," she said loud and clear.

And not even a lie.

Linda's eyes widened, and she covered her mouth with one hand. "Please forgive an old woman prattling on." She reached over and patted Annie's hand with her own, her skin almost translucent over fragile-looking bones.

"No worries." Annie smiled politely, then turned to the till, tapping a few buttons that brought up a summary display she didn't actually care about. Her gaze drifted back to the bay window.

Elisabeth, huh? Was she his ex? His lover? How long ago? Elisabeth's hand lingered on Conrad's shoulder, and he didn't seem to mind. Not long, then. Was he still in love?

A pang of unease twisted in Annie's stomach. She'd been in love a couple of times—blinded by it, missing what was right in front of her. Was it always like this, ending in tears?

"Oh, young love," Linda sighed wistfully. Annie turned back just as an older gentleman in a brown turtleneck sweater approached the bar.

"What can I get you, sir?" Annie looked at the man, ignoring Linda's comment yet hoping she'd say more.

"Two pints of Guinness, please, if you'd be so kind."

"Right away, sir. Anything else?"

He shook his head, his eyes drifting toward the window where Conrad and Elisabeth stood deep in conversation. "I thought they broke up?"

It seemed everyone in this darn pub knew about Conrad and Elisabeth.

Linda opened her mouth to respond, but Sophie beat her to it. "They did. And there's nothing going on between them."

"I don't know." Linda sucked the air in. "You're still young, Sophie. Those two have been on and off for years. Isn't that right, Victor?"

Annie finished pouring the golden liquid into the tankard and set the heavy glass down on the coaster in front of the man, then reached for another empty one.

"You're absolutely right, Lin."

"Here's your beer, sir. Cash or card?" Annie placed the second tankard next to the first.

"Card, please. As for Mr Brenman, I thought their last breakup was

... different."

Different how?

Annie entered the order into the till and handed the card reader to the man. He tapped his card, and the payment was accepted.

"Oh, just usual lovers' quarrel, I'm sure of that." Linda waved a dismissive hand, taking another sip. "They split during the pandemic, didn't they? COVID was hard on everyone." She sighed, her gaze drifting to the rows of liquor bottles behind Annie.

"Yes, I heard. I'm sorry for your loss, Lin." Victor touched her shoulder briefly before lifting his beers, and headed for a table in the far corner, away from the tourists.

Linda watched him go, then turned back to Annie with a wistful smile. "But you know, life goes on." She took a deep breath and looked at Annie, her expression brightening. "Would you make me an Aperol Spritz, love?"

Everyone had a history. The pandemic spared nobody. "Sure, on the house."

A wide smile cracked Linda's face. COVID long forgotten.

"You made my day, love."

Linda's eyes wandered back to the window, where Elisabeth's hand rested on Conrad's shoulder in an intimate gesture. "And look at them. What did I tell you?" She clapped her hands. "Love is in the air."

Sophie rolled her eyes and leaned in. "Linda, Mr Brenman is married now, remember? That's his *ex* out there. It's not what it looks like."

Linda blinked, then tilted her head with a knowing smile. "Right, right. Old habits die hard, don't they? But you can't tell me there's not *something* still there."

Annie forced a polite smile, hoping the topic would die down, but Linda's eyes sparkled with mischief as she took another sip of her drink.

Chapter 12

Elisabeth. His heart fluttered in his chest. Conrad had forgotten she would be here. For months, he'd managed to avoid her.

He took in the cascade of long, silky blonde hair and the high cheekbones of a woman who knew she was beautiful. All his mates had envied him. They had led a busy social life back then, and she'd been the crown jewel, the woman who turned every head when she walked beside him.

Conrad swallowed, watching her glide toward him with that mysterious smile on her perfectly symmetric face.

"Hi." Her voice was like a gentle breeze. "I'm surprised."

Conrad frowned. "Surprised?"

"To see you here today. I thought you were avoiding me." Her fingers brushed his shoulder, and he tensed involuntarily.

She wasn't wrong.

"Yeah, well." There was no point pretending otherwise. Besides, she might think he was here to make amends. Far from it. "We had an emergency, so I had to step in."

"Ah." The light in her eyes dimmed slightly, and she glanced out the window.

She seemed hurt. For a fleeting moment, he felt the urge to tell her he missed her, and that she looked as stunning as ever.

No. It was all for show.

He should know better. He wouldn't let her play him today. Or ever.

"Don't turn the tables around." Conrad's voice as tough as steel. "You're the one who bailed on me, remember?"

"If that's how you see it. My memory's a bit different, but it was a long time ago." A half-smile tugging at her full lips. "What emergency? Anything I can help with?"

"Stop pretending you care." His hostility should make her leave. He wanted her to leave. His life was better without her in it.

"I always cared, Conrad. Maybe too much." Her gaze focused on his eyes. "I don't know what you remember, but you can't blame it all on me. You never cared enough to stop me from leaving."

Now that was rich.

"The only thing you cared about was my money. The moment I went under during COVID, you dropped me in a heartbeat."

Her cheeks flushed. She pressed her lips together, but she didn't look away.

"I don't want to argue with you, but for your information, I was surprised you even noticed I'd left. You only remembered me when you needed to show off in town. With COVID, there was no need for me anymore, was there?"

"What a pile of rubbish."

Her eyes glistened, and she swallowed hard.

"Maybe to you." She looked away, gathering herself. "Anyway, I just wanted to say hello." She turned to leave.

Conrad took a deep breath. "Wait. I'm sorry."

Why was he so hostile? It had been two years since she'd left. He should have got over it by now.

"You're right. It was a long time ago."

Elisabeth looked at him with an unreadable expression. "Do you really believe I only cared about your money?"

Of course. What else? Conrad sighed, not sure what to say. She was right. There was no point arguing about the old days.

"It felt like that to me."

"I thought we had fun together. Sure, maybe our lifestyles were different, but when we were actually together, it felt right to me." A melancholic smile appeared on her face. "But clearly not for you."

He nodded. "It was great, as you said, when we spent time together. But in between … "

"In between, you were never there," she finished, almost to herself. She shook her head. "I get it now. I couldn't compete with your job. It was stupid to think I could."

Wait, what? He blinked. "My job? What does that have to do with you leaving me because I had no money for you to spend?"

"What?" Elisabeth chuckled, though he could see his words had stung her. Again. He was a real prince charming today. "You thought I left because of your money?"

Conrad cleared his throat. "Yes." He raked a hand through his hair, feeling a knot forming in his stomach. Had he been wrong all this time?

"I thought you knew me better than this." She shook her head, eyes dropping to the floor. "No. I left because you were not there. You were never there."

He had to strain his ears to hear her.

"Whenever I offered to help with the business to be closer to you, you'd just hand me your credit card and brush me off. You kept pushing me out. I was lonely."

He frowned, feeling the weight of her words. Memories stirred, half-buried under years of resentment. She was right—she'd tried to be involved, to support him.

"And when the COVID hit and you had to be at home, I thought I finally got my chance. Boy, I was wrong ... " her voice broke, and she glanced out the window.

Conrad touched her shoulder. She wasn't faking it now, and he remembered. Scotch. Lots of it.

"I'm sorry, Elisabeth. I remember now."

And he did. The past came back tumbling—the blurred days and endless nights, her hands holding his head over the toilet, pushing water into his dry lips, her tears as she begged him to get help. And then the silence when she'd finally left.

Conrad opened his mouth, gasping for air. "I'm so sorry. I—" What could he even say? That he'd forgotten? That his brain conveniently had blamed it all on her?

Elisabeth placed a gentle hand on his shoulder. "It's in the past now."

Conrad covered her warm hand with his. "But how can I ever make up for what I did?"

She smirked, but in a joyful way. "Well, you can stop avoiding me for a start. I'm not your enemy."

"Done" He managed a small smile, but his gaze grew serious again. "But that's not enough. Do you need anything? You're with the group today, right? Can I get you something to take away, or ... ?" His eyes darted around, searching for some tangible way to make amends.

She laughed. Out loud. He'd forgotten how much she liked that laughter.

"I'm fine, and you're trying too hard. I was serious when I said it's all in the past. Because—" Elisabeth cleared her throat. "Well, I met someone and—" Her eyes widened, locking onto his. "—we're getting married."

Conrad wasn't entirely sure he'd heard her correctly, as her voice was barely audible, like she was afraid of something.

"Are you happy?" It was the first thought that came to mind.

"Yes," she said, her voice filled with quiet conviction. "I am."

"Then it's fantastic news! I'm so glad you found the happiness you truly deserve." And for once, he meant it. Odd sensation. If someone had told him an hour ago that he'd be genuinely happy to hear Elisabeth was engaged, Conrad would have laughed.

"Thank you." She blushed. "I heard you got married too."

"Ah, yeah." He looked over at the bar, where Louise was expertly managing the till; her face lit up with concentration.

"She's pretty."

"What?"

Elisabeth nodded toward Louise. "Your wife. That's her, isn't it?"

"Yes, but—" He couldn't tell her it was fake. And pretty much over.

"What," she said, raising an eyebrow with a teasing glint in her eyes, "are you worried she doesn't love you as much as you love her?"

Conrad laughed, opening his mouth to say something, but what exactly, he wasn't sure. Deny? Admit? What?

"No need to worry. I saw how she looked at you," Elisabeth said softly. "And I noticed you checking on her earlier."

How was Louise looking at him? He wanted Elisabeth to tell him more, but without revealing it was a fake marriage, he wasn't sure how to ask. Besides, Elisabeth had been his girlfriend once. Wouldn't that make this conversation ... awkward?

"I'm happy for you, too. I truly am." Elisabeth hugged him, her lips brushing his cheek. "I need to go now, but let's not be strangers anymore, promise?"

"You got it."

As she turned to leave, he watched her walk away, a strange mix of nostalgia and closure settling over him. The bitterness, the anger—all of it finally began to ease. For the first time, he felt ready to let her go.

***

Annie glanced at Conrad and Elisabeth. They did look cosy. Was he still seeing her while being married? Heat crept up Annie's neck, and she turned away from the scene.

"Stop meddling, Linda," Sophie said, her tone sharper than before.

"I just say what I see." Linda clicked her tongue. "Well, it's time for me, anyway."

The screech of a bar stool dragged Annie's attention back to the room.

"Lovely to meet you, love." Linda nodded toward Annie while gathering her purse and her brown jacket that matched her scarf.

"Likewise." Annie forced a polite smile, struggling to keep her focus on the older woman as the scene by the window drew her back like a magnet.

Were they still there? Touching? What if he kissed her? No, he wouldn't. Would he?

Annie knitted her eyebrows. What should she do if he did?

Linda strolled out of the pub, waving at people as she passed. Once the door closed behind her, Annie risked a glance toward the window. Still there, Conrad's hand over Elisabeth's.

Stop. Annie shook her head, grabbing a cloth and wiping the bar top with such determination that her own reflection began to shimmer on the polished surface.

No, she couldn't just leave it like this. She *had* to know.

"Sophie, is it true?"

"What, Mrs Brenman?" Sophie's response was muffled, her cheeks bulging with a bite of blueberry muffin. Annie's stomach gurgled.

Sophie pushed a plate of pastries toward her. "Please, help yourself. The Hiker's Club will be here any minute, so we don't have time for a proper lunch."

Annie's hand hovered over the plate, her eyes flicking to Sophie's. "So, is it true what Linda said about Conrad and that Elisabeth woman?"

She nodded toward the bay window, even as her fingers selected a banana muffin with white chocolate.

"Well, some of it, yes."

Annie studied Sophie's eyes, framed by the eyeliner and fake lashes. "Which part?" she pressed, her tone deceptively light as she picked at the muffin.

"They used to date. But it's all over now, I can assure you, Mrs Brenman." Sophie blinked and swallowed, looking as though she feared saying too much.

"Look, I'm not going to get upset about the past." Annie dragged a stool from under the bar top and sat down as if the topic were casual. "I'm just curious. How long?" She broke off a piece of the muffin, pretending to be disinterested.

"They were dating for? Or since they broke up?"

"Both."

"Well—" The young woman licked her lips—her purple tongue dyed by the blueberries. "They split up during the first COVID year, or so I heard. I don't know exactly, as we were all on furlough until the year after."

Have they seen each other since?

Annie opened her mouth to ask but stopped, reaching for an almond croissant instead and breaking off a corner. If she said nothing, maybe Sophie would reveal more.

"As for how long they were dating—" Sophie looked away toward the pub entrance. "Ahem."

She clicked her tongue, clearly stalling. Annie waited for a moment longer, but it was clear that the young bartender needed encouragement to say more.

With her eyes on Sophie, Annie said, "Linda mentioned they were on-off, so I assume months at a time."

Sophie nodded.

"But how long since the very first time they hooked up?" Annie pressed.

Sophie cleared her throat and whispered something Annie couldn't hear as the door to the pub burst open, and the loud clang of the bell reverberated around the pub.

"Oh, look, the Hiker's Club is here!" Sophie brushed off the crumbs of her T-shirt and dashed toward the far end of the bar.

Annie grimaced. *Saved by the bell. Literally.*

A group of hikers poured into the pub, boots scuffing the floor and hiking sticks tapping the ground as they flowed toward a long wooden table. They looked more like a beer crowd than pastry enthusiasts.

Annie's eyes darted back to the bay window just in time to see Elisabeth leaning toward Conrad. Her eyes opened wider.

No, they wouldn't.

Not with so many prying eyes watching. Not in front of her. Annie swallowed, her heart thumping in her chest. What would she do if … What *should* she do as Conrad's wife, if …

"If they kissed," she murmured, unable to look away.

Elisabeth's lips brushed Conrad's cheek, and then she pulled back. Annie felt dizzy from relief.

She watched as Elisabeth weaved through the growing crowd, her blonde hair swaying. Annie's chest tightened. *I wish I could be like her to someone.* It was obvious Conrad loved Elisabeth. Annie had no doubts about it.

A wistful sigh escaped her lips, her shoulders sagging. Not only was this marriage nothing more than a financial transaction, but now she was also *the other woman*. Of course, she had no right to feel upset, given their arrangement.

But it stung anyway.

***

Conrad locked the door behind the last of the singing groups. Some patrons clearly hadn't realised it wasn't karaoke night. He stretched his arms, cracked his neck, and strolled back to the bar.

Louise was wiping the counter with a cloth, stacking coasters into a neat pile. Her face looked ashen, framed by dark circles under her eyes.

"Please, sit down, Lou." Conrad grabbed the nearest high-backed chair and placed it behind the counter. "You've done enough for one night."

He gently removed the dishcloth from her numb fingers, guiding her toward the chair, but she stumbled and fell into his arms. Not that he was about to complain.

"I don't know how we would've coped tonight without you."

Holding her in a protective hug, he tilted her chin up so he could see her face. "You seem tired. Ready to go home?"

She nodded but didn't pull away, resting her head on his chest instead. If it was up to him, they could stay like this forever.

"I'm sorry about the Isle of Wight trip," he murmured into her ear, simply to keep her close. "We can't go tomorrow either—I've got a meeting Thursday morning, so I need to be in town. But what about a long weekend instead?"

Conrad loosened his embrace just enough to see her face. Her green eyes had lost their spark. "What do you think?"

Louise's head bobbed in a half-hearted nod. "Yeah, fine."

"Oh, boy, let's get you into the car." Conrad gently released her and wrapped an arm around her shoulders to guide her toward the back door.

Colton and Sophie waited outside.

"Sophie, I've lined up a full squad for tomorrow from the local agency. Plus, Bob from The Swan will also be there to back you up, so you won't have to manage the rookies alone."

"Oh, that's fantastic news, Mr Brenman." Sophie beamed, visibly relieved.

It was great news indeed. He had called a few agencies before he secured a temporary replacement until the end of the week.

"Do you need a lift, Sophie?"

His bartender blushed. "No, I've got someone waiting for me."

Conrad hid his grin, knowing how embarrassed she'd feel if he joked about it. "Thank you for your great work today. You are a star."

Another blush, but with a smile. "I would've been lost without Mrs Brenman. She's the one who should be thanked, not me."

Conrad smiled. "I totally agree."

Louise stirred, raising her head as if snapping out of a trance. She shifted and stepped to a side, breaking the bond between them. His arm flopped uselessly to his side, and he rubbed his hands against his thighs, to give them something to do.

He tilted his head and looked into his wife's half-closed eyes. "If I didn't know you were majoring in art, Lou, I'd say you've been running pubs your whole life." He chuckled, watching Louise's eyes grow bigger.

"I just did what needed doing." Her cheeks flushed a deep red, a stark contrast to her pale complexion. It seemed not only Sophie had a hard time accepting compliments.

"Right, ready to go?" His comment wasn't directed at anyone in particular, but Colton nodded, retrieving the car keys from his pocket.

"I'll bring the car around, Mr Conrad. No need for Ms Louise to walk all the way."

"Good thinking, thank you, Colton," Conrad said.

The older man turned on his heel as Sophie chimed in, "I'll join you. It was a pleasure to meet you, Mrs Brenman."

"Likewise," Louise said, managing a faint smile.

As they left, Sophie glanced back and added, "Oh, and don't pay any attention to Linda's words. She doesn't know what she's talking about."

Linda's words? Conrad knitted his eyebrows, pondering this cryptic statement while watching his bartender and Colton disappear into the alley leading to the car park.

"What was that about?" he asked, turning to Louise.

His wife seemed suddenly more awake than a minute ago. "Well." She sucked the air through her mouth and looked away, so her words barely reached him. "She said you're in love with Elisabeth."

Wow.

That was a loaded statement. He was—and he wasn't. Truthfully, he wasn't sure anymore what his feelings for Elisabeth even were.

Louise's shoulders stiffened. She turned to face him, stepping closer until he could feel the warmth radiating from her body.

"Are you?" Her eyes searched his face, seeing through him like he was transparent.

Lying wasn't an option. But what was the truth? And would the truth shatter any chance this fragile marriage had of surviving?

"Honestly, I don't know anymore." He sighed, his voice softer now. "Until today, I resented her, but now … "

"Now what?" Her breath was tickling his face.

Exactly. Now what? Right now, he wasn't thinking about Elisabeth at all—just the emerald-green eyes locked on him and the full lips only inches away.

"Things weren't how I remembered them," he admitted. "But now, I think I can finally let go."

Conrad leaned closer, his hands finding her waist. He stroked her back, pulling her gently toward him. She didn't resist. His heart thudded as he tilted his head, their lips only a whisper apart.

She tensed in his arms. "Will you see her again?"

Ouch.

"Probably," he murmured honestly, and his wife shifted in his arms, increasing the distance between their lips.

"And you might too." He forced himself to keep his tone casual. "We've got an invitation to her wedding."

Louise blinked, her surprise evident. "A wedding?"

The moment was gone—maybe for the better. What was he doing anyway? This wasn't supposed to be a romantic relationship, was it? He didn't need it, anyway, did he?

"Yes, Elisabeth's getting married and invited us to her wedding."

His wife, free from his embrace, rubbed her arms, avoiding his gaze. "And how do you feel about it?"

"I'm happy for her." The words flew off his lips with ease.

"Really?" Louise's voice was quiet, almost wistful. "Because you looked like you wanted to be married to her, not me."

Her words carried a hint of jealousy, and it stirred something unexpected in him. A flicker of hope. Was she ... jealous?

A small smile tugged at his lips. "I mean it."

The feeling of calm and resolve enveloped him. He was now certain of two things: he was genuinely happy for Elisabeth, and he couldn't let this marriage—this chance with Louise—slip away. He'd already screwed up too much in his life. This time, he had to make it work.

Chapter 13

The barking of a dog woke Annie up. She turned in bed toward the window with a wide smile on her face, and with eyes still half closed, she listened to the sounds of nature—birds chirping, the delicate rustling of leaves in the breeze, and the staccato of a woodpecker. The dog barked again, quieted by a sharp whistle.

Annie inhaled the air, scented with lilacs and morning mist, sat up in bed, and stretched her arms. Sleep had energised her, filling her with this internal certainty that everything would be fine.

Watching the orchard through the window, still enveloped in a morning fog that turned it into a magical place, Annie's thoughts returned to the day at the pub.

Despite feeling afterwards as though a truck had run her over, she had this overwhelming sensation of being in the right place. Of belonging. After all, a pub used to be her domain, a place she called home. Where she had spent most of her days organising deliveries, coordinating staff schedules to fit their lives, ensuring customers had been looked after and dealing with anyone who dared harass her female employees without mercy.

Her locals had been like family to her, and she'd been family to them—celebrating babies being born, graduations, and first jobs. Supporting them through breakups or simply through bad days at work.

Her stomach ached as she thought of those times—the camaraderie, the sense of belonging, the ability to make someone's day better.

But COVID had ended that life. It had finished the pub and her career along with it. And when the world had reopened, before she had a chance to get back on her feet, Darren had entered her life. Quite literally.

One evening, during her server shift at a dingy pub—a job she had taken temporarily while searching for other opportunities—Darren had saved her from a nasty patron with a habit of smacking the bottoms of the female staff. And he hadn't been gentle about it. The poor sod had ended up in an ambulance with a broken nose, but Annie had lost her job.

Not that she'd liked it there, anyway. Plus, she'd genuinely thought she'd finally met a great guy, her knight in shining armour. Her protector.

Annie chuckled dryly and reached for the glass of water on her nightstand, gulping it down to wash away the bitter taste in her mouth. She'd never been more wrong about anyone.

What about Conrad? Was she wrong about him, too?

The way he'd stepped in yesterday at the pub—how he treated Sophie and the other staff with respect. And the way he'd interacted with his employees last Sunday at his other pubs. It reminded her of how she'd treated her own staff—with care and respect. That's why it had felt so familiar. Maybe Conrad wasn't such a bad guy after all.

Annie swung her legs off the bed, slipped on her bathrobe, and tied it securely. Barefoot, she tiptoed toward the wall and stroked the frame of the picture of young Grandma Ann.

"What would you do in my place, Granny?"

Take responsibility for your actions—that's what she'd say.

Annie's chest tightened. It wasn't her fault, though. None of this was. It was her parents who'd made the shady deal. They'd forced Louise into this mess, and Annie had only stepped in to protect her sister. She wasn't the one pulling the strings here. Right?

And yet, her gaze fell to her stomach. Her hand drifted to the faint curve, her fingers tracing it gently. She had to do what was best for her baby—the one she could still save. Her child deserved a safe, stable life, and she would do whatever it took to provide it.

You should have ended it back at the church.

Annie rubbed her face, trying to silence her inner voice. What was the point of dwelling on the past? She couldn't undo it now. The only thing left was to move forward.

She needed to come clean. Conrad had the right to know the truth. But when? Right now? Later? This weekend on the Isle of Wight?

She scratched her chin, her thoughts whirling. If only she could find a way to make Conrad let her stay. To keep the deal alive—or to strike a new one. She could offer him her skills and the inheritance money. She'd give up all of her alleged inheritance—her parents assured her it was waiting under lock and key—if it meant having a place to raise her child.

Would that be enough?

Her hand dropped from her chin as doubt crept in. Would he see through her desperation? Did she even have the right to ask him for anything?

Annie sighed and straightened her posture, as though physically lifting the weight pressing on her shoulders. It could work. She just needed a bit of luck. She crossed her fingers.

Well, maybe quite a lot of luck. And the right moment, the right mood, and the right atmosphere. A lot of "rights", but not impossible. She simply had to wait for that special moment.

Marching to the door, she whispered, "Granny, help me if you can."

***

With a cup of freshly brewed black coffee, Conrad sat at the kitchen table, waiting for his wife to appear. He'd heard noises behind the closed doors earlier and had put the coffee machine on, hoping to lure Louise out.

He tapped a complex melody with his fingers, rehearsing the conversation in his head.

Should he keep it casual, ask how she liked her toast, and maybe suggest a day out? Or go for something more serious—make her understand he was willing to put in the effort?

"Coffee?" He jumped to his feet the moment she appeared in the doorway.

Her eyes widened, and she took a step back.

"Sorry, didn't mean to startle you."

His wife pulled her bathrobe tighter, as if trying to shield herself within its folds.

"It suits you." He pointed at the fluffy fabric. "I think you should keep it."

"I thought it reminded you never to trust a woman?" Louise took a few proud steps forward, her chin raised high. It wasn't the reaction he'd expected to his compliment, but hey, he wouldn't complain. At least she wasn't retreating anymore.

With his eyes fixed on her, Conrad pondered the situation. If it was a rhetorical question, answering might start a fight. On the other hand, if he ignored it, focusing on coffee, she might feel disrespected and that could be even worse.

"It's a great question. How about I make you a cappuccino, and then we have a chat?" Without even waiting for her response, Conrad placed a mug under the coffee machine spout and poured milk into a small jug for steaming.

"Actually, yeah. There is something I'd like to talk about." Her tone softened, less feisty now. "I'll be back in a sec, just gonna change quickly."

The door opened and closed behind her, the sound barely audible over the coffee machine.

If she was planning to bail on him now, he had to stop her. Subtlety wouldn't cut it. As he waited for the milk to steam, Conrad emptied a pack of Digestives into a small bowl. By the time he'd poured the milk into the mug, the door opened again.

"Do you need a hand?"

He glanced over his shoulder to see her dressed in leggings and the jumper he'd bought her the other day. It seemed like the clothes had been designed specifically for her.

"Could you take the biscuits, please? I'll carry the coffee."

They ambled toward the patio without speaking, the creaking of the wooden floorboards filling the silence.

She perched at the edge of the sofa while Conrad took the lounger, angling it away from the sun so he could see her face. Louise took a small sip of her coffee, licked her lips, opened her mouth as if about to speak, and then closed them.

Now or never. If he waited any longer, find the words he wasn't ready to hear. That this wasn't going anywhere. That they'd tried and failed. That they'd be better off going their separate ways. No. He wasn't giving up without a fight.

"So, I was thinking ... "

Louise glanced at him with a spark of interest in her eyes.

Keep talking, mate.

"Yesterday you were an enormous help."

She waved her hand in a dismissive gesture.

"Honestly, woman, we wouldn't have coped without you. It was almost like you were born to do this job."

The moment the words left his mouth, Conrad regretted them. *Shit.* Now what? What woman wanted to hear she was born to be a bartender? Conrad tensed as he took a sip of his already cold coffee, bracing himself for an inevitable barrage of insults.

"It was fun." Her light chuckle made his jaw drop.

You lucky bastard.

Somehow, he was still in the game. Carefully now, he formed each sentence in his head before speaking. "I'd like to make it up to you for yesterday. Have a day of fun rather than work. What would you say to an art fair?"

"An art fair?" Her surprise seemed encouraging.

"Yes. Someone mentioned there's one happening this week in Bradford on Avon. Local artists showing their work."

She cocked her head, clearly interested.

"We could go now, have a wander, maybe even buy a piece or two, and then stop for lunch at The Canal Inn."

"Your pub?" Her tone turned hesitant.

"Yes—or we could do something else. There are plenty of lovely places nearby." Conrad barely took a breath between sentences. "We could go on a boat trip and have lunch on the barge. Or go to Bath. Or … " He was running out of ideas. "So, what do you think? Would you like that?"

Her head nodded slightly, but Conrad held his breath, unsure if it was a yes or a maybe.

"Yeah, that would be lovely, but I need to tell you something."

"Brilliant." He clasped his hands together and sprang up from the lounger. "We can chat later during lunch—unless it can't wait?"

With his feet already facing the house, he glanced back at Louise, who seemed to be working through something in her mind, judging by the number of wrinkles on her forehead.

She exhaled visibly, and the creases disappeared. "Yes, it can wait till lunch. No rush."

One point for him. He was still in the game.
Just don't screw it up, man.

***

It could wait till later, couldn't it? What difference would it make if Annie pushed for this conversation right now? Maybe it would be better to do it in public—but not at any of his pubs. Oh no, that would be a disaster.

Annie took another sip of her cappuccino, watching Conrad disappear through the doorway.

"Are you coming?" His voice called out from inside the house, snapping her out of her inertia.

"Sure." Holding the mug in both hands, she rose from her seat and glanced around at the cracked wooden rails and the patio planks, polished by years of shifting feet. The white and pink blossoms of the apple trees completed the magical picture, with morning rays of sunlight weaving between the leaves and branches. The fog had lifted, promising a sunny day with no chance of rain. It was almost as if nature had gifted her this one last beautiful day to enjoy before facing the future.

"Louise?" Conrad's head popped through the door.

Dressed in pale blue jeans and a navy polo shirt that accentuated his muscular arms, he could easily model for a magazine cover. Maybe he had? Annie wouldn't put it past him, given his empire and his love for luxury clothes and cars.

She placed her empty mug into his outstretched hand, his hard calluses contradicting the polished, model-like image he projected.

"Yeah, let me grab my bag, and we can head out."

Before she had a complete meltdown imagining his muscular arms on her waist—like the other day when they had danced a tango full of desire—Annie squeezed past Conrad, brushing against his chest and feeling the firmness of his muscles through the fabric of her sweater. Heat rushed up her neck.

What's wrong with you, woman?

She tilted her head away from Conrad, hurrying toward her room. It must be the pregnancy hormones.

Annie paused over her suitcase, scratching her chin. Was it, though?

She couldn't recall feeling this way during her first pregnancy—not with Darren.

Her shoulders tensed, and her body shivered as the memories flooded her mind. Darren's anger, the accusations over something she'd said or done, the feel of his fingers digging into her arms, shaking her, pushing her. Tripping over a chair behind her. The fall. The piercing pain, followed by that haunting numbness.

Annie inhaled deeply, filling her lungs with air, then exhaled slowly and deliberately, blinking the tears away.

No. That would never happen again.

She stretched her neck, mentally wiping the images from her mind, and focusing on the new life within her. Her hand stroked her still flat belly, while the other touched the picture frame on the wall.

"Louise?" Conrad's voice came again, faint and distant, with a tone of …

Of what? Annoyance? No. Worry? Yes, it sounded like worry.

Annie bent down and picked a pair of jeans and a white T-shirt, quickly changing into them. Her unzipped hoodie completed the look paired with trainers. She grabbed her bag and lunged for the door, to hesitate and turn back on her heel.

The camera. If she truly were her sister, she'd never miss the chance to take pictures.

Not for much longer, though. For better or worse, after lunch, she'd no longer be Louise.

***

Conrad stood at the open house door, dangling the keys on his finger, waiting. Where was that woman? How long could it possibly take to grab a bag? He glanced at his watch, starting to do some mental arithmetic, when Louise finally appeared at the end of the hall. A small rucksack hung over her shoulder, and she cradled his dad's camera in her hands.

I knew it.

A wide grin spread across his face, and whatever annoyance he'd been feeling evaporated without a trace. His dad would be over the moon knowing someone had so much love for his camera.

As she reached him, a wrinkle furrowed her forehead as she scanned the driveway.

"Is Colton not here yet?"

"No, he's looking after the business."

Someone has to while I'm having a day off.

And jumping through hoops to make sure his wife stuck to her part of the deal.

"Ah, so you booked a taxi?" She shaded her eyes with her hand, scanning the road for any sign of a car.

"Nope. We're taking my trusted truck." Conrad locked the door and strolled to the left side of the house, the crunch of her footsteps on gravel following close behind.

"I wouldn't have pegged you as a truck guy. You strike me more as a Bentley or S-Class type."

Me and you both.

Conrad swallowed hard and hid his thoughts behind a forced laughter. "Not today. We'll need something that won't get stuck in mud or on a country road."

Half the truth. The art fair was set in a meadow, with the parking lot likely situated in a nearby field.

As they rounded the corner of the house, his old red pickup truck came into view, tucked between the side wall and a tall wooden fence. The vehicle sat there like a relic, rarely used but still functional. Conrad stopped and turned to Louise.

"Wait here. I'll bring it around."

Without waiting for her answer, he squeezed through the narrow gap, unlocked the truck, and slid into the cracked faux leather seat. The door groaned in protest, but at least the old beast still worked. It was the last car he owned. It was a godsend that Colton never complained about driving Conrad's ass around in his Tesla.

He glanced through the windshield at Louise, who was staring at the truck with her mouth slightly open. Sliding the key into the ignition, he winced as the diesel engine roared to life—a stark contrast to the quiet hum of the Tesla he'd grown used to.

Conrad gritted his teeth.

Soon. It will be over soon.

Once he paid off the bank, he'd have more money to inject into the business, and from there, the luxuries he used to take for granted—like a better car—wouldn't seem so far off.

As the truck rolled forward, Conrad leaned over and opened the passenger door. "Hop in."

Louise scrambled into her seat and fastened the seat belt while Conrad searched for a radio station without a crackling static noise.

"This looks ancient." Her curious gaze flitted across the interior. She ran her fingers over the battered dashboard and paused at the window handle. "Does it even work??"

A bit of faith, woman.

"Sure. It might look old, but trust me—it's as good as new."

Louise laughed, the sound light and easy. "It's probably older than me, but I don't mind. As long as it gets us where we're going."

She nestled into the seat and rummaged through her backpack, pulling out a pair of sunglasses, which she perched on her forehead. After placing the rucksack on the floor, she rubbed her hands together. "Let's do this."

Her cheerful command jolted Conrad into action. He pressed the clutch and shifted into gear, and the truck rumbled forward.

Conrad grinned and let out a whistle. A woman who didn't mind being driven in an old beater? That was a first. She was a keeper—his mum would have said if she'd lived to see this moment.

Chapter 14

"Are you going to take this?"

Annie glanced at Conrad, expecting to see something in his hands, but they were empty. "Take what?"

"The picture, of course." His laughter carried warmth and amusement. "I thought you brought the camera for a reason."

Only now did Annie feel the heaviness of the camera strap pressing against her neck. Without a second thought, she lifted the camera and pointed it at the colourful stalls and tents dotting the hill, the river meandering at the far end. She squinted at the back of the camera, searching for a screen and the switch-on button, but couldn't find any.

Of course.

Conrad had mentioned it was a film camera. There was no screen, and she wouldn't see the results of her shots until the film was finished and developed.

Using her fingers to trigger touch memory, Annie traced the sturdy camera body, discovering the shutter button. Closing one eye, she peered through the viewfinder and settled on a scene, then pressed and released the button.

The satisfying click reminded Annie of her childhood—watching Grandpa meticulously setting up his shots and taking one careful photo after another. Then agonising hours waiting outside his darkroom as he developed his pictures. And even though Annie had loved watching the process and even had taken a few shots, it had been Louise who'd inherited his gift.

"It might come out better if you take the lens cap off." Conrad's amused voice sounded right next to her ear.

"Oh." Annie blinked and batted her lashes, her cheeks warming as she giggled.

What a stupid rookie mistake.

Louise would never have done that. She probably would've studied every aperture and setting, zooming in and out, experimenting with the camera to its fullest. Or not. She might have actually been more interested in experiencing it all for herself, so she could paint it later.

"I got distracted by the view. Shall we head down there? I can't wait to see it up close."

Without waiting for Conrad, Annie trotted down the pebbled path leading to the stalls and art displays. The reassuring sound of his footsteps followed.

The first stall she came across fit more into the craft than the art category—crocheted flower coasters and little bottle warmers. Annie glanced without slowing down. Not her cup of tea. Then she halted and Conrad bumped into her.

"Sorry. Found something you like?" he asked.

Good question.

Would Louise find this stall interesting and precious, or boring and beyond her? Well, probably not beyond Louise, but her pretentious artist friends would have dismissed it as quaint or amateurish.

"Not exactly. I spotted something that reminded me of my Grandma Ann. She used to crochet while she thought things through. The house was full of little doilies."

Annie moved on, glancing from side to side as she passed stalls showcasing handmade jewellery, carved wooden trinkets, and delicate ornaments.

Lovely items, but not what Louise would have deemed "real" art.

A flash of colour caught Annie's eye. She moved toward it, and soon rows of easels came into view, their canvases brimming with painted scenes.

With a fluttering heart, Annie stopped in front of the first painting, searching for words her sister would use to describe it. The scene seemed serene, joyful, sunny and holiday-like. It was the kind of image Louise's colleagues would dismiss as pedestrian, but it triggered that ache in Annie's stomach. The ache for a blissful, careless life. For family holidays and sand in the shoes. For sticky ice creams and reading a book under a parasol.

"It reminds me of my childhood," Conrad said, stepping beside her. His shoulder brushed hers as his gaze fixed on the painting. "What about you? Is it any good?"

Boy. A loaded question.

As an art student, she couldn't call it good, but as a human being, it made her connect with all the good feelings.

"Some of my colleagues would not spare it a second thought, but I admire the freedom in the brush strokes, the intensity of the ultramarines and ceruleans, and the precision of the strokes to make the foreground realistic with a fuzzy and fluid background."

There. She did it. Judging by the contemplative look on Conrad's face, she had used enough arty words to make it sound the way he expected.

"Right. So ... you like it?"

"Kinda." As she said the words, a woman in a colourful frock emerged from the shadows. With round cheeks and braided long hair, she embodied a classic image of a folk artist—except for her smartwatch and the sneakers peeking out from beneath her skirts.

"Oh, this one is my favourite." A tone as false as her nails. Her manicured fingers had no sign of paint, either. "But it's not for sale—it's already reserved by a wealthy gentleman" She brought a hand to her lips and whispered. "He offered two thousand pounds for it but as he is not here ... "

Her exaggerated wink left little doubt about her intentions.

"Interesting." Conrad's eyes focused on the piece, his fingers brushing the edge of the canvas.

Annie grabbed his arm and tugged him away. "Thank you for the information."

Caught off guard, Conrad let her pull him a substantial distance away before he protested.

"But you liked it, and she seemed keen to sell. I'm sure we could've negotiated."

Annie shook her head. "Maybe. But I don't think she painted it." She glanced over her shoulder. "And I doubt the money would've gone to the actual artist. I don't like sneaky sales tactics."

And the last thing Annie wanted was for this man to spend money on something like that and then find out how much of a con this marriage really was.

"Hmm, now as I think about it, I guess you might be right." He released his arm from Annie's grip but then rested it on her waist, pulling her closer. She could still walk even though she struggled to breathe, the touch of his fingers making her acutely aware of her own body needs.

"Conrad, my man!"

The cheerful voice startled them, and Conrad turned to greet a man who looked as though he had spent his life in the gym.

"Dicksy! Long time no see," Conrad said, shaking his hand.

Dicksy's gaze flicked to Annie, and a chill ran down her spine. She instinctively stepped closer to Conrad, and his arm tightened protectively around her.

"And who's this lovely girl you're hiding here?" Dicksy asked, his voice dripping with false charm, his sharp gaze raking over Annie like she was a prize to be claimed.

"Louise," Conrad said firmly. "My wife. So, back off."

Dicksy raised his hands in mock surrender. "Alright, alright." He turned back to Conrad. "Anyway, have you heard about Greg? Man, even I wouldn't have gone that far …"

Annie tuned out the rest, her attention drifting to the stalls ahead.

Conrad must have noticed a change in her behaviour as he said, "Go on, I'll catch up with you."

A peck on her cheek jolted her into a healthy pace. Just as well, as the conversation turned even more cryptic.

A few steps in, Annie slowed and let her eyes enjoy the crafts on display. She no longer had to filter it all through an alleged artist's mind. A row of necklaces on leather cords drew her in. Her fingers touched a polished emerald stone shaped like a tiny bagel.

"Feel free to try it on." A welcoming voice came out of nowhere, and a short lady with a head full of hay-coloured hair beamed at Annie. "Here, have a mirror." She shifted a few jewellery items aside and set a small mirror in the centre, right in front of Annie. It would be rude not to try it on.

The clasp clicked with ease, and the necklace settled around her neck, neither choking her nor hanging too long. The tiny pendant reflected the light, casting a warm green glint, and Annie couldn't stop stroking it with her fingers. It felt like it had been made for her.

"Shall I bag it?" The lady's tone suggested the deal was already sealed—which it would have been, if circumstances were different.

With a pang of longing, Annie unclasped the necklace and placed it back on the display.

"Here you are. I thought I'd lost you in the crowd." Conrad's voice startled her.

How much had he seen? Had he been standing there long? Annie's eye caught a glimpse of teardrop-shaped pendants strung together in healing chakra colours.

Perfect.

"I'll take this one, please." Annie pointed at the rainbow necklace, ignoring the surprised look from the seller. It would look great on Louise's long neck and match her outfits. More importantly, it was exactly what Louise would have picked if she were here.

"Let me get it for you." Conrad pulled out his card, but Annie blocked it with her hand.

The gesture felt genuine, far more natural than the clothes shopping—but she simply couldn't accept it. "Not this time." She smiled gently and offered her own card to the contactless reader.

The seller handed Annie a small velvet bag. "Enjoy, and come back anytime for anything else that might catch your eye."

Annie blushed and glanced at Conrad's face. Did he notice? The hint? Did he see through her masquerade?

Her shoulders relaxed when she realised, he wasn't even looking at the stall anymore.

"Shall we?" She nudged him and chuckled, watching his head jolt back as if he'd just woken from a deep sleep.

"Absolutely." Conrad slid his arm around her waist like it was the most natural thing to do—and strangely, it felt like it. "We have more of little Avinguda Diagonal to see."

"Little what?" Her stride matched his as they strolled between stalls filled with more of the same kinds of crafts she'd already seen.

"Avinguda Diagonal. You know, Barcelona? The famous art street."

"Oh. I've never been." Not there, not anywhere she'd always dreamed of. Liam had always picked their travel destinations based on whatever his gambling instincts told him to do.

"Oh, you'd love it there. It's not just the street—it's the buildings.

Even I couldn't walk by without gawking."

"Sound like it was lovely." She couldn't hide the misery in her voice. Travelling had been one of her greatest dreams.

Conrad must have read her mind. "Well, let's put it on our bucket list."

"A bucket list?"

"You know, a list of things people want to accomplish in their lives." Conrad pulled Annie closer as they squeezed through a narrow passage, the intimacy messing with her train of thought.

"Yes, but ... "

Should she tell him they wouldn't be together long enough? Or that no one had ever wanted to make a list with her before?

"But what? You want to go somewhere else?"

"No. Yes. I mean ... "

Oh boy, get a grip, woman.

Conrad directed Annie toward the path leading down by the river. "Well, where do you want to go?"

Good question.

"Oh, I don't know." Nowhere right now—not with a baby on the way and no money to speak of. But ..."There are so many places I always wanted to visit."

"Great. Pick the first one that comes to mind."

"Ice Hotel." The words flew out before Annie even formed the image in her mind. "And the northern lights."

Conrad laughed. "I hear it's beautiful in winter. Shall we go this Christmas?"

What?

Annie halted while Conrad continued ahead. His hand slipped off her waist, creating a void. Christmas with him? Scary? Wonderful? All of it?

"Did I say something stupid?"

She shook her head. "No, no. It's just ... Family."

"I didn't know you celebrated with your parents."

She swallowed, unsure whether she should confirm or deny it. But she didn't have to. Conrad pulled her into a tight embrace, his breath brushing against her ear, sending shivers down her spine. "No rush. Let's put it on our bucket list, and we'll find the right time and date for it. Together."

Annie nodded as a gigantic ball of something rose in her throat. None of her former boyfriends had ever wanted to do something *together*. With her. For her. It had always been about them and their dreams—not hers. Not once had any of them asked where Annie wanted to go.

Not until now.

***

With Louise, a few steps behind him, her backpack on his shoulder, the camera slung around his neck, and a chicken wrap in his left hand, Conrad waved with his only free hand. "Wait!"

A man untying a rope stood up and turned toward Conrad, who approached with long, purposeful strides, raising dust wherever his feet struck the ground. The sound of Louise's diminishing footsteps didn't slow his pace. As long as he stopped the boat from departing, it would buy her time.

The man, sporting a bushy beard and eyebrows, nodded and pushed his hat farther onto his forehead. Conrad reached the bank, stopping beside the moored narrow boat, and fished out two stiff tickets he had bought earlier at the information centre. He handed them to the bearded man.

With a screech, the man pulled the red-painted metal platform—already tucked away—to cover the gap between the boat and the canal bank, stomping on it to secure it in place. It clanged, but didn't budge. "Off you go." The man stepped aside as he stroked his beard.

Conrad glanced back toward the path they had just come down, shielding his eyes with his palm as he scanned for Louise. She was nowhere to be seen. Where had she gone? His forehead creased as his gaze searched past a family of four with a buggy taking up the entire width of the path.

"Are we boarding or what?" Her voice came from right beside him, making Conrad wobble.

"You alright, mate?" The boatman looked at Conrad with suspicion and sniffed.

"Fine, thank you." Conrad straightened up and gestured for Louise to board the boat. "Let's go to the front. I saw a bench there."

Louise's hair bobbed up and down in silent agreement as she

disappeared inside the boat.

"I don't need no trouble, mate." The bearded man pointed at the navy blue boat with a stern expression.

Like Conrad was some kind of drunk knucklehead. He gritted his teeth but kept his tone calm. "Yeah, sure, no trouble." Ducking, he entered the narrow doorway that led into the boat's interior, where only a few cushioned seats were occupied. Low season.

He caught sight of Louise's silhouette disappearing through an open door toward the front of the cabin. Squeezing through the narrow aisle, his shoes stuck slightly to something on the linoleum floor. The backpack bobbed from one headrest to another—unreasonably heavy despite its small size. Conrad pondered peeking inside but thought better of it.

A breeze from the open hatch mixed with oil fumes and bird droppings greeted him as he exited onto the boat's deck. He inhaled deeply and smiled. Life on the water—that was something else. He could totally do this.

"Here." His wife patted the space on the bench beside her. Conrad flopped onto it, the old wood creaking under his weight. Still holding the chicken wrap, he attempted to set the backpack on the adjacent seat.

"Let me." Louise plucked the wrap from his hand. "Strap it there." She pointed at the metal railing. It made sense—the bag wouldn't slide into the murky water or the wet bottom of the boat.

Unburdened, Conrad retrieved his sandwich from her hand. His stomach growled as he peeled back the foil and took a bite of the juicy, spicy chicken. "Have you—" He glanced at Louise's sandwich, already half-eaten. "Ah, I see you've tried it. How is it?"

His wife took another bite and murmured with appreciation. A kindred spirit.

The boat heaved, moving under their feet. A light breeze intensified, ruffling Conrad's hair, flapping the sides of his light jacket, and dislodging strands of lettuce from his wrap.

He used a finger to push them back into place and took another hearty bite, the spicy sauce igniting his taste buds and squeezing tears from his eyes.

"You've got mayo on your cheek and your nose." Louise tilted her head, watching him with a grin.

"Uh-huh." It was all he could manage without spitting food onto her dazzling white T-shirt.

After rummaging in her backpack, Louise leaned closer and extended her hand, armoured with a tissue. Conrad stopped chewing. Her delicate, warm fingers brushed his cheek and nose. Her intoxicating scent enveloped him, her mouth inches from his, inviting.

The thought of kissing her flashed in his mind. He swallowed hard—and choked when the bite got stuck.

A hearty pat on his back cleared all the romantic thoughts. A water bottle appeared in front of him, and he took a sip between coughs.

"You okay?"

He nodded, still unable to speak.

The boat wobbled as it turned, gliding under a bridge, splashes of water sprinkling the deck. Wrapping his leftover sandwich in the foil, he slid it into his pocket and moved to stand near the railing.

Louise joined him, their arms brushing as she stood close. She took a deep breath and cleared her throat as if to speak, but no words came.

Her knitted brows suggested she was lost in thought—and whatever she was thinking about didn't seem pleasant.

Now was the perfect moment.

Conrad took a step backwards, reached into his pocket, and pulled out a small velvet pouch. His fingers closed around the tiny, emerald-coloured doughnut pendant as his shoulders tensed. Crossing his fingers for luck, he lifted the necklace and clasped it around her neck.

"What?" Her wide-open eyes were unreadable. Was it a shock? Delight? Horror? Had he misread her?

"Um. I thought you liked it, so I got it for you."

Her eyes filled with tears.

Damn it. He should've asked her. She'd told him more than once not to buy her anything, but he hadn't listened, had he?

Stubborn idiot.

"Forget it. We can return it."

"No, I love it." She touched the pendant, and a sob escaped her lips.

Conrad's heart lurched toward her, but he'd never been good with tears—never known how to make them stop. Awkwardly, he touched her arms, and she fell forward into his embrace. With her head buried in his chest, her sobbing intensified.

He pulled her tighter, stroking her hair as the boat rocked gently on the water. He didn't know what had caused this sudden downpour of emotions, but he was damn sure he'd figure it out—and do whatever it took to make sure it never happened again.

***

Annie sat on the old, weathered sofa bench, watching the sunset as it cast the garden in shades of orange and purple. She inhaled the aroma of the night-scented stock planted next to the patio. The fragrance made her feel light-headed and a little reckless.

They had returned half an hour earlier after a lazy trip on the canal followed by dinner at a cosy local pub. Annie touched the round pendant hanging from her neck and stroked it with her fingers. It no longer brought her to tears. Instead, it reminded her of something no other man had ever done for her—notice what she wanted and surprise her with it.

She chuckled softly to herself. Who would have thought that this cocky showman of a man, the one she'd first met at the wedding, would tick most of the boxes on her perfect-man list? She sighed, the smile fading from her lips. If only the circumstances were different. If only.

And she still had to tell him.

Annie had been so close to saying everything earlier, but when Conrad had hung that necklace around her neck, the wave of emotion it had stirred in her had shaken her resolve. She would tell him, but not tonight. Tomorrow. She would tell him tomorrow.

The crickets chirped their evening melody as Conrad stepped out of the house, carrying two steaming mugs of hot chocolate. The sweet, rich aroma wafted toward her, mingling with the fragrant scent of the night.

After handing Annie a mug, he wrapped her in a soft blanket before settling next to her, his warmth seeping through the layers of fabric.

As they sat in companionable silence, savouring the velvety taste of the hot chocolate, Annie's phone buzzed. A text from her father lit up the screen, asking if Conrad had set a date for the cottage transfer yet.

Her stomach twisted with guilt, but she ignored it, unwilling to let the outside world intrude on this perfect fleeting moment. She tucked the phone away, her focus returning to the quiet garden.

The fading light cast long shadows across the garden, and a gentle breeze rustled the leaves of the ancient oak tree.

"So, what do you think we should do tomorrow?" Conrad asked, breaking the silence.

"Tomorrow?" Annie's fingers instinctively wrapped around the pendant.

"Yeah. I have a meeting in the morning." He waved his hand dismissively. "It won't take long. After that, how about a gentle stroll through the countryside? We could stop for lunch at that country club I told you about?"

Annie inhaled sharply, her curiosity piqued. "The one my parents want you to invest in using money from my fund?"

"Exactly. I want you to see it for yourself."

She nodded but frowned slightly as the memory of the waitress's cryptic comment at The Canal Inn resurfaced.

"Conrad," she began cautiously, "what did that waitress mean when she said I saved the inn?"

He hesitated, his gaze drifting toward the horizon. Then, with a half-smile, he said, "I suppose I was spending too much time at the inns with no family to keep me in check."

There was a subtle shift in his tone, a shadow of something unspoken. Annie noticed, but decided not to press further. Instead, she tilted her head toward the vibrant sky.

"Look at that sunset, all those fiery oranges and reds melting into purples. It's mesmerising."

"I'll grab your camera," Conrad offered, starting to rise. "You'll want to capture this moment."

She shook her head, her eyes never leaving the sky. "No. Moments like this should be lived in, not watched through a camera lens." Her voice was soft and earnest.

"Moments like this?" Conrad echoed, his voice low as he leaned closer.

Annie's heart raced as she nodded, captivated by his sky-blue eyes. Gently, Conrad brushed her cheek with his hand, his touch warm and lingering.

"These are the only moments worth living for," he murmured.

Their lips met in a tender, electrifying kiss that soon deepened, passion igniting between them like wildfire. Annie felt as though she was floating, the taste of the sweet hot chocolate on her tongue blending with the sensation of Conrad's powerful arms pulling her closer.

For one fleeting moment, she let herself get lost in it. But the truth crept back in, sharp and unrelenting. She wasn't Louise. She couldn't keep deceiving him like this.

With a sudden urgency, she pulled away, her breath coming fast. "I can't," she whispered.

Conrad's eyes softened, and he gently stroked her hair. "It's okay. I can wait."

***

With her heart still pounding and her cheeks hot from the burning need inside her, Annie closed the door to her bedroom before she could change her mind. Her fingers brushed her lips, recalling the kiss. Urgent, hungry—but not angry. Not like the surprise one at the wedding, or the mocking one after the ceremony. This one had been real. Deeper. Promising. Offering.

Annie sat on the edge of her bed and texted her sister.

Me: *Are you asleep?*

Lou: *No. What's up? Do you wanna talk?*

Annie tilted her head, straining her ears to listen—a distant sound of running water and humming. A chuckle escaped her lips. He must be in the shower. She hit the call button and pressed the phone to her ear, lowering the volume instinctively with her thumb.

"What's up, sis? Everything okay?" Louise's voice held a sleepy warmth.

Annie hesitated, then giggled. "We kissed."

"What?" Louise sounded wide awake now, her voice muffled slightly as she turned to someone. "Meggie also wants to know what on Earth happened."

"I know, I know. It's crazy." Annie buried her face in her palm, but her smile refused to fade.

"Does he know?"

Annie shook her head before realising her sister couldn't see her. "Not yet."

"Tell me you're joking." Louise's tone shifted—a seriousness that rarely surfaced. It should have made Annie pause, but that giddy, fluttery feeling in her chest refused to be silenced. It whispered, *Jump. Live for once.* And Annie wanted to live.

"It'll be fine. He's taking me to that country pub tomorrow. The one he's supposed to buy with your money. So, I'll tell him there."

And then ... what? He'd forgive her? Promise to stay by her side no matter what?

Yeah, right. Annie had always been good at imagining grand endings, but even she knew this one was a long shot. Still, maybe he wouldn't be *that* mad.

"You mean the money that doesn't exist. The money he was promised in exchange for the cottage?"

When had Louise become such a grown-up? The light feeling in Annie's stomach dimmed, replaced by something heavy and twisting.

"Yes, I know. But I have a plan."

"Oh, really?" Louise's voice dripped with scepticism. "Do tell."

"Well ... I'll offer him a new deal. My inheritance." Annie's voice carried enough to pique her sister's curiosity.

"What inheritance?"

"Father said the cottage would unlock some money for us. I don't know how much, but it has to be worth something, right?" Annie bit her lip, her heartbeat fluttering now for entirely different reasons than half an hour ago.

"Well ..." Louise paused, her tone softening just a fraction. "I hope you're right, sis, and that it's enough."

"I hope so too."

Annie's ears caught the sound of a door shutting somewhere in the house. Footsteps followed, growing louder, closer.

"Bye," she whispered and held her breath, the phone slipping from her hand onto the bedspread.

Was he coming here? Her heart raced, torn between anticipation and dread.

The footsteps stopped.

One minute passed. Then two. Silence stretched, taut as a drawn thread.

Annie stayed still, waging a battle in her mind, waiting for him to knock. Would she let him in? Should she?

The sound of retreating footsteps broke the stillness, fading into the depths of the house. A door shut somewhere far off, leaving the world quiet again.

Annie released the air trapped in her lungs, her chest aching from the strain.

It was better this way.

So why didn't she feel relieved?

Chapter 15

Conrad whistled a complex tune as he parked his truck behind the house. After switching off the engine, he waltzed toward the main entrance. Even the noncommittal behaviour of the two venture capitalists he had met earlier hadn't dimmed the spark in his eyes. If anything, the closer he got to home, the brighter it shone.

Why had he even bothered with that meeting? He didn't want to sell his business. It had never been his preferred option—more of a desperate, last-resort kind of solution. The meeting had been arranged weeks ago, so Conrad had gone out of courtesy, but he had a growing feeling it wouldn't be necessary.

Not only would he get the agreed money—he was now certain Louise would keep her side of the deal—but his fake marriage might even become a real one. Who would have thought? Chuckling, he turned the key in the front door lock.

With a hand on the handle, he paused, recalling last night's events. Maybe he should have tried harder. He could tell she'd wanted it, but her soft "I can't" after the kiss had held him back from knocking on her door.

Well, tonight would be different. The visit to the country club, paired with its delicious food, would clear any doubts from her mind. And if he'd read the situation correctly, the attraction between them was mutual. A wide grin spread across his face as he opened the front door, but before he could announce his arrival, his phone buzzed.

"Lovely to hear your voice, Maureen. Again." He couldn't resist the jab, though he knew it wouldn't faze his mother-in-law.

"Well." He wasn't wrong. That ice wouldn't melt even under the direct sun.

"Well, what?"

"Can I speak to my daughter now?"

Conrad scratched the back of his neck, tempted to suggest she call Louise directly if it was so urgent—Maureen had already interrupted his meeting twice. But there was no point antagonising her further.

"I just got back to the house. Let me check if she's available, and she can call you back."

"No, no. I'll wait on the line."

Of course she would. Conrad strode toward Louise's bedroom and knocked on the closed door.

***

Annie woke up, the memory of last night's passionate kiss lingering on her lips. She lay in bed for a moment, recalling the warmth of Conrad's body against hers as they had sat on the sofa, the fire they'd ignited in each other. Her gaze shifted to her phone on the nightstand, noticing several missed calls and texts from her parents. Choosing to ignore them for now, she slipped out of bed and headed for the shower.

Half an hour later, as she was towelling her hair, a knock sounded at her bedroom door.

Pulling her bathrobe tighter around her body, she called out, "Come in."

The door creaked open, and Conrad stepped inside. Annie's cheeks flushed as his gaze lingered on her, taking in her damp hair and the way the bathrobe clung to her curves.

In a deep voice that sent a shiver down her spine, he said, "Your mother thinks I keep you locked in the basement. The funny thing is, she doesn't even disapprove." A mischievous grin played on his lips as he held out his phone. "She wants to talk to you about something."

Annie rolled her eyes and accepted the phone. Conrad mouthed the word "coffee," and her eyes widened, making him chuckle as he left the room.

She pressed the phone to her ear, bracing herself for the conversation.

"Why aren't you picking up your phone?" her mother demanded sharply. "I've called you several times. So has your father."

"I was busy," Annie replied, a coy smile playing on her lips.

"Busy with what?" her mother snapped.

"I just got married, Mother. What do you think?" Annie grinned at her reflection in the mirror, enjoying the momentary silence that followed.

"You should be ashamed of yourself!" her mother finally spat.

Annie smirked. "I thought that's what a dutiful wife is supposed to do."

"A lady doesn't talk about that. You'd know if you were one." The ice in her mother's tone could have frozen a volcano.

"Well, you asked," Annie retorted, tracing her finger along the edge of a picture frame that held a photo of her grandmother. "So, what's so important? We're just about to head out."

"Head out? Where?" her mother demanded with interest in her voice.

"Hiking. Out and about. Conrad—" Annie's lips curled into a half-smile. "—my husband wants to show me the countryside."

"But what about the paperwork and the will signing?" her mother pressed. "It's booked for tomorrow."

"I guess you'll have to reschedule."

"Stop playing games. This is your future at stake as well! And I thought you wanted to be done with Conrad, not play house with him. Have you forgotten he thinks you're Louise?"

No, she hadn't forgotten. "I remember. Stop panicking. There's still time. In fact, we're stopping for lunch at the country club Conrad will be buying with my marriage fund money."

"Today?"

"Yes. And now, if you'll excuse me, my husband is waiting."

Annie ended the call and inhaled deeply, steadying herself. She gazed out the window, where the morning sun bathed the orchard and fields in golden light. Birds sang in the trees, their melodies blending with the distant rumble of the coffee machine and the enticing aroma of freshly brewed beans wafting through the house.

She rummaged through her suitcase, pulling out a pair of trainers and a clean T-shirt. The leggings and sweater she'd bought the day before completed the outfit. As she got dressed, her heart pounded—a mix of excitement and fear for what the day might bring.

Her eyes lingered on the photo of her smiling grandmother one last time, and she whispered, "Will anyone ever love me the way George loved you, Grandma?"

***

The narrow trail buzzed with life. Nettles and thorny wild roses surrounded them. When the path became too narrow for even one person, Louise cocked her head, casting a sceptical glance at Conrad.

"Really? Is this your idea of fun?" She gestured at the dense foliage ahead.

"Well, it wasn't like this last time I was here." Conrad rubbed the back of his neck.

"And when was that?" Her eyebrow arched.

"Good question."

Conrad still remembered that gloomy day in early March, all those years ago. He shook his head, clearing the memory of the despair that had consumed him on that day. "Let's go around."

He turned on his heel and retraced his steps until they reached an opening with a path leading into the field.

"So, when was it?" His wife persisted.

"When was what?" Conrad narrowed his eyes, unsure of what she was asking about. He pointed toward the edge of the farmer's land. "Here—be careful where you put your feet, but this should take us right to the country club's side gate."

"When was the last time you walked that bushy path?" She waved vaguely in the direction they had just come from.

"Ah, that. Well, it's been a while. Twenty-nine years."

"Almost thirty years?" Louise chuckled. "And you didn't think it might have changed?"

"I didn't realise it had been that long. Also, it was winter." Conrad picked up a tall blade of grass and rolled it between his fingers, watching a squirrel scurry up the trunk of a tree.

"Winter? Really? I thought you liked this club. I'd imagine you must have been here more recently than twenty-nine years ago."

"Of course, I've been to the club recently. I eat there at least once a month. I just don't take this path."

"So, why did you bring me this way? As punishment?" She cocked her head, leaving Conrad unsure whether she was joking or serious. Women and their faces—so hard to read.

"Of course not. In fact, this used to be my favourite route. It was our thing."

"Our thing? Whose thing?" Louise shaded her eyes with her hand, looking out at the field ahead.

"My family. My parents and I used to stroll from the cottage to the club, have lunch, and walk back. Sometimes Grandpa would join us, but not often. It was quite a hike for him."

She turned her face toward him. "Twenty-nine years ago was when they died, wasn't it?" Louise's expression softened as she touched his shoulder.

"Yes. That day. After the police told me what happened, I had to escape. I needed to get away from all the fuss, all the people telling me how sorry they were. I wanted to be alone, so I walked."

He paused, his gaze fixed in the distance as memories flooded back. The steel-grey clouds had hung low in the sky that day, in stark contrast to the light, fluffy clouds now overhead. The overgrown, colourful bushes and trees teeming with bees and birds were a far cry from the frozen ground and bare, lifeless branches of his past.

"And then, when it hit me that I'd never hike with them again, I sat down in one of those ridges on the frozen ground, and the sky fell on my head."

The horses' neighs near the country club fence seemed to resemble a wailing cry, echoing across the rural landscape.

Louise stood quietly, listening, her green eyes shimmering with empathy. Conrad exhaled and met her gaze. The furrowed lines on her forehead smoothed out, and she stepped closer, wrapping her arms around him in a comforting embrace.

Conrad welcomed her touch, the gesture filling the cracks in his heart. She was warm and soft, and the scent of her enveloped him like a balm. Although it was meant to be a supportive hug, Conrad couldn't help but be affected by it—the warmth of her body against his made him ache for her, emotionally and physically.

He stroked her hair, letting his fingers trace the curve of her cheek. She looked up at him, her eyes like bottomless emerald pools pulling him in.

"You are beautiful," he murmured.

A half-smile brightened her face. She licked her lips and parted them as if to speak, but Conrad couldn't resist any longer. He crashed his lips onto hers with a force that drew them together, his hands slipping under her clothes, exploring her warm, soft skin.

The taste of her, the press of her body against his—it consumed him, filling him with a desire he hadn't felt in years. At that moment, nothing else mattered. He wanted her more than anything.

She wriggled away, breathless. "I'm hungry," she said, her dilated pupils locked on his face as she grinned. "For food."

***

Annie crunched into a sweet potato fry, savouring its taste as she took in the breathtaking view from their secluded table at the countryside club. The smell of a charcoal grill wafted up, drawing her gaze to her plate, piled with a juicy, medium-rare sirloin steak smothered in thick, smooth peppercorn sauce.

"If only the countryside pub I worked in had such a stunning view." Annie inhaled deeply, letting the scent of the garden linger.

"I had no idea you worked in a pub like that. I thought you said it was some grimy place?" Conrad raised his glass of red wine, his eyes curious.

She gasped and gulped from her water glass to cover her reaction.

How would she wriggle out of this one? How, indeed, could Louise have worked in two different pubs while studying art? From what Annie knew, her sister had always been knee-deep in one assignment or another, barely having time to sleep, let alone hold a part-time job.

As she chewed on a juicy bite of steak, she reached for her linen napkin and dabbed the corner of her mouth.

"Oh, it was another one—just for the summer. The pub was on the outskirts of town, like this one." She gestured around, pointing at the rustic wooden tables covered with crisp white tablecloths. "But not as posh as this, and there were no outdoor tables. It was more of a local spot, with the same jolly crowd every day, coming for a pint and company."

A light breeze rustled the hedge fence, blowing a strand of hair into her misty eyes as she recalled the friendly faces.

"I still can't believe I had no idea about your grandfather, George." She quickly changed the topic, hoping Conrad hadn't heard about Louise's summers in Italy. But how else could she explain working at a countryside pub while supposedly studying in Bournemouth? "We spent countless evenings talking about the past, but Grandma Ann never mentioned him."

Conrad leaned in closer, his wicker chair creaking under his weight. "Some things aren't easy to share in casual conversation."

Annie waved her fork, agreeing with his point. "True, but I remember asking her once how she knew Grandpa was the love of her life."

She held her fork in mid-air, dripping peppercorn sauce on the pristine tablecloth.

"It was after I got a proposal." Her voice softened, growing distant. "I came home, confused about whether I wanted to get married or not, and I asked her how she knew."

"A proposal?" Conrad's eyebrows shot up. "You've been engaged before? I didn't know that." His tone was light, but curiosity glinted in his eyes. "When did that happen?"

Annie's eyes widened as she realised her slip. She'd shared a part of her own past, not Louise's. Again.

"Oh, it was a long time ago." Annie forced a fake laugh and waved her hand dismissively. "Nothing to write home about."

"Couldn't have been that long ago." Conrad chuckled, leaning back in his chair. "Unless he proposed in college. Was it that dude we met at the shopping mall?"

Louise had barely started college when Annie had got married and had still been at uni when Annie had got divorced.

"Well, yes, it was him, but it feels like ancient history now." She glanced down at her plate, focusing intently on cutting another piece of steak.

"Are you still in love with him?" His inquisitive eyes searched her face.

"God, no. I haven't seen the man in years. I mean, before the shopping mall encounter." At least she hadn't lied about that. "He turned out to be someone very different from what I thought."

Before Conrad could press further, Annie quickly shifted gears.

"The country club seems to be thriving. I'm surprised they want to sell."

Conrad wriggled in his seat, licking his lips before taking a long sip from his glass. He looked like someone trying to find words for a tough conversation, not answering a simple question. Annie scratched her chin. Now he'd piqued her interest. It seemed she wasn't the only one keeping secrets.

It was time. She took a deep breath, mentally rehearsing the sentences she'd been crafting for days.

"So." She swallowed hard and opened her mouth, but before she could say anything, a familiar voice cut in.

"What a delightful surprise! Who would have thought we'd stumble upon you lovebirds here?"

Annie's heart sank as her parents approached their table. Conrad's eyes bore into her, cold and accusing as if she'd betrayed him.

"Maureen, Richard, what a surprise!" Conrad rose from his seat, his smile strained as he shook hands with her father.

With her arms crossed, Annie gave her parents a stiff nod, avoiding her mother's hug. "What are you doing here?" she asked, her voice brimming with hostility.

"We came for lunch, of course." Maureen beamed. "After all, this is the place you'll own very soon. We wanted to check on our investment."

"Your investment?" Annie's eyes narrowed.

Her mother patted her hand. "I meant *family*, dear. We simply care about you and Conrad and want the best for both of you. We're in the catering business, after all, so of course, we have to offer our expertise."

Annie stared at her mother, her lips pressed into a thin line.

"Do you mind if we join you? It looks busy here." Maureen planted herself in the nearest chair without waiting for permission.

Conrad's icy gaze rested on Annie's face. She shook her head slightly, pleading silently for him to understand she'd had nothing to do with this.

But it was her fault, wasn't it? Annie's stomach twisted as she remembered telling her mother where they were going. *If only I had kept my mouth shut.* She bit her lip, guilt clawing at her chest.

"Conrad, darling, could you get the waitress for us? I'm starving."

Conrad nodded stiffly, turning on his heel, his movements rigid and tense.

"You had no right," Annie hissed through clenched teeth once he disappeared. "He'll think it was my idea—that I betrayed him."

Her mother smirked, tilting her head. "Oh, and now you're so concerned about him? Only a few days ago, you thought he was a ruthless, egotistical bastard, going after a trophy wife and her money."

Annie shook her head, her voice firm. "I didn't know him back then."

"And you do now?"

***

As Conrad strode toward the bar, his mind buzzed with conflicting thoughts. On one hand, he was annoyed that Louise's parents had crashed their date, but on the other, he couldn't help but feel relieved. Their intrusion might help speed up the paperwork for the cottage and bring them closer to the finish line.

With a determined spring in his step, he entertained the thought of escaping early and continuing their otherwise perfect day. If he committed to sorting out the paperwork by the end of the week, it should buy him enough time to reassure Louise that he was on her side.

He drummed his fingers on the wooden bar, waiting for a staff member to hand him the menus. The club buzzed with lively conversation, and the afternoon sun poured through the tall windows, casting a golden hue over the room. A server finally approached, smiling as they handed Conrad the menus and advised him to return to the bar to place their order after deciding.

The hedges separating the main dining area from the garden, where they were seated, obscured his view of their table, but Conrad knew the spot well. This place had been a family favourite for years, filled with memories of fresh countryside air and laughter against the stunning landscape. But the truth was, the club wasn't for sale—he'd asked more than once in the past.

Still, once they got back on their feet, Louise could have her pick of any pub or club she wanted, and he would find the money to make it exclusively hers.

As he neared the table, he heard his wife's voice—the soft, teasing tone he had grown used to was now replaced with hard steel.

"So, why are you here?" she demanded.

Conrad stopped, stepping behind a leafy plant where he could hear but remain unseen. He wanted to give her the chance to deal with her parents on her own terms. Her pursed lips and arched brows would have made even him think twice before crossing her.

Richard leaned back in his chair, his face tight with irritation. "Because you can't do a simple job, like getting Conrad to sign the paperwork. As unreliable as always."

Louise's eyes flashed with defiance. "Maybe because I don't want to do your bidding. It's his cottage and his right to decide what to do with it—and when."

My kind of girl. Conrad grinned. He could kiss her right now. The same fiery stubbornness he'd experienced earlier was now aimed at her parents.

"Well, the deal was clear, and he knows it." The finality in Maureen's modulated voice left no room for argument.

"Then I'm sure he'll honour it." Louise crossed her arms over her chest.

Richard's hand slammed against the table, rattling the silverware. "But when? Time is ticking!"

"I don't know. When he's ready," his wife snapped back. "Maybe if you treated him better and didn't pressure him, he would have done it by now."

Conrad took a deep breath. The conversation was getting heated, and he was ready to step in and back her up.

"Maybe if you treated him better, he would," Maureen scoffed. "You can't even play the role of a proper wife."

"What? Do you want me to sleep with him just so you can get your precious cottage?" Louise's face flushed crimson with anger.

"Don't be vulgar, dear." Richard clicked his tongue. "You know this isn't just about us. Your poor sister is counting on you."

Her sister? Conrad's ears perked up. There had been no sister at the wedding, and Louise had never mentioned one.

"Leave Lou out of it. This was your idea, not hers." His wife waved her finger at her father. "You know she'd happily give up her share if you'd just leave her alone."

Lou? Conrad's brow furrowed, his mind reeling with confusion. What was going on here?

"Be reasonable, Annie. There's money in this for you, too." Richard touched her shoulder, but she shrugged it off.

Annie? Conrad's heart pounded in his chest, and his eyes widened, his mind racing to catch up with what he'd just heard.

"I know that," she snapped. "But I'm not going to push him into doing something he's not comfortable with. And you can't force me like you forced me into this marriage."

Maureen leaned back in her chair, a sly smirk spreading across her lips.

"Well, that's on you, Missy. We had no idea you'd take your sister's place."

Sister's place? Conrad's heart slammed against his ribs. His jaw tightened, and a whirlwind of emotions churned in his gut—confusion, anger, betrayal. His fists clenched as the truth hit him like a freight train.

***

"You forced her, so I had no choice. And you … "

The words died on Annie's lips as she spotted Conrad approaching the table. She sprang to her feet, her napkin fluttering onto the table.

"We're leaving. Enjoy your meal." Her tone was as frosty as the ice cubes clinking in her glass.

Annie snatched the menus from Conrad's hand and slapped them down on the table. Her fingers closed around his wrist in a firm grip as she tugged him toward the exit, her heart pounding.

"What about the bill?" Conrad pulled on her hand, slowing her down.

She smirked, her lips forming a hard line. "They can pay for their daughter and her husband's meal. It's the least they can do."

"Remember what we talked about!" Her father's voice echoed after them.

Annie's footsteps faltered outside the club. Conrad, still clutching her hand, spun her around. His voice cut through the air between them like a blade.

"What were you talking about?"

She held his icy blue gaze, bright and unyielding, though her insides churned.

"They want me to force you to sign that paperwork on the cottage. I told them to shove it."

His chuckle was short-lived, replaced by a deep frown.

Annie studied his expression, trying to read him, to find a flicker of trust, but his features were stone. "I know why you're so angry."

"Do you, now?" His voice dripped with irony, as cold as a winter storm.

"You need to believe me. It wasn't my idea." Annie's voice shook, her free hand twisting her wedding ring nervously.

He shrugged, letting go of her hand, and pulled out his phone.

She furrowed her brows. "Who're you calling?"

"A cab company. I'm not in the mood to walk back." His fingers flew over the screen, the rapid tapping a harsh contrast to his chilled demeanour.

"I'm sorry, but it really wasn't my idea." A note of desperation crept into her voice.

"I'm not sure about that." His eyes remained glued to his phone.

"So, you don't believe me?" The words slipped out before she could stop them. "I thought you'd got to know me enough to realise I would never do that." She touched his arm, his muscles hard as steel.

"I don't think I know you at all." His words landed like a physical blow, and Annie took a step back.

Shielding her eyes from the blazing sun, she watched Conrad's hunched shoulders as he kicked at pebbles down the scorched road, raising a haze of dust.

What else could she say to break through the wall he'd built between them?

A rotten smell from a side alley mixed with the pungent odour of horse manure from nearby fields—a reminder of the reality she now faced. How could she make him believe that it wasn't her idea?

The taxi pulled up, and Conrad opened the door with a stiff, controlled movement.

"For what it's worth, I'm really sorry they destroyed our lunch," Annie murmured, her gaze fixed on the worn leather of the taxi seat.

"Me too." His words were soft but distant. She reached for his hand, but he pulled it away, the move starkly contrasting the passionate kiss they'd shared only an hour earlier.

As the taxi pulled away, Annie stared out at the vibrant countryside, her heart as heavy as the hot, still air around them. She rubbed her thumb over a small splinter she'd picked up from the table, the sting a welcome distraction from the harsh reality of her situation.

How could she ever teach her child to be happy if she couldn't find it for herself?

Chapter 16

The taxi's faux leather seats felt cold against Conrad's skin as he sat in the back, arms folded, staring out the window while the car descended the winding country road toward the cottage. The sharp scent of a pine air freshener filled the cramped space, making his stomach churn. He could still feel his wife's touch—her warm fingers on his skin. He was drawn to her, but she was a fake—an illusion.

How could he have been so blind? From the corner of his eye, Conrad watched her hunched shoulders, radiating misery. Her hand brushed against his arm but withdrew quickly, leaving him with a longing he couldn't shake.

That charm and warm laughter from earlier when they'd kissed … Those mesmerising emerald eyes and that hair, alive and dancing around her face … Was any of it real?

"Don't be like that," she said, her voice hoarse, raw with emotion.

With a deep sigh, he turned to face her, taking in her ashen face. The wrinkles on her forehead and around her eyes caught his attention—a more mature look he found oddly alluring. Was she older than she seemed? And what had her life been like before she became Louise? Maybe she was an actress. If so, a damn good one. She'd fooled him. They all had. How could he have been so stupid?

"I understand you're upset, but it was just my parents crashing our lunch, not a tragic disaster. I didn't like it either."

"You've got nerve." His jaw tightened, anger bubbling beneath the surface. "It's way more than that."

"And what do you want me to do? I didn't invite them. They showed up unannounced." Her voice was a blend of defiance and desperation, her green eyes now clouded. Her worried face was framed by hair that had lost all its shine. He wondered if it was all an act—a well-rehearsed performance designed to tug at his heartstrings.

The taxi came to a halt at the entrance of the cottage—a soft groan from the car engine marking the end of the journey. Conrad pointed at the door.

"This is your stop. I'm going to the inn. I have work to do." The words trickled through his clenched teeth.

"So, this is how you deal with problems? Run away from them?" Her voice was sharp, her green eyes flashing with anger and frustration.

He shot her a look, his tone as cold as the steel-blue sky outside. "What do you want me to do?"

"Come inside and talk. Straighten things out instead of burying your head in the sand." She crossed her arms. "Or I'm going with you."

"I don't think this is a good idea, but have it your way."

Conrad reached for his wallet, his fingers brushing against the rough edge of the plastic card as he held it over the card reader. As he stepped out of the car, the howling wind cut through his thin shirt, chilling him to the bone. Without pausing at her side of the taxi, he stormed toward the cottage. Behind him, she followed, her scent of jasmine and coconut filling the air when they stepped inside.

A dream catcher rattled outside while voile curtains whipped in a frenzy. Conrad leapt to the open windows, pressing against the old, rough wooden frames until they finally shut. Across the room, his wife slammed another window closed and silence enveloped them. The tension in the room was palpable, the air thick with unspoken words.

"So?" Her voice echoed in the quiet room.

Conrad turned to face her, hands on his hips. "So what?"

Her lips thinned, her green eyes blazing. "So, why are you so angry at my parents? Is it about the paperwork? You agreed to give them the cottage, and now you've changed your mind, so you want to blame it on them, right?"

A knot of guilt tightened in his chest. There was a bit of truth to her words, but that wasn't the point.

Conrad cleared his throat. "Oh, so you think I'm overreacting?"

She raised an eyebrow and scoffed. "Aren't you?"

He stepped closer, his voice low and measured. "No, I don't think so,

Annie."

***

Wait, what?

Annie blinked, her pulse tripping over itself like a clumsy dancer. Conrad's icy voice cut through the silence of the cottage, his words hanging heavy in the air.

"This is your real name, isn't it, Annie?" He enunciated her name like it was the punchline to a cruel joke. "And don't try to pretend this is what your parents call you. I know Louise is your sister."

A bubble of hysterical laughter threatened to escape her throat. Conrad's face was set in a grim mask of revelation, as though he'd just uncovered a state secret. The absurdity of the situation, combined with the relief of her secret finally being out, was almost too much to bear. No more pretending. No more guilt. But this was no laughing matter. She bit her lip hard, letting only a wry smile paint her lips.

"When did you find out?" Her hair tumbled into her eyes, but she made no move to brush it aside.

"I overheard your little chat with your mother today."

She nodded. They'd been shouting, so probably the entire restaurant had heard them.

"Then you know it wasn't exactly a friendly chat." Her voice sounded steadier than she felt, despite the chaos inside her.

His eyes, like liquid steel, bore into her, a stark contrast to the warm, rustic hues of the cottage interior.

"Is that your excuse? No apology? As if it's perfectly normal to impersonate your own sister?"

His hands clamped down on her shoulders, forcing her to face him. The move was so familiar, so reminiscent of Darren's controlling grip whenever she'd displeased him, that it sent an icy shiver through her. Sweat dripped down her spine, pooling in the small of her back.

"Conrad, you're hurting me."

"Sorry." He jumped back like he'd been burned, his hands dropping to his sides. His clenched jaw softened, and a flicker of regret darkened his eyes. Not like Darren. Darren would never have let go so easily, and would never have shown shame or regret. Darren would've made her beg for forgiveness.

Behind Conrad, a vase filled with lilacs wobbled and crashed to the floor as he bumped into the side table. Shattered china swirled in a pool of murky, rotten water, spreading in every direction.

"I meant to tell you." Annie stepped over the growing stinky puddle and hastened toward the kitchen area.

"Really?" The rapid staccato of his footsteps echoed on the wooden floor as he followed her. "Before or after I handed you my home?"

She rummaged through the cupboards, searching for a microfiber cloth. "Your home?" Her gaze fell on a colourful piece of fabric—an oven glove. Useless for mopping water.

"Yeah, that cottage you all want so badly." He leaned against the counter, inches away from her, his presence still intoxicating, his exotic cologne making her cheeks flush despite her anger.

"It's not your home. Your home is a posh mansion in Bath." She jabbed her palm against his chest, taking a step back. "And how dare you compare what you did to me with that?"

His eyebrows narrowed in confusion. "Compare what? Did what?"

Annie's eyes caught the shiny reflection of the metallic kitchen towel stand.

Her voice sharpened like a blade. "Buy a woman who could be your daughter with that damn cottage."

His face flushed deep crimson. "What? No!" He waved a hand in exasperation. "You know damn well this marriage was a means to an end. Your parents wanted that cottage, and they promised your sister's marriage fund in exchange. That's all it was."

A bitter taste filled her mouth, sour and metallic. It all made sense on paper, but the reality felt so much uglier. Conrad was no different from her parents. All he cared about was money.

"So, you ruined a young woman's life—not because of her, but because she was just part of a business transaction. You bastard!"

***

Annie yanked the kitchen towel roll off its stand and hurled it at him. He ducked, his mouth open in surprise, and the roll flew past his ear.

It bounced off the floor, unspooling mid-air, leaving the room littered with strands of paper towel. Combined with the shattered vase in the corner, the living area now resembled the aftermath of a stag party.

How on earth did she turn this around? Somehow, she was making him look like the villain while conveniently ignoring her part in this mess.

Conrad's gaze locked on Louise—no, Annie—standing on the other side of the counter with her arms crossed over her chest.

"And now I'm the bad guy?" He leapt around the counter, towering over his wife as he halted inches away from her. "Never mind the fact that you tricked me into this marriage."

She met his gaze head-on. "You were the one so eager to put a ring on it. I just stepped in to prevent a disaster."

"Oh, really?" His laugh was bitter. "Heard you were pretty eager to play the blushing bride. Not many chances left at your age, huh?"

Her cheeks flared crimson at his words. "My age? How dare you!" She jabbed a finger at his chest, her voice rising. "I'm still younger than you, but for you, it's probably too old. You need a young and beautiful wife to validate your status. Isn't that what men your age crave?"

Conrad curled his lips into a wry smirk. "Was it my charm that worked on you, or is it my bank account you find so irresistible?"

Her hands shot to her hips, her chin thrusting out defiantly. "Oh, really? Who's after whose money? You wanted to marry my sister to snatch her inheritance. I stepped in to stop that!"

A whirr from the coffee machine cleaning cycle filled the air, accentuating her words.

"I did this for Louise, you know. I couldn't let her be used like that—not by my parents, and certainly not by you."

Her eyes sparkled like the purest of emeralds while her hair danced around her animated face. Conrad swallowed hard, resisting the urge to end this argument by crashing his lips against hers.

"A sacrifice so immense you didn't think to stop the charade at the altar?" His tone was biting, his eyebrows furrowed.

"You were so wrapped up in your plans you didn't even notice your bride was a different person!" Annie's words stung, hitting the mark.

Conrad grimaced. "You know damn well I only met your sister once. But your parents? Oh, that's a different story. They knew exactly who you were and didn't stop the wedding."

"They must have been in shock," she murmured, her gaze faltering for a brief moment as her shoulders sagged.

Conrad kept advancing, jabbing a finger in her direction until her back pressed against the shiny white surface of the fridge. "I beg to differ. I bet they were thrilled to kill two birds with one stone—get their hands on the cottage and rid themselves of their biggest disappointment: their daughter from hell."

Something in her shifted. The fire in her eyes dimmed, replaced by a vulnerability that hit him harder than any argument ever could. Her shoulders drooped further, and her defiant expression crumbled.

In a trembling voice, she said, "You're right. I was never good enough for them. Always a disappointment. And I don't think that will ever change."

Her words hung in the air, raw and heavy. Tears welled up in her eyes, threatening to spill over. Before he could respond, she pushed him away and bolted, the slam of the bedroom door echoing in his ears.

Conrad stood rooted to the spot. His anger evaporated, replaced by a sour taste of regret.

Why the hell did I say that? He raked his fingers through his hair, pacing the room as guilt settled over him.

It was her fault. No one else had ever rattled him this much. But his wife—since the moment they had met—pushed his buttons like no one else, always finding a way to get under his skin.

But why now? Why those tears? They'd traded worse words than this before, yet he'd never seen her like that—fiery and defiant, yes, but never broken.

The harsh reality of the situation hung in the air like a thick fog of regret and confusion. He had wanted to corner her, to force her to face the truth, but his words had struck deeper than he intended.

He'd hit his mark, sure—but at what cost?

***

Tears streamed down Annie's cheeks, hot and stinging as they fell onto her trembling lips. Taking a deep, shaky breath, she crossed the room in two long strides, her heart hammering against her rib cage, her gaze fixed on the open suitcase lying on the wooden floor near the dresser.

Bending down with a swiftness born of desperation, she clutched the worn suitcase handle, her fingers trembling, the knuckles white from her grip. Using all the force she could muster, she heaved it up and hurled it onto the bed, her hands shaking with anger and frustration.

The sudden motion sent half of the suitcase's contents—bits of her old life, her past—scattering across the floor. Clothes spilt like fragments of memories, falling into a chaotic mess.

Muttering a quiet curse, Annie crouched to gather the scattered items, knocking the photo of her grandmother off the dresser. The wooden frame hit the hard floor with a dull thud that echoed in the silence.

Annie reached out, her fingers tracing the edges of the polished frame—its cool, glossy surface a stark contrast to her warm tears. Her thumb grazed over the familiar face in the picture, and a sad smile tugged at her lips.

"Wish you were here, Granny. I miss you so much."

As if triggered by a sensory switch, the subtle fragrance of lavender emanating from the dresser zapped Annie into a different realm. The scent was a one-way ticket to a past era, an era filled with warmth, love, and the unwavering presence of Grandma Ann.

In her mind, she was sixteen again, a naive girl in love, too insecure to say no when her boyfriend had insisted they be intimate. If only he had kept it to himself. But no, he had bragged about their encounter, and word had reached her mother.

Never before had she seen her mother's face twisted in such a potent mix of fury and disgust. The words had been few, but the message was unmistakable: the half-packed suitcase by the gaping front door said it all.

"You are dead to me," her mother had said, slamming the door shut behind her.

At first, Annie had stood her ground, banging on the door and begging her mother to let her in. But all she'd got was silence, punctuated by a sorrowful glimpse of her nine-year-old sister's tear-streaked face and smudged palms pressed against the cold glass of a window.

How long Annie had stood there, she couldn't remember. The shadows had stretched longer, and the streetlights had flickered on. That night had been the longest of her life.

The biting cold and descending darkness had not been her worst adversaries—it was the crippling loneliness, the overwhelming feeling of utter abandonment.

She had woken up stiff and shivering to a calm, soothing voice and the smell of lavender.

"Everything will be okay, honey. Let's go."

Grandma Ann had swept in like a guardian angel, wrapping her in a soft, pale blue blanket and helping her to the safety of a waiting car.

It had been eighteen years ago—almost to the day. Since then, until her passing earlier this year, Grandma Ann had been a safe port in Annie's tumultuous life. Despite Whether Annie had got into trouble with one boyfriend after another, lost her marriage fund to the gambler she'd married in haste, or barely stayed in touch because Darren had convinced her she was better off with him than her family, Grandma Ann had always had her back.

With trembling hands, Annie placed the photo in the centre of the dresser.

She could never forgive her mother. She wondered if her mother even remembered what had happened that day. And if she did, did she regret it?

But now, Annie was the one betraying someone. Doing her parents' bidding, she had deceived Conrad.

"Granny, how did I end up in such a mess?"

Annie looked out the window. Outside, the fiery sun sank lazily behind the horizon, painting the sky in hues of scarlet and gold—an ironic contrast to the turmoil within her. The ghastly wind subsided, replaced by a chilled evening breeze carrying the sweet aroma of night-scented stock.

Birdsong mingled with the faint rumble of a distant tractor. Annie closed her eyes and inhaled deeply, savouring the brief peace and quiet.

"Granny, it would be bliss to raise my child here." Her whisper was barely audible.

But she couldn't stay. Not here. A quiet sigh escaped her lips as she zipped the suitcase. There were only a few items left to pack from the bathroom, and she would be ready to go.

The sound of footsteps outside the door made her heart pound faster. Annie froze, unsure of what to do. She didn't want to face Conrad—not now. She needed to leave before he could stop her.

Suddenly, a familiar pain gripped her lower belly, forcing her to double over. A hot flush swept through her, and her knees buckled as she collapsed onto the bed, weak and powerless, like a newborn.

"Not now. It can't happen again. Please, God."

***

He rapped on the door once more. Silence.

"Fine." Conrad pursed his lips and marched toward his study. With his hand on the handle, he furrowed his brows, hesitating, then turned around.

The wooden wine rack, holding a few bottles of his favourite Merlot, shimmered under the artificial glow of a side lamp. His gaze landed on the shards of the broken vase scattered near the rack.

"Who cares?" Conrad smirked and shrugged.

In a few long strides, he reached the rack, grabbed the nearest bottle from the top row, and pulled a sizeable wine glass from the hanging cabinet.

He stomped back down the hallway, pausing briefly to glance at the closed door to her bedroom before disappearing into his study.

With one swift motion, he cleared his desk. Papers fluttered into the air, landing on the floor, the bookshelf, and the windowsill—the perfect mess.

Like my entire life.

Conrad planted the bottle and glass in an empty spot on the desk, then swung his computer chair around and sagged into it.

Women are nothing but trouble.

Why had he ever thought this was a good idea?

After unscrewing the bottle's cap, Conrad poured half a glass of wine and lifted it to his mouth. A slightly sour and bitter taste hit his tongue.

"Con artists, all of them!"

How could he have been such a fool, and not realise she couldn't be that young, innocent girl he'd first seen in that coffee shop?

"Because you didn't want to see it, you idiot."

From the moment she'd stood next to him in that church, smelling of coconut, he'd wanted to touch her, to know her better. He should have known. He would never be drawn like that to a woman that could have been his daughter.

Conrad poured another glass, his gaze drifting to a neat stack of letters sitting on the edge of the desk—brought in by Colton, no doubt.

The bold lettering on the top envelope made his stomach twist. Still, with an inexplicable urge to torture himself further, he dragged the stack closer.

The envelopes felt thin and cheap beneath his fingers. He sliced the top one open with his leather-bound letter opener—a gift from his grandfather—and pulled out the stiff, ink-stained paper inside. Bold letters stared back at him.

He swallowed hard and downed the entire glass in one go, refilling it instantly. The bank stopped playing around. No more reminders or polite requests to pay. Just a statement of fact. "Your house will be repossessed a month from the date of this letter ..."

With trembling hands, he tore open the rest of the envelopes. Six in total. Each with a similar deadline, each driving the dagger deeper into his heart.

Conrad didn't care much about the house in Bath—it was just his official residence. His home was here, in this cottage. The cottage he'd promised to his wife.

"Not a chance in hell." He threatened the air with his fist, sending the glass flying. Wine splattered across the papers like blood from a fresh wound.

"You're not my wife! Do you hear me? You're an imposter!" he shouted toward the closed study door, his voice echoing in the empty room.

He grabbed the bottle and took a long swig, his throat burning.

"There is no wedding fund for me, is there?"

The whisper barely left his lips, so quiet even he could hardly hear it.

He had promised his employees that they would keep their jobs. He had promised that he'd found a way to save the business.

And now? Now it was all gone. There was nothing he could do.

He clenched his fists and roared into the void. "You conned them all! Are you happy now?"

Chapter 17

The suitcase wheels rattled on the uneven wooden floor, producing an ear-splitting noise that echoed through the empty house. Annie winced, casting a glance over her shoulder. The room, bathed in the muted light of an overcast morning, painted everything in a dreary, melancholy hue. Still no sign of Conrad.

It's better this way.

She let out a sigh and tiptoed toward the front door, but the persistent clattering of the wheels sabotaged her stealth.

"Sneaking out in the middle of the night like a thief?" Conrad's gravelly voice cut through her thoughts. She froze, hand on the door handle.

So much for the grand escape.

"Actually, it's late morning." Annie turned to face him.

He leaned against the doorway of his bedroom, looking like he'd lost a wrestling match with his pillow. His eyes were shadowed by dark circles, his eyelids puffy, and the normally neat stubble on his jaw was scruffy and uneven—a dishevelled mess.

"I didn't want to wake you. I left a note."

Annie waved vaguely toward the bedroom with one hand while gripping the suitcase handle with the other—the vinyl cold and slightly sticky with her sweat.

"Oh, I wasn't sleeping."

The muscles of his bare chest flexed as he sauntered toward her, each step increasing her heart rate.

"I didn't know." Annie swallowed hard, her gaze skittering away as a flush crept up her neck.

"So?"

Conrad stopped just inches from her. His masculine scent, tinged with the sour tang of alcohol, made her nostrils flare. Annie wrinkled her nose but made no comment. She couldn't blame him.

"I'm leaving. The taxi should be here any second." She gripped the suitcase handle, her palm clammy.

He squinted at her, his body leaning closer. "Figured as much."

She didn't want another fight. There had been enough damage already.

"Look, for what it's worth, I'm sorry. I should never have let it get this far."

She reached out, her hand landing on his shoulder, more to keep him at bay than comforting. He flinched at her touch, tensing beneath her fingers.

"You're right," he said, his voice low and flat.

The pungent smell of alcohol on his breath hit her, making her stomach churn.

"I'll call the civic office today and get the marriage voided."

Conrad loomed over her, pinning her between his broad chest and the door. Annie's heart pounded so hard that she could feel it in her ears, her palms growing slick with sweat.

"What about your parents?" His voice dropped to a soft rumble that raised goosebumps on her skin.

She sidestepped, taking a breath. "Quite frankly, I don't care."

His eyebrows arched in faint surprise, softening the puffiness of his face. The expression prompted an unexpected chuckle from Annie.

The doorbell chimed, sharp and clear, slicing through the charged air between them.

"Must be your taxi." Conrad unlocked the door and swung it open with a flourish.

A cool breeze swept in, whipping her hair around her face. It was as if nature itself was urging her to leave.

"Good—" The word caught in Annie's throat as her eyes widened in shock.

"Here you are, you little slut."

***

A well-dressed man, a few inches shorter than Conrad, barged into the hallway, his predatory gaze fixed on Annie. She retreated swiftly, her back pressing against the unyielding wall, her eyes large orbs of sheer panic.

"What are you doing here, Darren?"

Her voice trembled, a vulnerability seeping into her tone that Conrad hadn't heard before.

Conrad scratched his chin, his brow furrowing. What kind of trouble had she got herself into, now? "I take he's not the taxi driver, then?"

Annie shook her head, her eyes riveted on the suit-clad intruder. Conrad sized him up. Perhaps he was another fella she and her family had conned. And now, he had tracked her down like a bloodhound on the hunt.

Taking two strides forward, Conrad extended his hand. "Conrad."

The man's gaze swept over him, up and down, before a smirk spread across his lips. He didn't extend his hand in return. Unfazed, Conrad folded his arms across his chest, his feet planted wide apart.

"A little privacy?" The intruder's icy words finally acknowledged Conrad's presence.

"Mate, you're in *my* house." Conrad didn't budge. His brows knitted together as his eyes studied the man, watching every subtle twitch of his face and hands.

Annie's whisper barely reached Conrad. "How did you find me, Darren?"

Darren's lips stretched into a predatory grin, but his eyes, made of steel, hadn't changed at all.

"You thought you were that clever, huh?"

She wrapped her arms protectively around herself, shrinking into her frame like a turtle retreating into its shell.

"You shouldn't have left the envelope behind," Darren sneered. "I found your sister's shabby pod, and my guys had no trouble tracking your folks' place from there."

His guys?

She must've really rattled his cage to make him go to such lengths.

Rubbing his immaculately trimmed beard, Darren flicked an imaginary speck of dust from his designer suit.

"Your mother put up quite a fight, though. From what you told me, I thought she'd grass you up without a second thought. Instead, she told me to bugger off."

He encroached further into Annie's personal space, his every move calculated to intimidate. Her breathing quickened, shallow and erratic. "And you know I don't like rude people."

"Leave my parents alone, Darren." Her voice might've trembled, but there was an unmistakable steel in her tone now.

Conrad's mind spun at the unexpected revelation. Her parents weren't part of the con? Weird.

"I couldn't care less about them as long as I have *you*."

Darren loomed over Annie. Her throat bobbed as she swallowed hard, her panicked eyes around like she was a trapped animal. Conrad's forehead creased.

"Luckily for me, your folks aren't the sharpest tools in the shed. My guys followed them to your little reunion at the country club yesterday and then here, to this dump."

His manicured hand gestured flippantly at Conrad's home.

"You should've left last night, you little skunk." With a swift movement, he grabbed Annie's arms. She gasped in pain as his fingers dug into her flesh. "Now you'll regret this."

A surge of protective adrenaline shot through Conrad. He closed the distance in a heartbeat, shoving Darren hard enough to free Annie from his grasp.

"Who the fuck are you?"

He stepped between Annie and the intruder, his broad frame shielding her. With a glance over his shoulder, he motioned for her to stay behind him. No matter who she was, no lowlife was going to threaten a woman under his roof.

"And what do you want from my wife?"

Darren's beady eyes met Conrad's, his lips twisting into a sardonic smirk.

"Your wife?" He sized Conrad up with a new appraisal.

"You've got a problem with that?" The words rumbled from Conrad's chest like distant thunder.

"She can't be your wife." Darren's smirk grew wider, more sinister. "She's mine."

Caught off guard, Conrad turned to Annie. Her face crumpled, terror stretching her features and dwarfing her eyes. Her lips quivered as she shook her head, her voice barely threading through the tension-filled air.

"No, I'm not. Believe me, Conrad. I'm not."

Conrad wasn't sure what to believe anymore, but this wasn't how he'd imagined the morning would go.

"Whatever, mate. You need to leave."

The scumbag chuckled, his fingers tracing the crisp white collar of his shirt.

"I wasn't planning on staying—" his gaze locked on Conrad, a dark glint in his eyes "—*mate*. But she's coming with me."

Conrad shook his head, his voice gritty with resolve. "The hell she is."

***

The first blow came out of nowhere. Annie shrieked, and Conrad ducked just in time, Darren's fist missing his jaw by inches.

"No, Darren! Stop it!" Annie's voice was raw, panic laced in every word. She had done enough damage. There was no way she would let Conrad get hurt because of her past.

She pushed herself in front of Conrad. "I'll go with you."

"Of course you will." Darren smirked, extending a hand to grab her arm.

He shouldn't have done it. Conrad's fist connected with Darren's face, landing squarely on that smug expression.

"You're not going anywhere, Annie." Conrad's voice was a low growl as he stepped in front of her again, his broad, bare shoulders blocking her view. She stumbled to the side and gasped as she caught sight of blood dripping onto Darren's white shirt.

We're screwed.

"And you—" Conrad jabbed a finger toward Darren. "—are leaving right now, or I'm calling the police."

Darren wiped the blood with a tissue and dropped it to the floor. "Oh, we're not done yet, pussy boy. After I'm finished with you, you can call whomever you like."

Her ex clenched his teeth and swatted Conrad's pointing finger away, but Conrad didn't budge. "I'm serious, man. Leave. Now."

Conrad looked like an ancient god with his muscular arms, but he stood no chance against Darren and his men. Ever since she had overheard that conversation—how her ex handled his affairs—she knew this wouldn't end well.

She shook her head and took a deep breath. *Better me than Conrad.* She had brought this onto herself. He didn't deserve any of it.

"Let's go, Darren," Annie said, her voice trembling but firm. "You don't have to do this. You've already won."

Annie took a step forward, placing a hand on Conrad's shoulder. Her eyes met his, pleading with him to stay silent.

"I'm not finished yet." Darren's low growl made her look.

Annie barely had time to register his words before she saw his fist rise again.

"No!" she cried, stepping forward instinctively to stop him.

The blow landed squarely on her face, jerking her head back. Her vision blurred as a sharp, ringing pain shot through her skull. She stumbled, colliding with the nearby wall before her knees buckled, sending her crumpling to the floor.

She hit the ground hard, her breath stolen by the sudden, searing pain in her abdomen.

Her hands flew to her belly, panic and dread twisting her inside. A piercing scream ripped from her throat. "Nooooooo!"

Chapter 18

"How're you feeling?"

"I'm—" Her voice cracked, parched and brittle like an old desert trail.

A hand appeared in her line of sight, holding a plastic cup. She latched onto the straw, the cold water rushing down her throat, tasting like an exotic holiday drink.

"Slow down. I'm not taking it away." The hoarse but warm voice sounded familiar. Annie turned her head, stopping abruptly as a sharp pain almost made her blackout.

"Easy, tiger. No sudden movements." His words wrapped around her like a safety net.

As she sipped the water, her eyes darted around the room. Crisp white sheets stretched over a metal-framed bed with railings. A white bathrobe hung on the back of a worn armchair in the corner. A machine to her left beeped, and something squeezed her left arm.

"Why am I in a hospital?" Her breathing quickened, making the machine beep louder in response.

"What happened? Was it an accident?"

A low chuckle seeped into her ears—warm, but with a hint of sadness. Annie looked up. Conrad's blue eyes, weary and rimmed with dark shadows, met hers. A faint purple bruise decorated one of them.

"You might say that." He smelled like coffee, the rich scent mingling with the cold sterility of the room.

She reached for the cup again, her hand shaking. "More."

Conrad placed the cup in her right hand, guiding the straw to her lips. Her eyes caught the scratches and dried blood on his knuckles.

"What happened?" Annie struggled to sit up.

"Let me—" The top of the bed whirred upwards as he helped her up, stacking two fluffy pillows behind her.

"Comfortable?"

She was, and oddly, she felt safe. Having this man here with her, guarding her, made whatever had happened better.

The armchair screeched against the floor as Conrad dragged it closer. He dropped into it with a deep sigh.

"What's the last thing you remember?"

Good question.

They'd argued. She'd packed her suitcase. And then … pain. Sharp, searing pain.

Oh no!

Her hand flew to her belly, but it felt no different. She wasn't far enough along to feel the baby kick. The slight curve reassured her that nothing seemed wrong—yet that pain …

"Is my—" The words caught in her throat. She needed to know if her baby was okay, but she couldn't let him find out about it.

Conrad cleared his throat. "Your face."

"My face?" Annie raised her hand, the cannula tugging at her wrist, and touched her cheek. "Wait." She patted her face with her fingers. It felt different—misshapen.

"It's not that bad. Really." His voice sounded uneasy. "I'm really sorry. I should've reacted faster."

The memories came flooding back. "Darren?"

"Yeah, he got you square on the left cheek. You should've stayed behind me."

Annie shook her head. "No. Darren would've had it his way, anyway." She ran her tongue over her teeth and froze, her heart sinking. "My tooth?"

He nodded, his expression apologetic. "You lost it. Once the swelling goes down, you can get an implant."

Her hand dropped onto the covers. Would she ever be free from that man?

She stared at the pale, bare walls of the hospital room, shadows dancing across them like faint scars. A lone potted fern on the windowsill served as the only oasis of vibrant colour.

Lifting the cup again, she sipped until the straw made a slurping sound.

Conrad raked a hand through his hair and smirked. "Damn, woman. You're quick."

Her lips twitched into a faint smile. "So ... where is he?" Her heart hammered in her chest, the familiar fear creeping up her spine. She didn't really want to know—but she would have to face it, eventually.

Conrad flashed a confident grin. "Somewhere he won't be able to bother you ever again."

Her eyes widened as she sat up straighter. "What? You didn't ki—"

Annie studied Conrad's face, searching for any hint of what he meant. She'd seen enough crime movies to know exactly what that could imply.

Even if he did, it was self-defence.

His laugh—a rich, hearty sound—dispelled her fears like a gust of wind scattering dark clouds.

"No, I didn't kill him. Give me some credit, woman. I'm not him."

Relief washed over her. "No, I know."

Of course, he didn't. What was she thinking?! "But you know, accidents happen," she added defensively.

"Well, yeah, but I've been in enough fights to know how to handle myself." He rubbed the back of his neck. "Once I got him down and locked the door to keep his thugs out, I called the cops."

"Oh."

Knowing Darren, he'd be out in no time. The thought sent a chill down her spine. But maybe there would be enough time for her to disappear if she left right away. Annie shifted her legs over the edge of the bed.

Conrad clicked his tongue. "And where do you think you're going?"

"Somewhere far away. Somewhere he can't find me."

Did I actually say that out loud?

Conrad's touch was firm but gentle as he tucked her legs back under the duvet.

"Don't worry. He won't be out anytime soon." His voice was calm, reassuring. "Turns out his fingerprints matched an old case—someone beaten to death. They've got him, Annie."

Her heart stuttered, then slowed as his words sank in.

"Plus, I filed for a restraining order."

"So … this is really over?"

The room spun a little. Annie sank back into the pillows, her lids heavy but her heart lighter.

"Yes, you're safe now."

His words were a soothing balm to her fears, his presence by her side lending her an unfamiliar, but not unwelcome, sense of security. For the first time in years, Annie dared to hope—hope for a better tomorrow, a life free from Darren's shadow.

Conrad touched her arm lightly. "I'm going to grab a coffee. Want anything?"

Annie licked her cracked lips. "A sparkling water, please."

***

His steps echoed in the empty corridor. A coffee vending machine came into view next to a set of chairs, a small table, and a palm tree in a pot. The smell of disinfectant mingled with an artificial pine air freshener, making him scrunch up his nose. He didn't mind the disinfectant, but that fake pine scent—he couldn't stand it, whether in a bathroom or a car.

Conrad placed a brown plastic cup under the spout and selected a double espresso. As the machine whirred and streamed hot coffee, he grabbed a bottle of sparkling water from the fridge beside it.

The selection of cookies caught his eye, and his stomach rumbled. When was the last time he had eaten?

Conrad scratched his chin. This morning? No. Last night? No, it had been earlier than that. The lunch at the country club—that had been his last proper meal. He'd spent last night drinking a couple of bottles and nibbling on a bag of peanuts.

Munching on a ginger nut cookie, he stuffed his pockets with a selection of biscuit packs. He took a sip from the cup—strong, just the way he liked it.

What next? Could he really leave her here like this? Would he?

Mentally counting the passing doors, Conrad strolled back toward Annie's room. He should call her parents.

No. He shook his head. *She would hate that.*

Maybe her sister? Where was she, anyway? He couldn't simply leave

Annie in this state and get on with his life.

The door to her room was slightly ajar, and a murmur of voices reached him from inside. His heart skipped a beat. They had found her.

"You had a mild concussion, so we'll need to keep you overnight for observation, Annie."

Conrad exhaled in relief. A doctor. Not one of Darren's thugs.

"What about my baby?"

He stopped mid-step, frozen in place.

A baby?

"Your baby is fine. But you need to take better care of yourself. You're malnourished. I'll give a list of supplements to your husband."

"No. Not to him. Please."

"He doesn't know? You should tell him. He'll be delighted, I can tell."

"Doctor, you don't understand."

"Oh?"

"We're not together. We're separated. And the baby—"

"Let me guess, not his?"

Conrad didn't dare breathe in the sudden silence.

"Well. He looks like a decent guy. He deserves to know."

"He is, but it's complicated."

"Like everything in life, my dear. Let's recheck your blood pressure."

***

"Here's your water."

A familiar voice made her look toward the door, her heart pounding fast in her chest. Conrad entered the room, holding a pack of biscuits in one hand and a water bottle in the other.

"Sorry it took me so long, but Colton—" Conrad stopped mid-sentence when his eyes landed on the doctor, who was scribbling readings from the blood pressure machine. "Oh, good afternoon." He hesitated a few steps from her bed. "I didn't know you had company. Shall I come back later?"

Annie shook her head. "No, the doctor was just checking on me. Please, stay."

She let the air out of her lungs.

So lucky.

A few minutes earlier, and it would have been awkward. Conrad didn't need to know about the baby. They would soon part ways and forget about this whole thing.

"Yes, as I was just saying to your—" The doctor pushed his glasses higher on his nose, his gaze shifting to her, like a wise teacher trying to say a lot without saying anything. His eyes urged her to do the right thing. *Not a chance.* "—wife, all results are normal, but as Annie had a concussion, we'd like to keep her here until morning."

"And then?" Conrad took two strides forward and placed the water and a pack of Digestives on her bedside table.

"Then, if nothing changes, your wife can go home."

"What time do you think I can pick her up, Doctor?" Conrad munched on a cookie that had somehow materialised in his hand.

"Conrad, I'll be fine. You don't need to—"

He dismissed her words with a wave of his hand, crumbs scattering over the duvet.

"I'll pick you up. So, what time, Doctor?"

The doctor checked the clipboard he held. "I'd imagine around 10 a.m. Everything should be clear by then."

"Excellent." Conrad shoved the rest of the cookie into his mouth, making Annie's mouth water. Suddenly, her stomach gurgled, loud and demanding.

"It would be good—" The doctor shifted his focus to Conrad, holding his gaze like he was issuing a command. "—if someone stayed with Annie for at least 24 hours after her discharge."

"Absolutely." Conrad waved his hand again, this time holding a fresh pack of biscuits. Annie snatched her own pack and ripped it open, stuffing two Digestives into her mouth at once.

"Not a problem at all," Conrad added. "I'll ensure Annie stays home for another day or two."

She swallowed quickly. "But—"

"No buts." Conrad turned to her, his intense blue eyes locking onto hers, a warm smile lingering on his lips.

The doctor beamed. "I shall leave you now." He nodded toward Annie and strolled toward the door. Just before stepping out, he turned back. "And Mr Brenman, dinner will be served soon. Would you like to eat with Annie here?"

Conrad laughed. "You must be a mind reader, Doctor."

"No mind reading necessary in this case." The doctor chuckled and closed the door behind him.

Silence enveloped the room, stretching from pleasant to awkward.

"You don't need to do this, you know," Annie said softly.

"I know, but I'm not chucking you out on the street while you're injured."

He wiped his mouth with the back of his hand and then fixed her with a serious look, his brows furrowed.

"Besides, I deserve the truth about Darren, and somehow, I don't think you'd want to talk about it in the hospital."

I'd rather not talk about him at all!

"You're right."

"About pouring your heart out at the hospital or about me deserving the truth?"

"Both."

***

Despite the distant voices, screeching trolleys, and nurses popping in and out to check her blood pressure or ask if she needed anything, Annie felt detached and alone. Not lonely as new life grew inside her, but rather left to her own devices.

There was no hiding behind the marriage masquerade anymore. The future she had dreaded was here now, and Grandma Ann wasn't around to rescue her this time.

Annie took a sip of blackcurrant squash from the cup a nurse had left on her table and unlocked her phone with her thumb. A text notification sat at the top of the screen.

Lou: *Just landed. Call me xx*

Annie opened WhatsApp and hovered over the video call button, but hesitated. The gap in her mouth where her tooth had been made her self-conscious. Without a mirror to check her face, she relied on the pain and her fingers to paint the picture. It wasn't pretty. Sighing, she opted for an audio call instead.

"Hi, sis. Happy to be back?"

"Yes and no." Louise's carefree laughter spilled through the phone.

Should she even bring up her predicament? "I'll miss the sun and the free cocktails, but I can't wait to start organising my *real* wedding, you know?" Louise giggled.

"I bet." Annie smiled faintly. One thing she had done right—she'd made it possible for her sister to have a normal life.

"Speaking of which," Louise asked, her tone suddenly serious, "have you told him yet?"

"Well ... "

Louise gasped. "Annie, I love you, sis, but this needs to end."

Annie glanced at the machine beeping softly beside her, its tubes tethered to her vein. "Well, it kind of did."

"It did?"

Where should she even start? The country club lunch? The argument afterwards? Or Darren's sudden appearance? Annie took a deep breath.

"Long story, but it involves my ex showing up and a fight landing me in the hospital."

"Oh my God! Are you okay?"

Annie winced at the high pitch of her sister's voice. "I'm fine. It was just a punch. I tried to stop them from fighting, and it landed on my cheek."

"What hospital?" Annie could hear hurried footsteps and a distant murmur. "I'm coming."

Annie shook her head before remembering it wasn't a video call. "No, Lou, no need. Conrad brought me here, and they're keeping me overnight as a precaution."

"Conrad brought you?" Louise's voice softened. "That's decent of him, given the circumstances."

More than decent. Her knight in shining armour. Annie sighed. Well, maybe not *hers*, not after everything that had happened.

"Yes, and there's more, but I'll tell you all of it when I see you." Annie cleared her throat. "And about that, Lou ... I'll need a place to stay. A few weeks, a month tops."

Her sister's warm timbre of voice cut in. "Hon, you know my home is your home. Stay as long as you need."

Annie nodded, unable to speak as an enormous ball of emotion lodged in her throat. She blinked rapidly, willing the tears back.

"Annie?"

She swallowed hard and took a sip of her drink. "I'm here. It's just ... you don't have to."

Louise laughed. "Are you kidding me? I'd love to have you around. And then I'd be close to my niece or nephew." Annie could hear a murmur of a distant voice in the background. "Oh, and Meggie reminded me you're a great event planner, so please, please—will you help me with the wedding?"

This time, Annie didn't bother to stop the tears from flowing. "Nothing would make me happier."

***

Conrad unlocked the door and stepped into the empty house. He flicked the light switch, banishing the darkness.

Colton followed, carrying two grocery bags.

"If you could put them here, please." Conrad gestured toward the dining table. "I'll unpack them in a minute."

Colton nodded but strode toward the kitchen instead, placing the groceries on the counter. Without hesitation, he opened the fridge and began emptying one of the bags, methodically placing eggs, cheese, and yoghurt on their respective shelves.

Conrad placed a hand on his shoulder. "Colton, I can do this. Go home, or your wife will give me an earful again if you're late for dinner."

"It's no bother, Mr Conrad. It'll only take a minute." His hands worked quickly, but with the same precision, he applied to everything.

Wonder if he does this at home?

Conrad watched his assistant for a moment, then reached into the fridge and grabbed a can of beer, nudging the egg carton with his elbow as he did so. A grin tugged at his lips when Colton immediately straightened the box without missing a beat.

"I'll be in the study." Conrad turned on his heel and strolled toward the room that had witnessed so many of his rises and falls over the years.

"A baby, huh?" he murmured to himself as he sipped from the can, his gaze drifting to the orchard shimmering in the moonlight. Was it Darren's? Or maybe there was another man in Annie's life who hadn't yet stormed through his front door.

"I've finished, Mr Conrad. I'll be leaving now," Colton called from the kitchen.

"Thank you. Good night, and pass my regards to your wife."

The sound of the door shutting behind the old man echoed through the house. The room fell silent. Even the clock seemed to stop ticking. Conrad stood still, listening. Nothing. Not even the creak of a floorboard or the groan of a bed frame.

"Better silence than a crying baby and his feisty mother." He chuckled, a nostalgic smile tugging at his lips as he recalled the paper towel fight. How different it had been from the chaos of the morning.

When Annie had collapsed on the floor, his heart had stopped. He'd reached her in a single, smooth motion, his fingers immediately checking her neck for a pulse. The relief of finding it strong and steady had nearly brought him to his knees. Seconds later, Darren had lunged at him from behind. Conrad's instincts had taken over. A few moments later, the scumbag had lain unconscious on the floor, which had given Conrad the chance to call emergency services.

A pair of cable ties had served as makeshift handcuffs, allowing Conrad to focus on his Annie.

"My Annie?"

Since when was she *his*? He tilted the beer can back, draining it in one long gulp before crushing the empty aluminium in his hand.

Another?

He shook his head. The stack of letters on his desk demanded his attention. The time for grief and anger was over. There was no hope left. Conrad had to start liquidating, or he'd lose all his inns. The mansion in Bath would be the first to go. The location was convenient, but he had never liked that monstrosity. And besides, he would always have this cottage—*his* home.

"Remember, gift it to the love of your life," his grandfather's words echoed in his mind.

Chapter 19

The coffee machine whirred, spewing dark liquid into the mug. The shower stopped. Conrad replaced his mug with another one for Annie and flicked the switch on the electric kettle.

The faint smell of coconut wafted into the room as she entered, adding to the aroma of baked almonds from the pastries they had picked up on the way back from the hospital.

Conrad took a deep breath, letting the mingling scents fill his lungs. He could get used to this.

"Feeling better?" he asked, glancing at her. She looked angelic in the white bathrobe, her curly hair framing her still pale face.

"Much." Her voice was raspy.

"Sounds like you need a drink."

Conrad poured hot water into her coffee to top it up, added a spoonful of cream, and carried both mugs to the coffee table near the sofa.

"How about the patio?" Annie opened the double doors, inhaling deeply. The fresh air brought in warmth and the fragrance of lilacs.

He nodded and followed her outside.

Annie shivered in her bathrobe. "Give me a sec. It's not as warm as I thought." She hurried back inside.

Conrad whistled softly as he followed her, picking up plates and the bag containing a selection of pastries. Among them was his favourite Palmier—a sweet, heart-shaped layered delight. While he was arranging the treats on the patio table, she reappeared in the doorway wearing the leggings and jumper he'd bought for her the other day.

"Better." Annie smiled as she strolled toward him. "Thank you for washing them."

Conrad chuckled. "Don't thank me. I'd be lost without Colton. I don't even know when he did the laundry."

She curled her legs beneath her as she settled into an armchair. Conrad leaned back on a lounger with a raised backrest, stretching out his legs.

Home. Great coffee, lovely weather, and a beautiful woman. Life's little joys.

"I talked to my sister. She's prepped the room for me."

The joy in him flickered and dimmed. "What's the rush? When I said you could stay for a few days, I meant it."

"Well, I don't want to intrude."

"Well, you need a quiet place to stay, and I won't even be here. I've got business to attend to." His forehead creased as he remembered his appointment with the estate agent later that day.

She smiled faintly and looked away.

Conrad swallowed, debating whether this was the right moment to ask. "So … "

Her emerald eyes returned, focusing on him with full attention. He cleared his throat.

"Tell me about this guy I put in jail for you."

The corners of Annie's lips curled up, but her eyes remained guarded. Maybe he shouldn't have joked about it. But how else could he bring the subject?

"Sorry, I shouldn't—"

Annie waved her hand, and this time her smile reached her eyes.

"No, it's fine. You have the right to know. After all, you fought him for me."

She invited a joke here, but it didn't seem like the right time to respond with a juvenile comment.

"Well." She took a sip from her mug and licked her lips. "There isn't much to it. We were together for a few years. I thought he was different when I met him."

"You're not married to him, are you?"

She chuckled. "No, I'm not marrying every guy I meet, you know."

"You can't blame me. I've had a *different* experience." He winked at her.

"Touché. But no."

Her gaze wandered toward the orchard, and for a moment, it seemed like she'd forgotten their conversation.

"You said he'd changed."

Her expression darkened.

"No, I don't think he did. I think I was blind. When I met him, Darren was charming, and I thought I'd finally found a good guy after my previous marriage disaster."

Conrad raised his eyebrows. "Marriage? So, you're actually married to someone else?"

Annie shook her head. "Not for a long time. Divorced. Remember that guy I was running from the other day?"

Conrad nodded.

"That was my ex-husband. Not only did I lose years of my life to him, but also all my money."

"Your marriage fund?"

"Yeah. He gambled it away." Annie leaned over and touched his arm, her warm fingers sending a tingle through his skin. "Please don't tell my parents. They don't know."

"About the marriage?"

"No, the money. I wouldn't hear the end of it."

"So, what did you tell them?"

"Bad investment."

He chuckled. "Can't argue with that."

She laughed, the sound bubbling out of her until tears formed in her eyes. But then the laughter shifted, turning brittle. Was she laughing or crying now?

"Annie?"

"I'm fine. Very bad investment indeed."

"Do they know about … "

"Darren?"

Conrad nodded. He wanted to ask about the baby, but maybe that would come next.

"They do now. He barged into their house a few days ago. But before that, well … one of the things he did was keep me isolated. It came on slowly, you know." Annie shook her head. "I missed the signs. At first, he kept telling me that he and I were family, that we didn't need anyone else, and that my parents didn't understand me. And I totally fell for it. Stupid, huh?"

"No, not at all. You had no reason to doubt his intentions, I guess."

"Then he became very controlling, upset whenever I left the house without him, so I stopped doing it. Visits to my sister or any friends were out of the question after a while."

"That must've been awful."

"Not really. My relationship with my parents is, at best, strained. The only person I was close to was my sister, and since we moved around a lot, I never built any work relationships."

"So, you worked?"

"Yes, bartending. Moving from pub to pub. Every time I got settled, we either moved or he made a scene, and I'd have to quit."

"I'm sorry to hear that, but it explains your skills. I thought you were a natural."

Her soft chuckle warmed him.

"Old story now. Anyway, I always thought he was just a normal businessman with a bit of a temper. But one day I overheard him on the phone, instructing someone to solve a problem with a person who had a funny name. A few days later, I heard that name on the news. The guy was badly beaten and in the hospital, while his house burned down."

"Oh my God, Annie." He took her hands in his.

"Yeah. I still convinced myself it was a coincidence, but I started noticing things. Finally, several days ago, when I was home alone, a post came through with an invitation to my sister's wedding. It said the wedding was on the 7th of May, literally a few days away, and in an attached note, she asked why I wasn't answering calls or emails."

"And why weren't you?"

"I lost my phone at some point. In hindsight, I think he took it. And truth be told, I had no money to buy a new one. As for the emails—"

"Let me guess. No internet?"

"No. I checked my emails on the only computer at home every evening. But there was never anything interesting."

"So, do you know what happened with your sister's emails?"

"Yeah. That day, I broke the rule and entered Darren's study when he wasn't there. And checked those emails again."

"And?"

"And still nothing. I checked spam. Nothing there. Then I checked the bin folder."

He narrowed his eyes. "And?"

Annie frowned, the green in her eyes darkening. "He hadn't cleaned it. There were many."

"Bloody hell, Annie."

"Yeah. When I saw it, I grabbed a few possessions, took some cash from his drawer, and left the house through the window as he always locked the doors before leaving."

Wow.

If he'd known, he would've thrown a few more punches at that scumbag.

"I'm so sorry you had to go through that. At least you're safe now."

"Yes." She leaned over and kissed his cheek. "Thank you."

She raised her mug and held it close to her chest. "I want you to know I will void the marriage and tell everyone it was my fault." Her tone carried a firm resolve.

Conrad opened and closed his mouth. "Thanks."

What else could he say? That it wasn't exactly helping him right now? It wouldn't save the people who would lose their jobs when the sale went through. Maybe he could cut a deal with the new owner to keep his staff.

He sighed. It was his problem, not Annie's.

"What about your parents? They'll be disappointed."

Her face lit up. "I count on it." Holding her mug in both hands, she took a long swig from it.

"They're still your parents. They did it for you and your sister."

She smirked and finished her coffee.

"Want another one?"

Annie glanced at her empty mug. "Tea, please, and then I think I'll be going."

Conrad got up, collecting both mugs. "Seriously, Annie, stay till tomorrow at least. Doctor's orders, remember?"

She looked up at him with those emerald eyes without saying a word.

***

A hoot from an owl yanked Annie from her nap. The late evening hum of crickets floated on the warm breeze, accompanied by the sweet, potent scent of night-blooming flowers.

Shaking off the stiffness in her neck, she stretched and pulled the soft blanket higher, wrapping it tightly around herself against the evening chill.

"Conrad?"

The patio lights flickered, casting a mellow glow across the space. The heater purred in the corner, bathing the area in a snug, cosy warmth. From the dimness, Conrad emerged, balancing two boxes of pizza. The scent of garlic and pepperoni wafted through the air, and her stomach growled.

"You must be a mind reader." Annie sat up straight, pushing the blanket to the side.

The corners of his mouth curled upward. "Hard not to be, considering you've been out cold all day. Colton even said you were snoring."

"I do not snore!" She feigned indignation, but the corners of her mouth twitched upward.

Conrad placed the pizzas on the patio table, undoing his tie in a casual, unhurried gesture. She couldn't decide if she liked him more in a suit or a T-shirt.

"You look smart. What's the occasion?"

His smile faded. "I went to see the estate agent."

"About that country club?" Annie picked up a slice with her fingers. "You're still going to buy it?"

"No." Conrad sighed, sinking into a lounger opposite her.

"No?" She cocked her head while shoving a slice into her mouth.

His gaze wandered toward the darkness, and it didn't seem like he'd heard her at all. Annie chewed on her pizza, listening to the leaves rustling in the wind.

Finally, he shifted in his seat and turned toward her.

"The truth is … " he began, his fingers fiddling with the pizza box. "I counted on that marriage fund money. It would've pulled me out of debt."

"What?" She nearly choked on her pizza, washing it down with a gulp of water.

"Please, before you say anything." He touched her arm lightly. "I would've paid it all back and made your sister a co-owner of the inns."

Annie licked her lips, the tingling sensation on her arm distracting her. "Wait, what about the country club?"

"I—" Conrad swallowed and averted his gaze. "I lied about the club, Annie. It was never for sale. I needed that money."

She furrowed her brows, trying to make sense of what she was hearing. "But I thought you were ... well, rich?"

His grim chuckle sent a shiver down her spine. "The pandemic hit hard, Annie. I was lucky I only lost money." He stretched his arms and put them behind his head. "That money would've solved everything."

Annie scoffed. "Your problem, but my sister's money."

He licked his lips and focused his deep blue eyes on her. "I would never deceive anyone like that if it were just about me. You need to believe me."

She clicked her tongue. "What do you mean?"

"My staff—" He raked his hand through his hair. "They might lose their jobs when I sell."

Oh, that's what the waitress meant!

"And it was a good deal for both sides. Your family would get the cottage, and I could save my inns while making your sister's life very comfortable."

The implications hit her like a sledgehammer. The marriage. Her parents. The inheritance. Her mind whirred, replaying her parents' words, ensuring Annie that Conrad wouldn't be worse off without the cottage. If anything, they'd claimed taking it off his hands would make his life easier.

Easier my ass. Her breathing quickened as she realised how close she had come to deceiving a person in trouble. Her parents. Damn greedy parents. A sour taste filled her mouth.

"My parents ... " She sucked in some air.

How much should she tell him? It didn't matter now, and sharing more might only make him feel worse.

"They don't care about anyone but themselves. As for Louise ... " Annie swallowed, watching his eyes darken. "You need to understand." Her voice trembled. "Louise couldn't go through with the marriage. She ... she's gay."

Conrad exhaled audibly and hid his face in his hands, his shoulders sagging. The silence stretched, the pizza forgotten.

"Was today about selling your inns?" Annie broke the silence, her voice barely above a whisper.

"No. It was about my house in Bath. There's a buyer." His eyes met hers, a spark of determination in their depths. "It might help delay the foreclosures."

"But that's your home!" Her protest was met with a shake of his head.

"No, Annie." A hint of a sad smile appeared on his lips. "Haven't you guessed it yet?"

Guessed what?

She tilted her head, puzzled.

"This *cottage* is my home. It always was."

***

The suitcase rattled on the wooden floor as Conrad pulled it toward the door, with Annie strolling beside him. He inhaled her coconut-infused scent for the last time before opening the cottage door and letting the morning air sweep in. The sun still hung low over the horizon, and mist wove through the trees.

"You're sure you don't have time for breakfast?" Conrad's eyes pleaded, even though he knew it would only delay the inevitable. Breakfast or not, she would still leave.

Annie shook her head. "No, I can still feel that pizza from last night sitting in my stomach." She laughed, patting her belly.

"So, this is it." Annie's words ricocheted off the silent walls, her figure framed by the open door, the suitcase handle resting firmly in her hand.

An unexpected wind blew in from outside, weaving its chilly fingers through her hair, creating a playful disarray. She tucked the strands behind her ears in a manner Conrad had already come to recognise, and pushed the suitcase to one side, stepping closer to him.

"Yes. It was—" Conrad cleared his throat.

Great? Horrible? All of it.

"An eventful week."

She laughed in that carefree way of hers. He wished he could do the same.

"So, what now?" he asked.

"As I said, I'll void the marriage tomorrow, and you can forget all about us."

"Yeah."

He didn't want to forget it. Or her. He didn't want to forget her.

A murmur of an engine caught his attention, and he turned toward the road. A silver car approached, winding its way toward the cottage.

"Must be your taxi."

Annie shivered and rubbed her arms. "Yes, it must be."

"Cold?" Conrad pointed to the suitcase. "Do you need your jumper?"

She shook her head. "No, I'll be fine. The cab is almost here."

"Annie—" Conrad swallowed hard. He wanted to say so many things, to ask her to stay, but he couldn't. Not yet anyway.

She looked at him with those emerald eyes, sighed, and said, "I guess this time it's an actual goodbye."

Conrad wanted to hug her, to feel her body against his, her head resting on his shoulder. Instead, he extended his hand. She took it, shaking it firmly. "I guess it is."

The taxi's wheels screeched on the gravel outside the cottage just as his phone buzzed.

Conrad glanced at the notification bar. It wasn't a text. The phone buzzed again, displaying an unknown number—a déjà vu. His heart beat faster.

Annie touched his arm. "What's up?"

"Not sure," he said, answering the phone. "Hello?"

"Good morning, Conrad. I trust you're well."

"Good morning, Richard. How are you?"

Annie's eyes widened. In a hushed tone, she asked, "Is it my dad?"

Conrad nodded.

"I thought I'd check when we could book that reading of the will. Time is not on our side, you know." Richard's tone had a high pitch, hinting at his impatience.

"A will reading?" Conrad glanced at Annie, silently pleading for help.

She covered her mouth with her hand and whispered so softly he had to strain to hear. "Tell him to book it for Tuesday."

He furrowed his brows and mouthed, "What?"

"Conrad, are you there, my boy?"

"Yes, Richard. Just checking my schedule."

Covering the receiver, he turned back to Annie. "Why would I go to the reading?"

"We both will." She giggled. "And I'll tell them there that I've voided the marriage. So, they'll be left with nothing and no time to do anything about it."

Devious woman. He chuckled.

"Right, Richard. I think Tuesday would work. Will that be fine for you?"

"How about Monday? You know, Tuesday is the last day, and I'd hate for something to go wrong at the last minute."

Ah, that's why Annie suggested Tuesday. Conrad shook his head, smiling.

"I'm very sorry, but I can't possibly be ready by Monday. I hope you understand."

He heard an audible sigh on the other end.

"Tuesday it is. I'll email you the arrangements."

"Excellent."

The car door opened, and the driver stepped out of the cab.

"May I speak to my daughter?"

Annie shook her head firmly.

"Not now, Richard. She's—" The taxi boot opened with a thud. "At home. And I'm at work. Sorry, have to go."

Conrad disconnected the call a second before the driver called for Annie and grabbed her suitcase.

"Let's get you packed."

"Thank you." She smiled, walking beside him to the car.

"I'll see you on Tuesday, then?" He shoved the suitcase into the open boot.

Annie nodded. "Would you pick me up from Louise's place? I'll be staying there."

"Absolutely."

"See you then." She rose on her tiptoes and kissed him on the cheek. His heart somersaulted.

Chapter 20

Red or black?

Annie cocked her head, studying her reflection in the built-in wardrobe mirror. She wore a black shirt with skinny navy jeans—an outfit more suited for a night out than a will reading. Black court shoes with sensible heels would make it more appropriate for the occasion, but her red high-heeled pumps gave her more confidence.

"What do you think?" Annie turned to face her younger sister, Louise, who was perched on the edge of the sofa.

"Red is more sexy."

Annie sighed. "Black then. It's not a date." She turned back to the mirror, smoothing down her shirt.

"Oh no, I didn't mean it like that." Louise looped her arms around Annie's shoulders. "What would Grandma say?"

Annie furrowed her brow. "What do you mean?"

"It's her will reading. You knew her much better than anyone else. What do you think she'd say if you asked her?"

"Do what you want and to hell with everyone else." Annie chuckled softly. "I miss her, you know."

Annie sank onto the mocha leather sofa, worn from years of use, and slipped off her shoes, stretching her toes. "I wish I'd been with her when she passed away."

A gust of wind whipped through the wide-open windows of the living room, scattering multicoloured post-it notes from the desk. Annie watched as they danced across the room before settling on the wooden floor like fallen confetti.

Turning the red pump over in her hands, she looked up at Louise. "I should've been there."

"Don't beat yourself up about it." Louise plopped down beside her, the sofa releasing a little sigh and sending up faint puffs of colourful dust—remnants of one of Louise's projects. Her tanned skin glowed in the afternoon sunlight, the rays painting warm highlights on the floor. "You couldn't have known."

"If only I'd had my phone back then." Annie sighed, shaking her head. "Do you know that I actually found it? When I searched his drawers for cash. It was there, buried under a stack of paperwork."

"I'm so sorry, hon." Louise squeezed her hand. "But it's all over now. Thanks to your ex-husband."

Louise clapped her hands and cracked a wide grin. "I wish I could see their faces when you tell them you voided the marriage, and they can say goodbye to that inheritance."

Annie offered a half-smile, her fingers tracing the aged lines in the leather. "It was the right thing to do. But I'm sorry you'll lose out on the inheritance money. Dad said we would've got something out of it."

Louise scoffed. "Since when do you believe Dad's promises when it comes to money?"

"Yeah, you're right." Annie raised her hands in mock surrender. "And Conrad's a good guy. I just couldn't do it to him."

Louise placed a hand on Annie's shoulder. "So, what's your plan after this? Are you going to tell him?"

"Tell him what?" Annie's phone buzzed, drawing her attention. She glanced down at the message flashing on the screen. "He's downstairs."

"About the baby." Louise's eyes drilled into hers, pinning her in place.

"No, I don't think so. It's better he doesn't know." Annie slipped the red pumps onto her feet and glanced around the room, searching for her purse.

"Why not?"

"He's got enough of his own problems, and it's not even his kid. Not that we're getting married or anything, you know." She winked at her sister and danced toward the side cabinet, where she spotted the little black bag.

The doorbell rang. Annie pointed at the door, but Louise shook her head and bit her lip.

"You'll be fine. He's not a monster," Annie whispered as she reached for the door handle.

***

The door groaned open on rusted hinges, and Conrad was greeted by a radiant Annie, backlit by the golden light filtering through the wide-open windows. The afternoon sun highlighted her chocolate hair, giving it an ethereal halo—a sight that captivated him.

Her lips curled into a mischievous grin.

"You clean up nicely, Mr Brenman."

Conrad blinked and raked a hand through his hair, his grin widening. "You're not so bad yourself, ex Mrs Brenman."

Annie gestured toward the woman hovering by the brown leather two-seater. "I believe you've been introduced already?"

Louise looked different, nervously twiddling her thumbs. "Hi." Her voice was quiet and shaky.

Conrad took two strides toward Annie's sister and extended his hand, offering a firm handshake. "Great to see you again, Louise."

Her cheeks flushed a delicate pink, and her gaze shifted to her feet. She seemed so fragile. And so young. How could he ever have mistaken Annie for her sister?

As she reached out to shake his hand, her fingers trembled slightly. "Conrad, I'm sorry for what I've done. I shouldn't have."

Conrad offered a reassuring smile. "Water under the bridge, Lou. It wasn't meant to be. Also—" He glanced back at Annie, a playful glint in his eye. "According to your sister, I dodged a bullet."

Louise's brows knit together in confusion. "What do you mean?"

"Oh, I'm sorry. I didn't mean it that way." He chuckled, running a hand along the back of his neck. "Not about you—you're lovely. I meant your parents."

Annie's laughter chimed in, and the room seemed to brighten, the atmosphere less charged.

"You're not her type, anyway." Annie pointed at a framed photo on the desk, drawing Conrad's attention. The photo showed Louise embracing a woman with striking dark eyes and a confident smile that lit up her face. Her strong jawline and the determined tilt of her head gave her an air of quiet resolve, while the flowers in her hair added a playful, joyful touch.

Conrad gestured toward the frame. "Is she your ... "

"Yes, that's Meggie. We—" Louise's voice cracked slightly, and she swallowed hard. "We're engaged."

Conrad gaped at the revelation. "Wow. Congratulations!"

His thoughts whirled, untangling the past confusion and creating a clearer picture. He hadn't seen that one coming. Well, he should have.

Running his fingers through his hair, he felt a hint of embarrassment creeping up his cheeks.

"I was such a fool. I should have guessed when you talked about your friend with such admiration back when we met for coffee." He shook his head. "What an idiot."

Annie lightly punched his arm, her grin never faltering. "Well, now you know."

She tapped her watch. "We should get going. Showtime."

"Let's do it." Conrad offered her his elbow like an old-fashioned gentleman. Annie threaded her arm through his, her fingers gently brushing his arm, sending a shiver down his spine.

Louise waved them off, the tension easing from her expression. "Have fun, kids."

Annie made a face. "Oh, we will."

***

Annie checked her reflection in the tinted window of the sleek Tesla, which seemed out of place in the gravel driveway of her childhood home. But it was certainly better than Conrad's old truck. The woman staring back at her had the same auburn hair, the same freckles peppered across her nose, and the same lipstick-smudged smile, but it felt like she was looking at a stranger. Annie was just a girl playing a grown-up, a kid dressing up in her mother's shoes—red or black, still unsure—on a playground she no longer recognised.

A chill breeze whistled through the towering maples lining the driveway, sending shivers up her spine like a horde of ants marching across her skin. She reached out to steady herself on the cold metal of the car roof, her fingers brushing the silver surface, the chill seeping into her bones.

From the corner of her eye, she watched Conrad standing beside her, his casual elegance in a smart black jacket and jeans radiating quiet confidence that seemed to contrast starkly with the nervous flutter in her belly.

He reached over and gave her hand a comforting squeeze, his thumb tracing soft, reassuring circles on the back of her hand—a silent promise that he was with her, even if just for the moment.

He caught her gaze, his eyes sparkling with concern. "You ready?"

She nodded, her throat too tight to squeeze out any words.

"Annie," he began, his voice barely above a whisper, "Remember, it's just news. They'll get over it."

She let out a dry chuckle, her gaze drifting toward the house, toward the ghosts of her past. "This isn't about the marriage, Conrad. It's this house. The last time I walked through those doors …" she paused, swallowing hard. "I was 16."

His eyes softened as he gave her hand another squeeze, a quiet show of support in the face of her haunting past.

"You're not that 16-year-old girl anymore, Annie," he said firmly. "You're a woman who's made her own choices, stood by them, and is about to kick some old-fashioned butt. You've got this."

A small smile tugged at her lips, his words kindling a spark of courage in her heart. "Thanks, Conrad."

She wasn't powerless anymore. Darren was gone. Those fears couldn't hold her hostage. What was a house full of overbearing, judgemental relatives compared to that?

With renewed determination, she stepped forward, her red pumps adding a splash of bold defiance against the monotonous greys of the mansion's stony path. Together, they crossed the threshold, stepping into a world teeming with memories of the past and anxieties of the present.

The scent of too many perfumes mingled with the smell of old wood and expensive scotch—a heady cocktail that was the signature of the Simmons family gatherings.

A sea of familiar faces, painted with warm smiles and hungry eyes, turned toward her.

Conrad's grip on her hand tightened as Aunt Agatha, her father's sister, started toward them, her eyes gleaming with juicy gossip and insincere praise.

"I'll find the will executor," Conrad said softly, releasing her hand. He vanished into the crowd as Aunt Agatha's shrill voice cut through the murmur.

"My darling girl, how long has it been?"

Annie's hand felt cold, abandoned without Conrad's touch. She glanced down at her empty ring finger, the lack of a band a blatant symbol of her impending announcement. Her gaze then travelled to her red pumps—once a bold choice, now the only splash of colour in a world that had suddenly gone cold and grey.

With a fake smile plastered on her face, she took a deep breath, bracing for what was to come.

"Agatha, how lovely to see you. Shame you couldn't make it to my wedding … "

***

"Ah, Mr Brenman. I was expecting you." The will executor, Mr Avanti—as indicated by the name tag pinned to his grey-striped suit—stretched out his hand and gave Conrad a vigorous handshake.

"Mr Delavoure explained what's supposed to happen, but are you sure?" Mr Avanti pushed his glasses up the bridge of his nose, his sharp gaze narrowing on Conrad with an intensity that made him shiver as if something terrible was about to unfold.

"Are you absolutely sure this is what you want, sir?"

Conrad took a deep breath and pulled a stiff, cream-white envelope from the inner pocket of his jacket. "Yes, I am."

But the will executor made no move to take the envelope.

"You know, you can still change your mind, and no one would be any wiser. This decision will have a tremendous impact on a lot of people."

Conrad nodded, his gaze drifting toward Annie. She was pinned against the wall by a tall woman in a Merlot-red evening gown that glittered in the chandelier's light. The woman waved her arms dramatically while speaking, towering over Annie like a willowy tree swaying in the wind. Hunched and visibly uncomfortable, Annie looked as though she was searching the crowd for an escape route.

Conrad's jaw tightened. He should be there at her side, not here having a pointless back-and-forth with a man he barely knew. He extended the envelope with a steady hand.

"Thank you for your insight, but I've had enough time to think it through. I'm absolutely sure this is what I want to do."

Mr Avanti raised his hands in a defensive gesture. "It's your right, sir."

Finally, he accepted the envelope, sliding it into a leather-bound folder on the mahogany desk beside him.

"The will reading will begin shortly. You're welcome to join us, sir."

"Thank you, but no. I'll stay only for Annie's speech and then head off."

The will executor tapped the folder with his finger. "Given the stir this might cause, I totally understand. Well, good luck to you, sir."

Conrad nodded. "Thank you." He shook Mr Avanti's hand and turned on his heel.

In the short time he had been gone, the dynamics in the main room had shifted.

The Merlot woman shifted toward the window and towered over a barrel-shaped man who stood at least four inches shorter than her. Meanwhile, Annie, cornered between a cushioned high-back chair and the fireplace mantel, looked like a trapped animal scanning the crowd for another predator.

Conrad sighed. Why had he even agreed to let her come here? If he'd known what this would mean for her, he would've insisted on delivering the news to her family over the phone—less chance of bloodshed.

He strode toward his ex-wife.

Was she ever his wife? He scratched his chin. His ex? Or had voiding the marriage erased everything like it had never happened?

Extending a hand to pull her out of the corner, Conrad shook his head. "No. I want to remember."

"You want to remember what?" Annie raised her eyebrows, the haunted look in her eyes replaced by curiosity.

Conrad chuckled. "Didn't realise I said that out loud."

"So, what is it you don't want to forget?" Her eyes sparkled, her tone teasing.

With a half smile, still holding her hands, he locked his gaze on Annie. "Us."

Her mouth opened, but no words came out. She didn't deny there had been "us", nor did she claim it wasn't real. Instead, she bit her lip and nodded.

"I'm glad we met. I won't forget you either." Was that a blush on her cheeks, or was it just his imagination?

Maureen's overly cheerful voice shattered the moment.

"Here you are, lovebirds!"

Did she really just say that?

Conrad nearly laughed out loud. The woman had no shame at all. Any lingering doubts about Annie's plan evaporated. Her parents deserved what was coming to them.

"Maureen, so thrilled to see you. And—" Conrad nodded toward Annie's equally beaming father. "And you, Richard."

"Likewise, likewise, my boy." Richard patted Conrad's shoulder like he was a racehorse he'd bet on and was confident would win. "You've kept us on our toes till the very last minute, haven't you?" His chuckle carried an undertone of disapproval.

"Solicitors. You know how they are. Always checking the fine print." Conrad shook his head, then stepped aside to offer Annie his arm. "I think it's time. Shall we?"

Annie swallowed hard but nodded, slipping her arm through his. Their walk to the room where Mr Avanti waited was far more in sync than it had been on their wedding day when he'd practically had to drag her out of the church like a sulking child digging in her heels.

Inside, the will executor sat behind a mahogany desk in front of three short rows of burgundy-upholstered high-back chairs, arranged like a classroom.

"Miss Simmons." Mr Avanti inclined his head.

"Oh, Mrs. Call me old-fashioned." Maureen jingled her fingers, glinting with multiple rings.

"My apologies." Mr Avanti bowed deeper. "I was addressing your daughter, Mrs Simmons. And yes, welcome, Mrs and Mr Simmons. Please, have a seat."

Conrad hovered near the desk with Annie, watching as relatives poured into the room. He recognised only a few faces from the wedding. The rest were strangers—though, given the Simmons family's penchant for grand displays, he doubted anyone had been excluded. The will reading, it seemed, attracted even the most distant of relatives.

"I didn't know your family was so big," Conrad murmured.

"You and me both." Annie shrugged. "I've only heard of half of them. Never seen them in person."

Maureen waved them over and pointed to two chairs in the front row. "Come here. We saved you seats!"

Annie cleared her throat. "Thanks, Mother, but I'd like to say something first."

Richard rose from his seat as if to join her, but Annie raised a hand to stop him. "I can handle this on my own, Father. Also—" Her emerald eyes landed on Conrad's. "I'm not alone."

"You bet," he whispered, his voice barely audible. But the reassuring squeeze of his hand said enough. He was on her side. For better or worse.

Well, certainly for worse.

And this could very well be the last time he saw her.

A shiver ran down his spine, and his jaw tightened.

No. Not if he could help it.

Chapter 21

She might have enjoyed this moment if her stomach wasn't in knots. Her parents, with their quizzing eyes, fidgeted restlessly in their seats. Yet, surrounded by relatives and bound by the weight of the occasion, they couldn't demand answers outright. For once, they were at her mercy, and Annie would leave this house on her terms—not at her mother's command.

"Miss?"

Annie turned to Mr Avanti, who held a document stamped with the official seals of the municipal office. She nodded and took it, knowing it might be needed to convince her family that this wasn't some elaborate joke. Clearing her throat, she straightened her back, sensing Conrad shift slightly by her side.

"Good afternoon, everyone." A few nods and grunts rippled through the room before silence fell, the gathered relatives eager to hear if their names would be mentioned in the will.

"Thank you all for coming to hear my grandmother's last words. I only wish it were under happier circumstances."

Letting go of Conrad's warm, steady hand—her lifeline—was the hardest part. But this was something she had to do alone. She needed to show them the separation was real. He didn't move, though, standing behind her like a solid rock—or better yet, a mountain. If only they'd met under different circumstances.

Annie gritted her teeth. Her parents had ruined that for her, too. For the last time, though. There was no reality in which she would raise her child around such despicable people.

"You've all heard about certain conditions in Grandma Ann's

inheritance. Mr Avanti, would you please read the statement?"

Almost as if they'd rehearsed it, he stepped forward, cleared his throat, and, in an official tone, began reading from the parchment he held in both hands.

"If you're hearing this, it means I've gone on to greener pastures. I know you're not here for my rambling, so let's cut to the chase."

Mr Avanti blinked behind his glasses and looked up. "These are Mrs Ann's words, not mine."

As if anyone would believe that an old-fashioned gentleman would use such colloquial phrases. Grandma Ann, on the other hand ...Annie's lips twitched into a faint smile. She was never big on appropriateness.

After a murmur of confirmations reached him, Mr Avanti straightened his tie and continued. "I have appointed Mr Avanti as the executor of my estate, and the will has been sealed under his care."

Annie's breath hitched. So that was why her parents didn't know exactly what was in the will.

"My last wish is for my childhood cottage—" Mr Avanti paused, picking up another paper from the desk. "The cottage mentioned in Mrs Ann's letter is The Lilac Croft, located in Wiltshire and currently owned by Mr Conrad Brenman."

The murmurs rose again as the crowd was eager to skip ahead to the moment the will was fully revealed, but Mr Avanti stood quietly, waiting for the room to fall silent once more.

"As I mentioned, please note that the cottage in question, at the time of Mrs Ann's passing, belonged to Mr Conrad Brenman—" The will executor turned toward her ex-husband and nodded. "Present here with us today."

"Reading on." Mr Avanti took a sip from a glass of water on the desk and brought the parchment closer to his eyes.

Annie scanned the faces in the room. If this man weren't the only way to access the will, they would have torn him to pieces. She found it quite amusing, watching them squirm like that.

"My last wish is for my childhood cottage to be returned to the family so that my great-grandchildren may play in the orchard as I once did. The cottage is the key to unlocking the will. You have six months from the date of my passing to make this happen, or everything will be lost."

Annie pursed her lips to stifle a laugh. Even in death, Grandma Ann had found a way to make everyone dance to her tune.

Mr Avanti placed the parchment on the desk and looked up. The room waited.

Annie waited. *Surely, there must be more?*

"Miss?" Mr Avanti gestured toward her. "It's your turn."

Annie shrugged and stepped forward.

"As some of you know, Conrad Brenman—" she glanced toward him, offering a soft smile "—joined our family by marrying me. What you may not know is that the only way for the cottage to return to the family was for Conrad to gift it to his wife, a condition passed down through his grandfather's will."

Almost like they orchestrated it together.

The thought flitted through her mind, making her realise how similarly challenging the will requirements from their respective grandparents had been. In a way, since Annie had discovered they not only knew each other but had once been in love, it made sense. They must have shared a flair for drama and a love of a good mystery.

Annie cleared her throat and focused her gaze on her parents, her tone sharp and unwavering. "But what Conrad didn't know was that he married me."

Her father's eyebrows knitted together as he shook his head, silently begging her to stop talking. Oh, she was just getting started.

Smiling as if delivering a punchline, Annie continued. "He thought he was marrying Louise."

Gasps filled the room, though Annie rolled her eyes. She was certain that, for most, the shock stemmed more from her revealing the truth to Conrad than from the mischief itself. She could bet the gossip had already made its rounds, and everyone here had known about the switch but kept quiet until the will was read—just in case there was something in it for them. Greedy bastards.

"To make things right by Conrad, I have voided the marriage." She held up the document, silencing any potential objections.

Placing the paper on the desk, she clasped her hands together, her smile unwavering as her mother slumped in her seat, mouth agape.

"Thank you all for coming, but I'm afraid you'll be disappointed. Today marks exactly six months since Grandma Ann's passing, and the cottage still hasn't been returned to the family. So—" Annie paused, taking a breath, when Mr Avanti interjected.

"It has."

Annie froze and turned to Mr Avanti. "What do you mean?"

The will executor picked up a bulky envelope from the desk and handed it to her. "The cottage is yours, Miss."

***

"What?"

Conrad couldn't tell if the shock on her face was from delight or horror. Annie turned the envelope in her hands without opening it, shaking her head as she tapped the letter with her index finger.

"It can't be true!"

Horror, then. Well, he'd hoped for a more positive reaction.

"I take it you're not pleased with the gift." A half smile tugged at his lips as he touched her shoulder, trying to draw her gaze away from the envelope and back to him.

Her head kept shaking, her wide eyes fixed on the envelope. "This wasn't what we agreed. Why would you do that?"

Seriously, one couldn't please this woman. Why? It was a good question with a great answer, but this wasn't the time or place. Besides, she'd probably just laugh it off.

"It was part of the deal, and I never break a promise." Half the truth. Conrad cleared his throat, hoping she would accept the answer without prying further.

"But you said you'd have nothing left."

He sniggered and shrugged. "Better you have the cottage than the bailiffs."

A lonely buzz of a fly and the distant chime of a clock accentuated the room's silence. Someone in the back coughed and was promptly hushed by their neighbour.

Annie's eyes scanned the room, and he followed her gaze. Her parents were practically glowing, basking in their apparent victory. That was the one downside to this whole thing. Still, it was worth it. Annie needed a stable place to stay, somewhere to raise her child—just as her Grandma Ann had wished.

Mr Avanti shifted from one leg to the other, his fidgeting breaking the stillness.

"Shall we proceed with the will reading, Miss Simmons?"

Annie cocked her head, biting her lip. Conrad could see the wheels turning in her mind.

"But this changes nothing," she said finally.

What?

Conrad frowned, his forehead creasing, but before he could ask what she meant, Annie's face lit up with triumph.

"It's not binding," she said, her voice tinged with elation. "I'm not your wife."

She looked like she'd just hit the jackpot, her face glowing and her emerald eyes sparkling.

So adorable. If Conrad had harboured any lingering doubts about Annie being in on her parents' scheming, they were gone now. Her reaction made it abundantly clear—she wasn't part of their game.

Conrad stepped forward, positioning himself so everyone in the room could see him. He took Annie's hands in his. For a brief moment, it reminded him of their wedding day, the same way he'd held her hands back then. But the emotions? Vastly different. She'd been a stranger back then.

He took a deep breath. What he was about to say would reveal far more about himself than he was comfortable sharing in a room full of people. But it had to be said.

"That was never a condition. My grandfather's last wish never mentioned marriage specifically. That was simply your parents' interpretation."

Annie's eyebrows arched, her eyes widening in surprise. Those vibrant, jade-green depths drew him in like a sea threatening to pull him under.

Without thinking, Conrad pulled her closer. His fingers traced the line of her jaw as he lowered his head. She didn't flinch.

"The note inside explains everything," he whispered, his voice soft. Then he touched her lips with his in a lingering kiss.

His body ached to pull her even closer, to lose himself in her entirely. The blood in his veins pumped fast, his fingers tingling. Somewhere in the distance, the crowd erupted in cheers.

Panting, Conrad forced himself to pull away. He took one last look at her flushed face, her breath coming in short gasps, before turning and heading for the door.

One day.

One day, but not today.

***

Annie stumbled and touched her lips. She almost followed Conrad, but Mr Avanti's polite cough brought her back to the room, full of prying eyes and ears eager for gossip.

The envelope in her fingers beckoned her. With shaking hands, she ripped the edge off and opened it. As she pulled out a stack of documents related to the transfer of cottage ownership, a small card slipped out and floated to the floor. Annie placed the cottage title on Mr Avanti's desk without glancing at it and bent down to pick up the lonely card lying under her feet.

The text on the card appeared to be a scanned copy. The crease marks from where the original paper had been folded gave it a wonky look, but the handwritten lettering remained clear and easy to read.

"... As for the cottage, I leave it to you, Conrad, under one condition: Don't ever sell it, my boy. It's a treasure that can only be gifted to the love of your life."

To the love of your life? The words made her heart thump faster in her chest. No, that couldn't be true. It was just a saying. Or ... could it?

She swallowed hard and glanced at Mr Avanti, who stood holding a much larger, stiff envelope. His eyes were fixed on hers, like a musician awaiting a sign from the conductor.

Annie licked her dry lips and nodded.

"As the cottage now belongs to Miss Ann Simmons, I pronounce the requirements for unsealing the will fulfilled."

Annie blinked. Mr Avanti missed his calling. With his formal tone, Mr Avanti would have made an excellent officiant at weddings—far more cheerful events than this ... at least most of the time.

When he opened the envelope with a vintage letter opener, even the fly stopped buzzing, allowing the sharp tear of paper to echo through the room.

The will executor removed a stiff, A4-sized parchment and carefully placed the now-empty envelope on his desk, aligning its edges with the other documents—most likely bringing murderous thoughts to the minds of her relatives, who were grinding their teeth in impatience.

Annie had to admit, despite not caring much about the contents of the will, this theatrical mystery reveal put her on edge, twisting her stomach into knots.

No, scratch that. Mr Avanti shouldn't officiate weddings. His dramatic pauses would send brides and grooms fleeing in panic.

"Shall we begin?" Mr Avanti adjusted his glasses and extended the parchment before him.

The crowd remained silent. Mr Avanti cleared his throat, and still, nothing happened.

"For the love of God, just start reading!" her father barked, breaking the silence. The room erupted into murmurs, voices urging the will executor to get on with it.

"Apologies," Mr Avanti said, raising a hand to restore order. "But I must ensure everyone can hear, and I cannot proceed under such conditions. Shall we take a recess, perhaps?"

Annie burst into laughter, and the room fell silent faster than she finished cackling, drawing all eyes to her in dismay. She raised her hands in defence and nodded toward Mr Avanti.

"Go on, please," she said with a smirk.

She could swear a fleeting smile flickered across his face, but when she blinked, his expression was as distinguished and collected as ever.

"Dear family," he began, his tone solemn, "I believe the cottage has returned to whom it belongs or otherwise, you wouldn't be hearing these words. Well done. Richard and Maureen, as I'm certain you had your hand in retrieving it, I, therefore, leave to you approximately £500,000 in investments. A detailed list is stored safely with Mr Avanti. To all relatives and extended family gathered here, you will each be granted £10,000, to be allocated at Mr Avanti's discretion. To my beloved—"

The crowd drowned out the rest of his words, cheering and clapping as though they had just witnessed a standing ovation-worthy performance.

Mr Avanti waited, but this time, it was impossible to silence them. They had got what they came for, and the only thing they were interested in now was which investments they would receive.

"Miss Annie, shall we move to the office, where I can finish the reading in peace?"

"Absolutely," her mother chimed in. Somehow, her parents had already managed to sneak up on her. Her father patted Annie's back with a self-satisfied grin. "A superb job, darling."

Annie scoffed. "I had nothing to do with it."

"Don't be so modest." He waved dismissively.

Her stomach twisted. This was the worst part. Now her father probably thought she had manipulated Conrad into giving her the cottage. Jaw clenched, Annie followed her parents and Mr Avanti into an adjacent room, closing the door firmly behind her.

Inside, Mr Avanti motioned for them to sit in the chairs before his less extravagant desk, piled with papers. Somehow, he'd already grabbed the will documents without her noticing.

After they sat, he raised the parchment again and continued reading, this time with no interruptions.

"To my beloved granddaughters, I leave the remainder of my estate to be shared equally between you. I trust you girls will not fight over it and will put it to good use."

"That's outrageous! She must have lost her mind!" Richard shouted, rising to his feet and flailing his arms.

Mr Avanti removed his glasses. "Are you challenging the will, Mr Simmons?"

"You bet I am."

"And why is that, may I ask? Do you not believe your daughters deserve their grandmother's wealth?"

"Well—" Richard blinked, crossing his arms.

"So, do you?" Maureen's steely voice sliced through the air, raising goosebumps on Annie's arms. Her father visibly deflated under its weight.

"I mean, of course, they do," he muttered. "But they're so young and inexperienced. Surely, we should be appointed to manage their financial affairs."

Mr Avanti plucked another document from his desk. "Because if you were to challenge this will, there is a statement here, one so ironclad that you wouldn't stand a chance. It specifies that, in such a case, all assets would be left to charity."

Annie could swear there was a hint of satisfaction in Mr Avanti's voice. She wondered how long he and Grandma Ann had known each other—he was clearly more than just a random attorney.

Richard gasped, his face turning pale as he sank back into his chair.

A sudden thought struck her. "Is that what would've happened if the cottage hadn't been returned to the family?"

"No, Miss Simmons," Mr Avanti said, his tone softening as he touched her arm reassuringly. "There was a separate clause for that. In that case, your parents would not have inherited a single penny."

Annie bit her lip. That didn't sound like a bad outcome at all. She had to read that letter from Conrad. Maybe she could find a way to return the cottage and—

"What about the cottage?"

Only now did she realise it wasn't actually part of Grandma Ann's estate.

"We'll take care of it, don't you worry." Richard brushed her question off in a sulking voice.

Over my dead body.

Annie hadn't said it aloud, but her expression stiffened, and she crossed her arms, ready for a battle. There was no way in hell she'd let the cottage fall into their greedy hands.

"Oh, but that's not up to you, Mr Simmons. The cottage legally belongs to Miss Ann, so it's her decision what to do with it."

"Come again?" Her father's face turned red. "As far as we were told, the cottage was returned to the family, so we are the family, and we will decide its future."

Mr Avanti's tone didn't change. If anything, it grew more mellow, as if he were speaking to a child.

"I'm afraid that's not true. Mr Brenman was very clear in his instructions: the cottage's legal owner would be his wife."

"Aha!" A wide grin cracked Richard's face.

"Yes?" The will executor looked up from under his glasses.

"First of all, they are no longer married." Richard pointed an accusatory finger to emphasise his words, but Mr Avanti sighed audibly. Even he had his limits.

"Apologies, my mistake. To his ex-wife."

But Richard waved it off and continued, "But most importantly, he married Louise, poor sod, so the cottage clearly does not belong to Annie."

As much as Annie hated to admit it, her father had a point. She'd impersonated her sister, so anything referencing their marriage could easily be challenged. Maybe she could buy them off? Depending on how much Grandma had left.

"Don't you worry, Mr Simmons. There is no confusion about the ownership. The cottage title states it belongs to Miss Annie Simmons."

Mr Avanti picked up a few pieces of paper and handed a copy to each of them. "I thought you might want to see it for yourselves."

The only word Richard managed when he stared at the document with his mouth agape was barely audible: "How?"

"As I believe that matter is closed, would you mind if I finished the will reading so we could make the arrangements?"

Her parents nodded, speechless.

"The costs of the will execution and £10,000 as a thank-you to Mr Avanti for his service shall be paid from the estate."

Annie nodded. It was the least they could do.

"My lovely girls, Annie and Louise, I leave it to you to decide what should happen to my house. Take your time, don't rush it. Mr Avanti is an excellent estate manager, and I trust there is a decent monthly income from all the investments for you two to enjoy your lives without worrying about the future. He will also be able to provide a rough estimate of the estate's value after deductions."

An income?

Until now, Annie hadn't quite grasped what inheriting Grandma Ann's investments really meant for her and Louise. She'd been so focused on making things right with Conrad that she hadn't even thought about how much might be left for them.

Would it be enough to live on? Or, if not, maybe she could sell some assets to buy herself a year with her baby without worrying about finding a job.

"And now, for my last farewell, Mr Avanti, thank you for your help." The old man's voice trembled, and he cleared his throat before continuing more briskly. "My dear family, lots of love from your old Granny Ann. And behave, or I'll haunt you. Just kidding."

Annie chuckled.

Mr Avanti placed the parchment down on the desk and picked up yet another envelope.

"Here, Miss Annie. A personal letter from your grandmother to you. There is one for your sister as well. I shall pass it to her when we meet to discuss the estate details."

The envelope smelled faintly of Grandma Ann's perfume, stirring memories. Annie felt a hot flush rising to her neck, the air in the room suddenly too thick to breathe. Still, Mr Avanti hadn't indicated that he was finished, so she sat quietly, waiting.

After a few moments of silence, her mother asked a question that would normally have come from her father, who was still lost in his brooding.

"So, how much are we talking about here?"

"The value of the estate, you mean?"

Maureen nodded, and the question seemed to snap Richard out of his daze, his eyes now locked on Mr Avanti's face.

"After deductions, I estimate it would come to—"

The will executor tapped a key on his laptop, and the screen lit up, revealing an open spreadsheet. Scrolling to the bottom, he nodded, confirming what he already seemed to know.

"About five million each, give or take."

"Five what?" Annie stared at Mr Avanti as the room spun around her.

"Five million pounds at the close of the market yesterday." The words seemed to come from far away. "You should understand that much of it isn't easily liquidated, but we'll discuss the details with Miss Louise present."

Five million pounds?

The world elongated, her vision blurred, and a tingling sensation spread through her fingers and toes.

"Miss?"

Chapter 22

The umbrella over Annie's table at the country club wobbled in the gust of the afternoon breeze that ruffled her hair. She zipped up her hoodie as the wind chilled her to the bone.

Turning Grandma's letter in her fingers, she brought it to her nose. The scent of home engulfed her, a bittersweet wave of comfort and longing.

"Wish you were here, Granny."

A butter knife sliced through the stiff envelope with ease, and a single sheet of cream-coloured paper slid out onto her awaiting hand.

Her grandma's last words.

Annie's chest tightened. She wished she had called more often. She could have used Darren's phone after losing hers, but it had never felt like the right time—not with him listening to her every word.

Her mouth felt dry. She put the envelope on the table, took a sip of caramel cappuccino, and smoothed the paper in her hands.

Dear Annie, if you're reading this, I failed to rescue you from your oppressor. He's not a good man, that Darren, but I trust you know that by now.

Annie gasped. "She knew about him!"

A few people glanced her way from a nearby table, but only briefly, as it would be impolite to stare, even if someone seemed to be having a conversation with themselves.

How did she find out?

Annie's gaze drifted to the trees in the distance, their waving branches seeming almost alive, as if they could answer her questions. Maybe Mr Avanti would know? She glanced at her watch—half past 2 p.m. There was still time before her meeting with Louise and the will executor.

Her eyes returned to the neat handwriting in vivid blue ink.

And if the cottage made its way back into the family again, I suspect you met young Conrad. He's something else, isn't he? I only hope his feelings aren't misplaced, as Louise will never give him the happiness he deserves.

Annie shook her head. "How?"

How had Grandma known Conrad would be involved with Louise?

You were out of the picture, a gloomy voice whispered in her head, and she found herself nodding. It wasn't hard to imagine her parents roping Louise into the scheme, and Grandma had known her son-in-law well enough to predict he'd cook up a plan.

Annie took a sip of her now lukewarm cappuccino and focused on the letter, wondering how many more surprises it held.

And she deserves to be happy. Oh, I know ... There was nothing more written on the page.

Annie raised her eyebrows, turning the page over. *About Meggie, that is.*

She chuckled, covering her mouth with her hand. That was classic Grandma—nothing escaped her all-knowing eyes.

Please look after your sister and ensure she chooses her happiness over your parents' shenanigans.

"You bet, Grandma." That she could do. With pleasure.

As for you, my dear child, if you need help with that vile creature, Darren, I'm sure Conrad will be able to help.

"You have no idea, Granny." Annie shook her head, remembering the fight. A smile brightened her face as she thought of Conrad's care—how he had puffed the pillows for her at the hospital, how he'd made her comfortable on the patio afterwards. "My hero."

"Miss?"

Annie blinked and looked up at a server standing next to the table, his expression politely neutral.

"Oh, sorry! I was talking to myself." She tapped the letter, then glanced at her watch again—only ten more minutes until the meeting. "I'm waiting for someone."

"No problem, Miss. I'll come back later."

Shifting in her seat, Annie took a last sip of her cold cappuccino and spotted Louise waving to her from the restaurant's entrance. She waved back and glanced down to scan the rest of the letter.

One last thing. If you can, stay in the cottage, at least for a little while. It was

always filled with love, and I have a hunch I'll be able to watch over you there.
All the love, Grandma Ann.

Annie stared at the closing words, hearing the warmth of Grandma Ann's voice in her mind.

"It's such a lovely place."

Her sister's vibrant tone snapped her out of her thoughts. Annie blinked her tears away and folded the letter, slipping it back into the envelope.

"The vivid greens of the countryside and intensity of the wooden furniture, contrasted by the whites of the linen and cushions. What a feast! I wish I'd brought my brushes."

Louise's laughter bubbled out like a child's, light and carefree, drawing smiles from a few nearby tables.

"Do you think they'd mind?" Louise pulled out a chair and sank into it, her eyes still scanning the surroundings.

"Mind what?" Annie waved at the server to return.

"Me painting here. Maybe over there." Louise pointed to the far edge of the seating area, where a thick, low hedge bordered the row of tables. "I'm so glad Mr Avanti chose this place for our meeting."

Annie nodded. "Yeah. I wonder why, though."

She had pegged him as a man of purpose—meticulous and exact, yet full of compassion and an intriguing sense of humour. She had no objections to keeping him on as their estate manager, just as Grandma had suggested.

"Ladies?"

The same server from before stood tall, waiting for their orders.

"My apologies for being late." Mr Avanti emerged from a side path, bowing slightly. Annie glanced at her watch—a minute to 3 p.m.

"Your timing is perfect. Please, have a seat." She gestured to the chair opposite hers before turning to the waiter. "I'll have another decaf cappuccino—vanilla this time, please. Lou, hot chocolate for you?"

Her sister nodded. "And a slice of carrot cake."

"Great idea." Annie beamed. "I'll have one too! Mr Avanti, what about you?"

She pictured him as the type to opt for a no-frills espresso and a simple croissant—efficient, minimalistic, and to the point.

"A latte, please. And indeed, that carrot cake sounds like the perfect way to celebrate."

He settled into his chair, placing a laptop at the table's edge. "If I may, Miss Louise, I'd like to introduce myself. I'm Bartholomew Avanti, your late Grandma Ann's estate manager and the executor of her will."

Louise's face lit up as she shook his hand. "Yes, Annie mentioned. So, why here?" she said in one breath.

He adjusted his glasses. "I beg your pardon?"

Louise chuckled. "Why this glorious place, of all places? Not that I'm complaining, but wouldn't your office be more appropriate for discussing estate matters?"

"Ah, yes." Mr Avanti opened a leather folder and pulled out a few sheets of paper. "I thought it would be fitting to introduce you ladies to your investment portfolio here." He handed each of them a printout, neatly organised, with columns of names and figures.

"I have a digital copy as well, but I thought it might be easier to review the printout while we discuss."

"I still don't understand." Louise waved the sheet lightly with her fingers, almost losing it to the wind.

"I'd like to draw your attention to the first item on the list."

Annie's eyes fell on the top entry. *Whispering Pines Country Club.*

"No way!" Louise exclaimed, expressing exactly what Annie was thinking. "Eighty percent ownership. That's a lot, right?"

"Yes, Miss Louise, it's a controlling stake. The former owner, Mr Baker, retained the remaining twenty percent and, in exchange, manages this place." He gestured to the surrounding property with a small wave of his hand. "And he's doing a sterling job, I must add."

"Totally," Annie murmured, her gaze following the sweep of his hand.

Suddenly, she started giggling. Memories of her parents' aspirations to own the country club flooded her mind.

"Lou, can we agree on one thing here?" Annie asked between bursts of laughter.

"Sure, as long as you tell me what's so funny." Louise cocked her head, curiosity clear on her face.

"Let's agree never to sell this place and never let anyone know who owns it."

"Okay ... " Louise's tone was wary, but intrigued.

"Oh, you'll love this." Annie leaned forward, still giggling. "Our

THE BIG DAY DECEIT

parents cooked up this elaborate scheme to use Grandma's inheritance to buy this very place. They even considered hiring Conrad to run it." She paused, savouring the punchline. "And all this time, it was already in the family."

Louise burst into hearty laughter. Even Mr Avanti allowed himself a soft chuckle.

Their drinks and cakes arrived, and the sisters fell silent, focusing on the rest of the list.

"Bloody hell. This is astonishing." Annie scanned the document, overwhelmed by the sheer scale of the investments. Her grandma had quietly amassed stakes in what felt like half the local businesses.

"But why never more than eighty percent ownership?" Louise asked, voicing the question Annie had already guessed the answer to.

"Because your grandmother believed in empowering others. She wanted to help businesses thrive without taking control away from their struggling owners. She believed no one knew their domain better than the people who built it. By investing, she offered financial support, guidance on budgeting and profitability, and the freedom for them to keep doing what they loved."

Annie nodded so hard she nearly spilt her cappuccino. That was Grandma Ann to a T—always helping, but never overstepping or smothering.

"So, what happens now?" Louise took a bite of her carrot cake. She groaned with pleasure. "Oh, this is divine."

"Ah yes, the cakes here are delivered by Little Mermaid Bakery."

"We should invest in them as well," Annie mumbled through a mouthful of cake. It was simply too good to ignore.

Mr Avanti tapped the paper in her hand. "Position thirteen, if you would."

Of course. Grandma wouldn't have missed that opportunity.

"As for what happens next, it's entirely up to you, Miss Louise and Miss Annie."

"Can we do nothing?" Annie tilted her head thoughtfully. "I mean. Everything seems to be running smoothly. Can't we just let it continue as is?"

Louise nodded in agreement, her mouth too full of cake to speak.

"If that's your decision, then we simply need you both to appoint a portfolio manager—"

"That would be you, Mr Avanti," Louise blurted out. "If you agree, of course. I can't imagine anyone knowing Grandma's plans better than you."

Annie smiled, grateful they were on the same page. This was something they had agreed on before coming to the meeting—to keep things going, at least until they understood the full picture.

Mr Avanti swallowed as if something got stuck in his throat. "I would be honoured." He gave a small bow.

"And what about Grandma's house?" Louise asked, her voice soft with emotion.

"Ah, yes." Mr Avanti flipped through his folder. "Your grandmother left the house to both of you to use as you see fit, but she asked that you wait at least six months before considering selling it."

"I could never sell it," Louise said, her tone resolute. She turned to Annie, her soulful eyes pleading.

"Of course not," Annie replied. Then an idea struck her. She raised her cake spoon for emphasis. "I have a suggestion."

Louise tilted her head, curious. "What kind of suggestion?"

"You should have it," Annie said.

Louise's eyes widened. "What do you mean?"

"I mean, the house should be yours. I had my time there, and now it's your turn. Let's make Grandma's house fully yours."

"I couldn't," Louise gasped, her voice thick with emotion.

"Why not? I have the cottage, and besides, I bet that the conservatory at the back has amazing light for your paintings."

Louise's hesitation was written all over her face, but before she could respond, a thought crossed Annie's mind. She scanned the list again, searching for any mention of Conrad's pubs. Nothing.

"Mr Avanti. Are we investors in any of Mr Brenman's pubs?"

"No, Miss Annie."

Her chest tightened. *What a shame.* She had to find a way to bail him out. "Could we be?"

Louise raised her eyebrows, clearly intrigued.

"Sorry, Lou," Annie said. "I should have mentioned this earlier, but … I need to do something to help him. I can't let Conrad go under. He's …"

She trailed off, unsure how to explain. How could she convince them this was important without delving into emotions she hadn't fully processed?

To the love of your life.

The words from her grandmother's letter echoed in her mind.

"You don't need to say anything else, sis. I get you." Louise turned toward Mr Avanti. "What could we do?"

Mr Avanti chuckled as though he'd heard a great joke. "I suspected this might come up, so I took the liberty of speaking with the bank manager. It seems they would halt the repossession if we paid off half of the loan."

Annie's stomach churned. Could they afford it? She still didn't fully grasp how wealthy they had become, but Mr Avanti seemed to read her mind.

"I would suggest liquidating one of the assets." He tapped Annie's list. "Position twenty-four. The former owner has expressed interest in buying back his controlling stake. That would free up enough cash to resolve the issue."

"Let's do it!" Louise declared, raising her mug of hot chocolate. "To Conrad's bright future."

"And ours!" Annie raised her cappuccino mug with such enthusiasm that half of the liquid splashed into the air. But she didn't care.

For the first time in what felt like forever, things were looking up.

Chapter 23

The lazy morning sun shone through the trees, bathing the cottage in vibrant light. The wisteria and lilacs fought for attention, as always, but at this time of year, the lilacs won hands down with their overindulging scent of pure joy and freedom.

Annie filled her lungs with the fragrant air while stretching her legs after the nerve-wracking drive through the narrow, unfamiliar lanes leading to the cottage. It had seemed so easy when Colton or Conrad had driven those roads, but for her, it was an exercise in patience and sheer will.

Conrad stood leaning against the red truck parked a few meters away on the side of the gravel path. He wore a white T-shirt under his light brown leather jacket, paired with classic blue jeans and brown leather shoes. He dangled a set of keys from his finger—an open invitation for her to come and take them. The keys to her grandma's childhood home. To her home now.

Shading her eyes with one hand, Annie strolled toward the man she had met only a few weeks ago. Yet, somehow, it felt like they had known each other forever—like they were old, close friends.

"How was the journey?" he asked.

No hug. Not even a handshake.

"Fine." Annie glanced at her rented Honda, holding all her possessions in the trunk. That single, lonely suitcase she had salvaged before leaving Darren for good. But for now, she didn't need more.

"I took the liberty of stocking the house with food so you wouldn't have to worry about it."

That raspy, warm tone of his voice—it had soothed her in the hospital and thrilled her when it whispered close to her ear before their kiss. Annie blinked, pulling herself out of the memory.

"Thank you so much. You didn't have to."

"Well, to be fair, it was Colton's idea, as you might imagine."

Of course. Since they'd met, Colton had been the one looking after their every need. Hopefully now, with the cash injection into Conrad's business, Colton could keep his position. Should she tell him now?

Annie bit her lip, nodding, but before she could say anything, the keys jingled in the light breeze just in front of her face.

"Here, your legacy, my lady," he said, his tone teasing.

She extended her hand and accepted the keys in silence. Words eluded her. Here was a man giving away his home, and she stood like a mute.

"Enjoy," he said simply.

Conrad turned on his heel and opened the truck's door, making it clear the conversation was over. Annie stood in place, staring at the keys in her hand. Maybe she could call him later?

"Go, enjoy your new home," his voice urged through the open window.

"Right. Thank you. Will you wait?"

"For what?" The corners of his lips curled up, but his tone wasn't cheerful. "Worried I gave you the wrong key and will leave you stranded?"

"Of course not."

Did he? No, he was just teasing her, that cheeky bastard. She marched toward the door without a second glance. If he wanted to drive away, that was fine by her.

The door was slightly ajar, so she pushed it open without slowing down. It swung wide, bouncing off the wall.

The overpowering scent of lilacs filled the air. Vases stood everywhere, overflowing with purple, white, and violet blossoms.

Her annoyance melted away as she inhaled the aroma and scanned the familiar space. It looked just as it had the last time she'd seen it—furniture and all. Yet, there was a faint, fresh scent of paint coming from somewhere. Nothing around her screamed renovation, though.

Maybe a paint container had tipped over in his office—the one room she hadn't seen—while he packed his belongings. She chuckled to herself and strolled toward the closed door.

An image of Conrad in his boxers and bare chest, standing in the doorway to his bedroom, suddenly invaded her thoughts. She licked her lips.

"It wasn't meant to be."

She passed Grandma Ann's room on the way. Its door was wide open, beckoning her with a promise of peace and love emanating from the walls. It would be her bedroom now.

Annie reached the closed office door. The scent of paint tickled her nose. Acrylic? Definitely not oil-based—she would know after all those hours spent with Louise.

Pressing the handle down, she eased the door open a few inches. Nothing fell or hit her in the face. It seemed safe enough.

Annie sighed. Why did she think he'd prank her? With her lips pursed, she pushed the door fully open and gasped.

The first thing she noticed was a cot—a baby cot, complete with swirly toys hanging from a mobile above it.

He knew.

Her throat tightened, and her eyes filled with tears as her gaze swept the room. Animals painted on the walls, a night sky on the ceiling, and a squishy play mat covering the centre of the floor. She stepped farther in, drawn toward the wall obscured by the door.

"No freaking way!" The words bounced off the walls, and in response—or maybe because of the sudden breeze—the banner hanging there jiggled, mocking her.

Annie pulled out her phone and jabbed Conrad's number. "The nerve!"

He answered after a couple of rings.

"Are you serious?" she demanded, skipping any pleasantries.

"I take it you found my little surprise?" His relaxed, cheerful tone left her speechless for a moment.

"So?" His question hung in the air while Annie pondered her answer.

She should thank him for the baby's room. Nobody had ever done anything like this for her before. Well, except Grandma Ann, when she'd rescued her from that kerb. But Grandma was family. And Conrad? They barely knew each other, and he had just handed over his home.

"So, what?" she shot back.

"Well, I thought you might be calling to answer the question from the banner."

She cleared her throat. "Yes."

"So, you *are* calling about the banner?" Amusement laced his voice, but there was an undercurrent of hesitation.

"No, you dummy. *Yes* was my answer to your question."

The sudden silence on the other end made Annie chuckle as her eyes flicked to the vivid pink letters.

"Yes?" he finally asked.

"What? Do you want me to change my mind?" Now, she was in charge, and she liked it. Things would definitely change around here, whether he liked it or not.

"No, absolutely not. I'm coming."

The line went dead, and moments later, hurried footsteps echoed through the quiet space like a summer storm. Annie's heart pounded as she watched him approach—his hair in disarray, his biceps straining against the sleeves of his T-shirt.

Before she could prepare herself, Conrad pinned her against the door, his piercing eyes locking onto hers, just inches away.

"Say it again." His hoarse, low tone made her tingle.

Annie stared back at him. "Yes."

"Yes, what?" He wouldn't let it go. She could feel the intensity of his body radiating against hers, magnetic and overwhelming.

Her gaze flicked to the letters bouncing on the wall, spelling out the most unexpected question.

"Yes, I *will* marry you."

"That's what I wanted to hear." The words were merely a whisper as he lowered his head and crashed his lips onto hers.

Your next read from Ann Fairway

The Elephant Umbrella

A Chance Meeting, an Unexpected Connection, a New Beginning

Only available to subscribers with a special link.

Get it today at https://read.annfairway.com/bdd-eu-subscribe

In a world of missed chances, sometimes fate brings the right people together at exactly the wrong time.

Caught in the storm of their lives—one literal, the other figurative—Rob Jenkins and Angie Walker share an unexpected moment of connection on the rain-slicked streets of Tossa de Mar. Rob, with an umbrella painted in vibrant elephants, carries the weight of grief he's never dared to unpack. Angie, dressed for sunshine in a town of downpours, struggles to rebuild her life after betrayal. Their meeting is fleeting, but the impact runs deep.

Back in England, both embark on journeys they never saw coming—Rob toward a long-overdue reckoning with his past, and Angie toward a bold reimagining of her future. Little do they know, their paths are far from finished crossing.

www.ingramcontent.com/pod-product-compliance
Ingram Content Group UK Ltd.
Pitfield, Milton Keynes, MK11 3LW, UK
UKHW030923060425
457073UK00001B/56